Confessions from the Dark

CONFESSIONS SERIES BOOK 2

A novel by

T. B. MARKINSON

Published by T. B. Markinson

Visit T. B. Markinson's official website at
https://lesbianromancesbytbm.com
for the latest news, book details, and other information.

Copyright © T. B. Markinson, 2017

Cover Design by Erin Dameron-Hill / EDHGraphics
Edited by Jeri Walker and Karin Cox
Proofread by Kelly Hashway
Book layout by Guido Henkel

This book is copyrighted and licensed for your personal enjoyment only. All rights reserved. No part of this publication may be reproduced, stored in a retrieval system, or transmitted in any forms or by any means without the prior permission of the copyright owner. The moral rights of the author have been asserted.

This book is a work of fiction. Names, characters, businesses, places, events, and incidents are the product of the author's imagination or are used fictitiously. Any resemblance to actual persons, living or dead, events, or locales is entirely coincidental.

Prologue

"Kat, I'm home!" I entered the front door of our redbrick home. When I had moved in several years ago, my mother, the flamboyant author, joked I'd moved into a retirement community. It wasn't an insult. I preferred modest over showy. Order over chaos. Boredom over drama. Not that I had a boring life. At the moment, my life buzzed with anticipation.

No lights were on in our home blocks away from Boston College, and it was deathly quiet, even though it was only a little after eight in the evening. Confused, I closed the blue front door, removed my hooded, down puffer jacket, and hung it on the coat rack affixed to the wall in the entryway. Then I set my canvas satchel on the bench. There wasn't a message scribbled on the board, unless Kat's hand-drawn

Christmas tree was some kind of code. She must be home. "Kat? Are you here?"

The kitchen was off to the left, and I stopped at the fridge to fill a glass of water, the whirring of the ice machine grating on the headache that'd started to form behind my eyes. I chugged half, dehydrated from drinking beer since three that afternoon, and then grabbed a banana to replenish my body with potassium. I peeled it and bit off a third.

"Kat?" I called again, holding a hand over my mouth so I wouldn't dribble banana onto the floor.

Still no answer.

"Why are the lights off?" I asked the empty hallway as I wandered to the back of the house. I was still gripping the water glass in one hand, the banana in the other, as I inspected her studio, my office, and our bedroom—Kat's usual haunts.

Odd.

The doorbell rang, and I stopped mid-step, nearly upsetting the water glass.

"Jesus, Cori. Pull your shit together," I chastised myself, unable to get my pulse rate to slow.

The light in the front room came on. "Kat?" I called from the end of the hallway, one foot in the nursery door.

"Cori?"

It was a male voice. "Roger?" I reached the end of the hallway in seven long strides.

"Yes, I'm sorry. I didn't mean to startle you." He stood in the entryway, looking like a ghost of my usually cocky uncle.

"Everything okay?" I asked.

It was highly unusual for Roger to stop by my house. A blistering cold wind forced the temperamental front door open and slashed through the house like a knife. I'd been meaning to have the door shaved to make sure it closed properly. Some snow drifted onto the welcome mat. Eyeing the mess, I realized I hadn't taken off my shoes, and there were pools of water marking my trek through the house. Kat, the uber housewife, was going to kill me.

Roger slammed his weight into the door to shut it completely. "I'll bring my tools over this weekend, so we can fix this door. Can we sit?"

"Oh, God. Is it Aunt Barbara? Is that why Kat isn't here? She's with—?" I stopped. My legs wobbled as if they understood it wasn't, but I couldn't bring myself to ask what my body clearly already surmised.

"No." He signaled for me to sit on the couch in the front room. I did, placing the water cup on the glass coffee table on a Salvador Dali coaster. I continued to claw onto the half-eaten banana.

"Mom? Dad?"

He studied my face as if he was trying to break the news to me without having to verbalize anything.

"Kat?" I finally said it, although my voice quavered.

He shifted uncomfortably on the arm of our newly purchased charcoal-gray, stain-resistant couch to go with the new stain-resistant carpet. For the past few months we'd been prepping our lives, including the house, for the new arrival. Just last week I'd purchased over thirty power socket protective covers.

"Please, Roger. Is she okay?"

He nodded, eyes filled with sadness, not alleviating the million thoughts rifling through my mind, the worst being death. The second worst was almost too unfathomable to think.

Roger sighed, clamped his hand over mine, and said, "She's going to be fine. She's in the hospital. We've been trying to call you."

"I dropped my phone on the way to class. The screen is shattered," I explained. It was the third phone in six months I'd either lost or destroyed.

Roger squeezed my hand.

"What happened? Why are you here?" I wriggled his hand off mine.

He didn't flinch. Usually, Mom or Barbara delivered messages.

"Looking for you." His steely blue eyes glistened. "You weren't in your office."

I shook my head. "Had drinks with some professors to celebrate the end of the semester."

He swallowed.

I was going to skip the end of semester ritual, but Kat had insisted I go, saying we'd both soon be up to our necks with responsibilities.

"We should get you to the hospital." He yanked the banana out of my hand and set it on the table; my squeezing had rendered it almost unrecognizable. My uncle wrested a silk handkerchief out of his suit breast pocket and wiped my fingers, staring at the messy cloth before shoving it into his coat pocket. He stood and waved for me to get off my ass. Light from the street outside danced on his silver, helmet-style coif.

I wasn't able to move. He tried to pry me off the couch, but I wrenched him back. We stared each other down.

"Tell me what happened," I demanded.

"She was in a car accident."

"No, that can't be." I jiggled my hand free from his grasp. "No… no." I darted up and paced the small space in the front room, pausing to straighten a baby Jesus ornament on the Christmas tree. "When I left for class, everything was fine. Kat told me she was going to curl up in bed and read all afternoon and evening." I stopped to gather my thoughts and then snapped my fingers. "That's right. *The Paying Guests* for next week's book club discussion. They call the club The Smut Patrol, but I don't think Waters's book counts as erotica. Sexy scenes, yes. Erotica, no. Mom and Kat love to get under my skin, though. That's the reason behind the club's name." It was like I couldn't stem the absurdity leaving my mouth, afraid that if I stopped saying inane things, reality would hit me hard. The news Roger didn't want to tell me would slice me like a karate chop to the throat.

Roger's face was sympathetic but stern. In four steps, he reached me and drew me into his arms. "I'm so sorry."

"The baby?" I whispered into his black Burberry trench coat.

He squeezed me tighter, unable to say out loud what I'd known in my heart the moment I gazed into my uncle's eyes at the front door. At six foot two, Roger only had a few inches on me, but I dissolved into a small child enveloped in his embrace. My body shuddered with sobs.

"Nooooooooooooooooooooo!" I wailed, banging his chest with my fists. It didn't seem possible that our baby had died before ever taking a breath.

He didn't let go.

***

As soon as the glass doors to the hospital slid open, both my mom and aunt rushed to console me. I didn't want consolation. I was desperate to see Kat. The thirty-minute stop-and-go car ride through the slushy streets of Boston was the longest half hour of my life. A small pond on Storrow Drive was particularly vexing, considering several timid drivers were afraid to drive through in fear of their car stalling. Roger, in his Jeep Grand Cherokee, had plowed right through the center.

"Where is she? Is she alone?" My eyes panned the waiting room needlessly, but I couldn't stop searching for Kat.

A woman across the room perked up in her seat, catching my interest, but it waned quickly when I saw a meek-looking individual, not Kat.

Aunt Barbara encircled an arm around my waist and led me past the front desk. "Your dad is sitting with her. She's asleep."

"What happened?"

"It was a hit and run…" Mom shuddered. "Someone skidded into her car on the ice and pushed it off the road. Didn't even bother stopping to help her."

"They tried, Cori." Barbara patted my arm. "She had a caesarean, but—" Barbara couldn't utter the unspeakable either.

I sucked in a ragged breath, trying to staunch the flood of tears, but they streamed down my face anyway.

"Is Kat okay?"

"She'll be fine," Mom said, without her usual moxie. She rested her head on my shoulder. I wondered what we looked like, walking arm in arm down the OBGYN corridor, sobbing. I imagined this wing was used to jubilation, not sorrow of this

Confessions from the Dark

magnitude. I wasn't even sure how I managed to move one leg in front of the other. My system operated on autopilot, and my sole mission was to find Kat.

"Has anyone called her parents?" I asked.

"I left a message saying to call me back. I stressed it was important, but I haven't heard from them yet." Mom's stiffened spine indicated she didn't expect a response. Kat's family situation was complicated, and all contact was on her father's terms, which usually consisted of getting together for dinner once a month.

Dr. Wicks stepped out of a room and motioned she wanted to speak. Both my mom and aunt gave me a look that said *Be strong*. Barbara handed me a wad of Kleenex. I dabbed my eyes and nose.

How in the world could I be strong when the woman I loved more than life itself had just gone through hell while I was out having drinks with colleagues to celebrate the end of the fall semester? While I was drinking, Kat was… I was gripped with a sudden wave of guilt.

"The placenta was torn from the inner wall of the uterus." Dr. Wicks's words drifted into my ears, alerting me to the fact that she had been talking to me for some moments. Maybe she'd noticed the blankness in my eyes, because she halted. "I'm so sorry. There was nothing we could do."

"Will she be able to—?" I shook my head, angry at myself for even thinking about trying again. Our baby was gone, and nothing would ever bring her back.

Dr. Wicks clasped a hand on my shoulder. "I'm sorry. There was too much trauma. It's more than likely Kat won't be able to fall pregnant again, or be able to carry to term." A deep well of sadness dulled her eyes, and the tremor in her voice conveyed how much she hated having to inform me of the brutal truth.

I bobbed my head, feeling like I should say something—what, though? Should I try to comfort her? Thank her for trying? No words came to me, so I just stood there awkwardly.

"Would you like to say good-bye?" asked the doctor.

"What?" I said, her words shattering my insides when I realized what she meant. Say good-bye to our daughter, Charlotte, Lottie for short, who we were expecting to officially welcome to the family in mid-January.

"Uh, y-yes. Yes, I would." I smothered my quivering mouth with a palm, sniffled, and said, "Can I see Kat first, please?"

"Of course." She chaperoned me to Kat's hospital room. "Go inside." Dr. Wicks withdrew down the hallway.

My beautiful wife was asleep, hooked up to a machine I assumed was keeping track of her heartbeat and other vitals. Minor cuts marred her face and her left eye was swollen with bruising already starting to show. Was that the side that had struck the car? My eyes roamed to her midriff, and my legs started to tremble.

An IV was inserted into Kat's left hand. Dad held her right hand and glanced up when he detected the shuffle of my feet toward the bed. Only the whirring machines and the beeping heart monitor disturbed the eerie quiet.

Dad rose, paused, and then glanced between Kat and me as if trying to fix the situation, like he had when I'd broken a favorite toy as a child. The pain etched crinkles around his soulful brown eyes and made me catch my breath. On the way out, he gave me a rib-crushing hug, and it took every ounce of energy to lock my emotions deep inside. *Be strong, Cori*. I wanted to be there for Kat.

"I love you, kiddo," he whispered as he exited.

He hadn't called me *kiddo* since I was ten, when I'd accidentally smashed a gravy boat during Thanksgiving at my grandparents, ruining both the gravy boat and a tablecloth that'd been crocheted by my great-grandmother as a wedding gift to her only daughter. After I'd received a harsh dressing down by my grandfather, Dad, who was soft-spoken and never quick to anger, had whisked me aside and reassured me everything would blow over.

This, though, would not blow over.

I forced some bile back down and steadied my nerves.

Sitting in the chair my father had vacated, I took Kat's hand in mine. She stirred and slowly opened her good eye.

"Hi there," I said.

She blinked.

Carefully, I lifted her hand to my mouth and kissed it. "I love you, Kit Kat."

She burst into tears, grimacing from the pain.

That was the moment I lost it too. Our tears wet the pillow as Kat tugged me to the crook of her neck.

***

It was three o'clock in the morning, but I refused to close my eyes. When I did, I pictured Charlotte in her mahogany casket, her tiny body shrouded in satin, as if she was just sleeping.

Forever.

I bolted upright in bed.

Kat lay on her side, clutching a pillow. Her furrowed brow and restlessness led me to believe her sleep was troubled, and even though her injuries hadn't healed, I imagined the source of discomfort resulted from similar images running through her mind.

I kissed Kat's cold forehead, soaked with perspiration, and tried closing my eyes, only to be haunted again by Charlotte's image. Her perfectly formed body, never taking a single breath of air. All of her tiny fingers, none of which ever had a chance to grip mine. The hollowness inside as her casket was lowered into the frozen ground.

My eyes snapped open, and a singular thought flew through my mind. Run.

I needed to run, to keep moving, or the memories would never leave me in peace.

In the bathroom, I changed into thermal running pants and a fleece jacket, not thinking, just doing. I had to run.

Outside, no one stirred on our street. No cars. No people. No signs of life.

Some houses still had Christmas lights twinkling, and I made a mental note to set up a time to help Old Man Henderson remove his, like I did every year.

I loped off toward the reservoir. Vapor seeped from my mouth, but at least the cold hadn't yet infiltrated my skin or my boots as my feet crunched through freshly fallen snow.

Numb. I'd been numb for weeks. Since the hospital. Yesterday, the sun had blared down on me as I walked to and from the university. Yet it wasn't until my mother greeted me at home, remarking about the weather, that it had dawned on me it hadn't been dark out. Both Mom and Barb had been switching off staying at the house to help me with Kat. I'd been encased in darkness for days on end, and I didn't see any end in sight. Perhaps, I didn't want to see one. Darkness—I craved it. So did Kat, who hadn't decamped from our bedroom since the funeral.

Moonlight skittered along the water's surface as I completed the first mile and a half lap. "Go away!" I shouted at the shimmer. "Leave me be!"

The moon ignored my plea.

I lowered my beanie, nearly covering my eyes completely, and ran six more laps.

***

Inside the house, light streamed from the kitchen.

"Kat?" I whispered.

Barbara appeared around the corner. It was her turn to stay over, helping out simply by being present. "Cori, what are you doing up?"

"I went for a run," I said as if it was perfectly normal to run at this time of day. "Why are you up?"

"I thought I heard Kat cry out."

I started down the hallway, but she pulled me back.

"No, don't wake her. She settled down. I didn't even have to go into the room."

I wilted against the wall in the front room. "I don't know what to do, how to ease the pain for her."

"Ease the pain? I don't think that's possible for either of you." She motioned for me to take a seat on the couch. "She needs time. That's all we can give her." She eyed my running gear. "How long did you run? Your clothes are soaked."

I shrugged, checking the digital clock on the DVD player. It was after five. It'd been well over an hour. I should have been exhausted, but all I wanted to do was go back out. Keep on running.

Chapter One

"You ready, Kat?" Mom's shrill voice hollered from the front room.

Kat's head emerged from our bedroom. As she inserted a dangling earring into her left lobe, she said, "Two minutes."

"What's on today's agenda?" I asked Mom.

"Massages, manis and pedis. You want to go?" She jammed an elbow into my side.

"Thanks, but I have plans with Sam and Lucy." My eyes roved to the front window, where a Christmas tree should have been standing. Neither Kat nor I had the heart to set it up this year. "Besides, I need to shower." I tugged my running shirt away from my skin.

"How many days in a row now?"

"Close to a year."

"You run even in the snow?"

I nodded.

Mom's beady eyes darted around the room, as if she was trying to find a way to tell me the truth—the truth about the running and about the darkness I'd never be able to escape.

I placed a hand on her shoulder to let her off the hook. On some level, my brain had grappled with the knowledge, but I didn't know how to stop. Couldn't stop.

"Okay, I'm ready." Kat brushed her lips against my cheek. "Let me know if you're going to be late for dinner at Barb's tonight."

"Will do. Have fun."

A horn blared outside.

Mom rolled her eyes. "I think Barb is demanding we get the lead out."

Kat rammed one arm through her pea coat and then the other. "Ever so subtle." She blew me a kiss.

I had an hour to kill before my lunch date, but my feet remained rooted to the floor. I was unable to tear my eyes off the empty window, and my mind off what the emptiness symbolized. I hugged my chest with both arms and got an unexpected whiff of my running clothes. Time to shower.

After a quick rinse, I wandered through the house in my bathrobe. The nursery, untouched since last year, didn't have a speck of dust. All of the onesies were neatly folded and powdered in the drawers. That didn't surprise me, even though I'd never witnessed Kat cleaning Charlotte's room. A breeze worked its way through the room, jingling the mobile over the crib. I gazed out the window, where Kat and I had planted an apple tree the day we'd found out she was pregnant with a girl. It was to provide our daughter with privacy. Apple trees symbolized youth, happiness, and health. I let out an anguished sigh and flipped the light off.

In Kat's studio, several works in progress were propped up on easels. In the past, her paintings always had a frantic but colorful, hopeful vibe. The ones before me were reminiscent of Goya's black paintings, although not as bleak. At least there wasn't one of Satan devouring his son, but Charlotte's loss existed in every dark brushstroke that slashed across the canvas. Not all were dreary—only the ones she was prepping for an upcoming show. It was as if she needed to proclaim to the world how much she hurt, even without uttering a word. Kat was Bostonian to the core. Her strength helped me face each and every day, but I knew she was in silent agony.

My phone buzzed, reminding me about my lunch plans.

***

Samantha Clarke and I sat in our usual rickety booth for four in Mulligan's, an Irish sports pub in the heart of Boston, where we'd been meeting every Sunday. The Pats pregame was on two of the three screens directly behind Sam's bouncy blonde head. SportsCenter was on the third. I focused on the ticker that listed the games for week fifteen. My brain was constantly glomming onto things it could understand, like team names, kickoff times, rankings—anything but *why did my daughter have to die before she even had a chance to smile or laugh at least once?*

"Do you want to go someplace less... cheerful?" Sam's sincere amber eyes tormented me.

Moments earlier, a herd of runners dressed in Santa suits for a charity event had swarmed the pub, eager for brewskies to slake their thirst and maybe to dull the soreness of running in fifteen-degree weather, minus the wind chill. The Santas had racing numbers pinned to their costumes and their faces were scarlet from the cold and the blustering wind gusts off the Atlantic.

"What? No." The carols on the radio and the blinking Christmas lights along all the walls were an excruciating reminder of what had occurred the previous year, and the Santa invasion amplified it—not that I would admit that aloud, though. "We've watched every game this season here." My eyes scanned the cheerfulness. "It's okay…" My mouth and brain ceased cooperating.

"How's Kat doing?"

I sighed and tried to smile, which I feared looked more like a grimace. "It's harder on her."

It'd been nearly a year since we'd buried our daughter, Charlotte. I rubbed my forehead in an attempt to blot out the memory of the tiny casket. Baby-sized caskets are an evil abomination; they should not exist.

My thoughts flashed back to cradling Kat's broken body in my arms as Charlotte vanished into the ground. The sense of hopelessness swirling around the two of us, the smattering of cold snowflakes that never reached the ground.

"I suspect it's hard on both of you." Sam hoisted a pint glass to her pink, glossy lips, observing me with sympathetic eyes. I could tell she was trying to figure out how far to push me. I still hadn't opened up much, even to my closest friend.

Tears formed. "Would you excuse me?" I blurted before making a beeline for the restroom.

I hid in a stall and wiped my eyes. Taking several deep breaths, I tried to bully my resolve. I was here to cheer on the

Pats with Sam and her girlfriend Lucy, not to have a breakdown. *Come on, Cori. Be strong.* I blew my nose on the coarse toilet paper, straightened my black Polo sweater, and fled the confines of the graffiti-covered stall, stepping over pools of suspect liquid and half-disintegrated tissues that were smeared into the gray cement floor. Before the accident, I'd never set foot in such a mess. But I'd been finding myself hiding a lot, and in increasingly darker places. My nightmares forced me out of bed at all hours, seeking anywhere that would keep my mind busy.

Lucy had arrived during my absence. She stood and gave me a quick hug, the scent of her rose-petal perfume invading my nose. I didn't wrap my arms too tightly around the skinny brunette, afraid my gangly but strong arms would sever Sam's girlfriend in half. Lucy ended the hug with a peck on my cheek, something out of the norm for the reserved novelist of conspiracy thrillers, who spent most of her days locked up in her office, alone with her Mac. It seemed that no one, not even the off-the-charts intelligent Lucy, knew how to handle the situation.

The situation—had I really just referred to Charlotte's death that way? The callous ploys and mental gymnastics I had to utilize to survive day after day made me shudder.

"Shall we order a pitcher of PBR and a shitload of greasy food?" Sam rubbed her palms together in a brave effort to pull me out of my funk.

"Yes!" Lucy and I said in unison.

When suffering, eat and drown your sorrows in cheap booze and food. The girls had been dragging me out of the house at least once a week to do just that. Before the accident, we'd met regularly, but now, the meetings were like clockwork and I'd come to rely on them. Kat wasn't your typical dyke. She abhorred sports, despite showing an interest lately, for my benefit. My mom and aunt had been taking her out for pampering while I let my inner-jock out in an effort to escape the darkness for a few hours.

"What'd you think? Will the Pats win the Super Bowl two years in a row?" Lucy asked, while Sam ordered at the bar.

I nodded, appreciating her attempt to divert the conversation from reality. My reality, at least. Sports had become the safe topic for the three of us. Several years ago, the Red Sox had played a role in rekindling my friendship with Sam, a former high school classmate, and now any sport was preserving my sanity. The other day, Kat had wandered into my office and found me watching synchronized swimming on YouTube. I was taking it almost as seriously as the competitors were.

I used any method I could to keep it together. I had to, for Kat's sake. Or so I kept telling myself.

Sam returned and launched full-force into debating the Pats' odds.

"Carolina is strong this season." I stopped nibbling on a hangnail for a moment to toss out that nugget.

Lucy shoved her tortoiseshell glasses back in place. "Where in the hell did the Panthers come from this year? I can't remember the last time they were still involved in the conversation after week three."

Sam tapped the tip of her nose. "Who knows?"

A server set a large platter and a pitcher of beer in the middle of our table and then forced her way past another wave of Santas, who'd just finished the race. This pub, on normal days at least, was spacious, even when every table was taken. Today was anything but normal. Christmas was right around the corner, the end of the NFL season was quickly approaching, and then there were the Santas—even one with an inflatable palm tree. That couldn't have been easy to run with in the howling wind.

"What's up with Harold? I heard there's a new girl in the picture. Did he and Amber break up?" I dipped a fried cheese stick into the ranch dressing.

Sam bit her upper lip in an attempt to stop her mouth from twisting into a grin. She placed both hands on the table, indicating the importance of the conversation. "Harold, Amber, and new-girl Simone have officially become a throuple."

"Throuple?" Lucy poured beer into a spotty pint glass; Mulligan's was not known for its cleanliness.

More Santas joined the throng of other red-suited runners behind us. Several did chest bumps, and a couple of them stumbled into the back of the booth, but Lucy managed not to spill a drop from the pitcher as she refilled my glass.

Sam glared over her shoulder but then relaxed into a smile. "Hey, Rick. I didn't know you were running today."

Rick raised a glass victoriously. "Just finished. You should join us next year. The company has a team."

"Really? Send me an email."

Sam and Rick nodded to each other as a way of ending the conversation.

I pantomimed for Sam to continue about throuples.

She rolled her eyes. "What, you haven't encountered throuples in any of the British novels you teach?"

"Not to my knowledge. Unless you mean the Bronte sisters," I said without thinking.

She covered her mouth so she wouldn't spew her beer. "Nope—not unless Charlotte, Emily, and Anne were in a committed sexual relationship with each other." She shrugged and then ripped apart a buffalo wing dripping with blue cheese.

I tried not to focus on the name Charlotte. I sipped my beer to wash away the memory. It took several seconds before I said, "Who would have thought? When I met Harold, he was a twenty-something virgin living with his mom. Now he's the hippest one out of the group—hipper than Kat, and I never thought anyone could outdo my wife."

Both of them fidgeted, picking up on the warble in my voice. I sensed Sam was mentally kicking herself for mentioning the name Charlotte. It was no secret Kat had named our daughter after the author. Handmade wooden animal puzzles, in the shape of letters, still spelled out the name on the dresser in the nursery.

Lucy gnawed on her bottom lip, and Sam quirked an eyebrow, imploring her girlfriend to divert the conversation to safer waters. "If you ask me"—Lucy paused for a sip of PBR—"the throuple is doomed to fail. Please pass the ketchup."

I scooted the sticky plastic Heinz bottle, which had clearly been refilled repeatedly, across the table.

"Why's that?" Sam forked a jalapeno from the nachos and popped it in her mouth.

"Harold's head over heels in love with Amber. Sure, it'll be exciting for the first few weeks, but can sexual exploration sustain a loving and equal relationship among three individuals? It's hard enough having two people in a relationship—the compromises, tiffs, misunderstandings, and such." Lucy immersed a cheese stick in the ketchup. It made my stomach lurch, but Lucy loved ketchup on almost everything. She even put it on Kraft Macaroni and Cheese, which was truly repugnant in my opinion.

"Sexual exploration?" Sam giggled, but I wondered whether it was forced, considering the angry glint in her eye when she glanced at Lucy.

It was my time to divert the conversation. "How'd they meet this Simone?"

"Your mom's erotic book club, where else?" Sam's wicked smile worked wonders on a Santa who was passing the table. The Mrs. Claus on his arm noticed and pummeled his shoulder. Ignoring them both, Sam added, "She's a librarian."

Sam meant Simone, not my mother, Nell Tisdale. Mom and Kat had formed the erotic book club before Kat and I married, and I still wholeheartedly believed they'd only done so to get under my skin. It had worked then, and it still worked today.

The club had halted for many months after the accident. Kat recovered physically within weeks, but it was closer to six months before she was mentally on the road to dealing with the loss. We hadn't made love all that winter and most of the spring. When we finally broke through the barrier, we realized we only experienced sparks of life during those intimate moments.

"Of course she is. Harold has probably had a million wet dreams about librarians. What does she look like?" I asked.

Sam pulled an iPhone out of her back jeans pocket, fiddled with it for two seconds, and then whirled it around on the laminated tabletop for me to have a look-see.

"Jesus!" I whistled. "Harold's my hero." In the photo, Harold had his arms around two women. Amber, the paralegal Kat had fixed Harold up with years ago, was attractive in a mousy kind of way. But Simone's image conjured up nonsensical phrases, such as *bada bing.* She was blonde, curvaceous, and drenched in sex appeal.

"I know, right?" Sam grinned.

"She looks familiar." I stretched my fingers on the screen to enlarge the photo.

"*Married with Children* ring a bell?" Sam asked.

I snapped my fingers. "Yes. Christina Applegate, but not as slutty—on the show, I mean. Or…" I swiped the photo to enlarge it even more. "Slutty with a touch of class."

Lucy shook her head. "Still, I give it two months."

"Even if that's the case, it'll be the best sixty days of Harold's life." Sam glanced at me out of the corner of her eye and winked. I suspected she didn't want Lucy to see, to avoid a "discussion" later that night. Sam had confessed to me last week that "discussions" were happening regularly.

The Santas erupted into a jolly cheer, and my eyes briefly hunted for Rudolph, until I realized the Pats had scored a touchdown.

The three of us clinked our glasses and took healthy swigs.

"Do we get to meet Simone?" I asked.

Lucy snorted, which was her signal it was time to move on to a new topic. I wondered about the level of trouble in paradise. All couples experienced ups and downs, true, but was I witnessing the beginning of the end? Again. They'd been broken up when Sam and I had reconnected a few years back.

"I'll ask Harold the next time I see him. Maybe he'll bring both girls to our Christmas soiree this Saturday."

"About that—"

Sam shot a palm into the air. "Nice try, but you're coming. It's our first holiday party, and we're hoping it will become tradition. You are one of my oldest and dearest friends, so you have to be there." She brandished a half-eaten wing in my face. "Oops, sorry," she said, dropping it back onto the plate, clearly having remembered I was a vegetarian.

Lucy shot Sam an admonishing look that would wilt most people's resolve, but not Sam's. Sam had a smile that'd charm the horns off Satan, and she carried on grinning.

"I'm not trying to wiggle out of it. Kat asked me to casually inquire what we should bring, even though the invite says only our *presence* is required, not 'presents.' Cute." I made quote marks. "So how about it?"

"This is your definition of casual?" Sam smiled.

I hoisted one shoulder. "I'm not good at fishing for intel. That's usually my wife's department."

"True." Sam leaned over conspiratorially and half whispered behind a hand, "I won't refuse a bottle of Dom."

I laughed. "Duly noted."

Lucy's mouth dangled open.

"What? I was just kidding," Sam said, not meaning a word.

Luckily, another torrent of cheers distracted Lucy. The Pats had intercepted the Titans on their five-yard line.

The interception roused Lucy's mood, and Sam volunteered to order another pitcher from the greasy-haired and overly tattooed bartender. Moments later, she returned with the pitcher and a tray of tequila shots.

"Does anyone need training wheels?" She gesticulated to three lime wedges and a saltshaker.

"Training wheels?" I scoffed. "If Harold is man enough to be in a throuple, I can at least do a proper shot of tequila." I boosted my shot glass, waiting for Sam and Lucy.

Lucy eyeballed the wedges. Clearly losing her nerve, she admitted she needed the lime and salt to make the Mexican liquor more palatable.

We tossed them back, each of us waving our arms and puckering our lips at the sourness.

"Yowsers! No more shots. I have my weekly family dinner tonight at my aunt's." I pushed the shot glass toward the end of the table. Even the smell was unsettling.

"Can you ask your mom what book they're reading next month?" Sam fluttered her lashes.

"Since when did you join The Smut Patrol?"

"Wow, you really don't approve of the group, do you?" Lucy asked with wide eyes.

"That's the name of the group, actually." Sam came to my rescue.

"Really, I expected it to be—"

"Less obvious?" I interjected.

"Yes, and clever, considering your mom's literary awards." Lucy ran her finger along the top of her glass, and I had a vision of her developing a mania for making music with water glasses.

"Mom has always preached that writers should ignore the hundred-dollar word for the more effective one that everyone knows the meaning of."

"So, slutty instead of salacious?" Lucy swallowed a jalapeno pepper smeared in ketchup. "She'd get along great with my editor."

"Mine too."

"I don't know how you two do it." Sam motioned to me with her drink, and then to Lucy. "It takes me hours to craft a simple work email, yet you two crank out books. When's your next one coming out, Cori?" She drunkenly slurped her beer.

"February." My publisher wanted to release it before the holidays, but I had my agent push it back. This wasn't the time to hit the road promoting a novel. No way could I abandon Kat to deal with the one-year anniversary alone.

"Harold says it's your best yet. Very *Bell Jar*-like."

I laughed, ignoring the comparison to Plath's masterpiece. "Harold's paid to say that." After the success of my first release, I'd hired Harold, the ultimate book nerd with an amazing Twitter following, as my assistant.

"Trust me, Harold doesn't lie when it comes to books."

"What does he lie about?" I separated a portion of cheesy fries. Strings of gooeyness elongated before snapping off and kinking back to the greasy mound on the plate. Harold was prone to exaggeration, but deep down, he was a kind and simple man.

"Usual guy stuff."

I lived mostly among women, except for my father and uncle; luckily, they both shielded me from men talk most of the time, unless you counted sports. Harold didn't really count as a man's man in my book, prompting me to query, "Which is?"

"Gosh, you're such a super-dyke sometimes. You know—conquests, penis size—stuff that matters to them. Maybe you and Kat should consider a throuple. Expand your horizons." Sam waggled her brows. "What about Clementine?"

I nearly choked on my beer when Sam mentioned Clementine, but I quickly spat out, "Puh-lease. No way would I share a woman like Kat. Besides Clementine isn't a dude."

"Who is *she*?" Sam pushed.

Lucy shifted in her seat.

Weeks ago, Sam had eavesdropped on a private conversation between Kat and me, and since then she had been trying to figure out who or what Clementine was. Her pursuit was useless: Clementine was a secret weapon that even my sexually confident wife would never reveal.

My glare silenced Sam's fishing expedition. Instead, she focused on the conversation at hand. "Harold's sharing Simone," she countered.

"Only because he met her after falling for Amber, who popped Harold's cherry, by the way."

Lucy indicated she wanted Sam to let her out of the booth. "I need to pee."

When the restroom door closed, I asked, "What's going on with you two?"

"Well, she hasn't come out and said it, but I think Lucy suspects I'm having an affair."

"Really? Why?" I wanted to kick myself for putting Sam on the spot and for inserting myself into the middle of their relationship. It was none of my beeswax.

Sam squirmed in her seat. "Let's meet for lunch this week. Does tomorrow work?"

Was that why Sam brought up Clementine and the throuple? To make having an affair seem like something everyone did? If that was Sam's agenda, she was barking up the wrong tree. Clementine wasn't a threat to my marriage.

I nodded and tried to extinguish any trace of guilt from my face. I wasn't the one who was cheating. Allegedly. Lucy must have espied my efforts to obliterate all judgment from my features, because she paused outside the bathroom door for a moment before returning to our booth.

Cheating was a topic that plagued my family. Not that I'd ever cheated, nor had Kat. It wasn't in her DNA. But Uncle Roger was more promiscuous than Tiger Woods, even if that was a closely kept family secret.

Sam stood and Lucy scooted into the booth. She had a thing about sitting in the corner.

"What I'd miss?" Lucy asked.

"N-nothing. Why?" I stammered.

"Because the score is different." Lucy pointed to the TV above my head with a scowl.

"Oh, that. The Pats scored"—I glanced at the screen above Sam and Lucy and made a quick calculation—"a field goal."

Sam's tight smile didn't alleviate the tension. We all drank beer, not looking at each other, staring at the television screens.

Chapter Two

"Cori, want to shoot some hoops?" Roger pounced soon after Kat and I arrived for the weekly family dinner.

My uncle had introduced me to basketball when I was a kid. It turned out to be my sport. A knee injury in college meant I hadn't played much after graduation, except for an occasional game of horse with Roger.

The path and half court had been cleared of snow, which wasn't normally the case this time of year. The edges of the court were lined with small hedges that were buried under half a foot of snow. The effort put into shoveling the court was proof positive I was about to receive one of Roger's pep talks.

"How are you doing?" Roger's three-point shot was all net. He hiked up the sleeves of his cashmere sweater, revealing defined forearms. His black down vest remained zipped, though, and I wondered whether he wore tights or bike shorts under his corduroy pants, restricting his movement, since they made a *zip-zip* sound with each step.

"Nice!" I said, referring to his bucket, and dribbled the ball to shoot from where Roger had just scored. I planted my feet, raised my arms, and released. It was even prettier than Roger's basket.

Roger retrieved the ball, tucked it under his right arm, and with a stern frown, prodded me to answer.

"I'm okay. I promise." I put two palms up.

"I hear you aren't sleeping. And from the bags under your eyes, you haven't been for quite some time."

Kat worked with my aunt at the studio, and it didn't take a relationship expert to divine Barbara probably received a daily report about anything and everything under the Tisdale-Finn roof.

I looked down at my Nikes. "I… I'm working on it."

"Has your doctor given you sleeping pills?" Roger dribbled to the free throw line and the ball effortlessly banked against the board and sailed through the hoop.

"In the beginning. She's worried about addiction, though. On the bright side, I'm getting a lot of writing done. Two novels in eleven months." I smiled half-heartedly.

"How about Kat?" He tossed me the ball.

I bounced it a few times. "It's killing me. She's trying to put on a brave face, but I see it."

"I wish I could say it gets easier, but it doesn't. Not really. The pain never goes away." Roger motioned for me to pass him the ball. I did, and he tried a hook shot à la Kareem. The ball ricocheted off the rim and landed in my waiting arms.

It wasn't the first time I'd been told the heartache never disappears; truth be known, hearing it didn't spark a lightbulb moment. Instead, it solidified my fears. *I'll never recover.* Of course, no one in my circle wanted to hear that, so I never confirmed their fears.

"Some days are better than others. This month, though… I can't escape reminders of the time…" I let my voice trail off.

Roger concentrated on the hoop, and I studied his handsome face, his profile marred only by a crooked nose, broken during his boxing days. "Barbara and I suffered four miscarriages in seven years."

I was about to shoot, but I lowered my arms and cradled the ball. "I didn't know that. I thought she couldn't get pregnant."

He shrugged. "Back then, people didn't talk about it. Still don't, really. Even now it's still difficult to remember. Maybe I should have talked about it with you earlier, helped you understand." His distraught eyes didn't leave mine, and I wondered what the confession would help me with. Dealing with my loss or understanding the reason for his infidelities? "I won't tell you to get over it, but I will say you need to get back into the game. Not just for you. Kat needs you. This family needs you."

I nodded. "I know." My voice cracked. "The guilt from that night. If I'd been there—"

His hand waved through the air. "No. You can't do that to yourself. It was not your fault. Not Kat's either. Someone else made an awful decision on an icy night that had a terrible—"

He stopped himself from saying *consequence*. It was almost as cold as me referring to Charlotte as *the situation.*

The other driver had never been found, and no witnesses had come forward either. It left me with no one else to blame —only myself.

Roger's cell phone buzzed, saving both of us from continuing the thread. He peeked at it, momentarily looking pissed, but then his easygoing grin slid back into place. He put a hand on my shoulder. "If you ever need to talk, I'm always here for you." He freed the ball from my grasp and attempted another skyhook. This time it was nothing but net. "I better put the steaks on the grill. How do you like your veggie burger cooked?" He winked. It was his usual joke regarding my vegetarianism, and it was his way of telling me he'd said his piece.

It was time for me to act human again. Responsible. Time to stop running.

"Crisp," Kat answered him, appearing around the corner.

"One crispy veggie burger coming up." Roger patted Kat's shoulder as he breezed past.

"Did you two get a chance to talk?" My wife slumped against the pole supporting the hoop.

I laughed. "Apparently, a little birdie said I wasn't sleeping."

"Those damn birds. Can't trust them." Kat crossed her arms over her expansive chest. Her long, silky raven hair was tucked behind her ears, and she wore a deep-plum hand-knitted hat.

"You know, Harold's started calling beautiful girls 'birds.' The other day, he bumped my arm and said, 'Check out the fit bird at seven o'clock.'"

Kat laughed. "Was the woman hot?"

I nodded, and she punched my arm playfully.

"He's been watching tons of British television shows and reading more English authors than normal. Have you noticed?"

Not answering, Kat pried the basketball from my hands and made a show of attempting a basket. It was nowhere near the hoop.

"Maybe you shouldn't wiggle your ass so much when shooting," I said with a grin.

"Maybe my intention wasn't to make a basket." Kat wheeled around and playfully nudged my shoulder with a finger. She licked her full lips.

"If your *intention* was to get my *attention*, you succeeded the moment you stepped into the light." I tweaked the drawstrings on her hooded sweater and met her eager mouth. "Have you ever thought there might be another reason I can't sleep at night?"

"Such as?" Kat put one hand on her hip and fluttered her lashes, making it nearly impossible for me to think straight.

"You'll have to wait until we get home for a thorough explanation."

She captured my lips and laid one on me. When I tried to deepen the kiss, she backpedaled.

Kat placed a cold finger against my lips. "Don't forget you promised we could stop at your aunt's studio for a bit."

"Haven't forgotten," I replied. She was shivering from the cold, so I twined an arm around her waist.

"Can you do me a favor?"

"Besides the studio favor?" I teased, burrowing my face into the crook of her neck.

"Yes."

"Anything for you. Shoot."

"You need to start sleeping." The pad of her thumb probed the black circles, as if trying to draw out the darkness. "I'm worried about you."

"Don't be, Kit Kat. I'm doing okay."

"Don't add liar to my list of concerns." She peered at me with murky, soulful eyes.

I kissed her forehead. "I love you."

***

When we waltzed back into the kitchen, my mom and Barbara stopped talking and failed miserably to banish the worry from their faces.

It made me angry. Not at them, but at me. I needed to get my shit together for everyone's sake. How hard was it to fall asleep? Even babies…

"Did Roger clean your clock?" Mom tugged on each end of her scarf, doing her best to comport herself.

"As usual," I replied with a forced smile.

"Let me put the kettle on and make you a cup of tea. Your cheeks are redder than Rudolph's nose. I told you to put on a jacket." Barbara flipped around and filled the kettle with tap water.

I wished people would stop reminding me of the time of year. Not that I thought any of them did so with malice.

Mom rubbed my cheeks and then pinched one with an evil relish in her eye. Oddly, it settled me some. Maybe I wasn't overly delicate. Leave it to my mother not to go overboard with coddling.

"So what's this top secret project Kat's working on?" Barbara asked in a flat voice, her back to me.

I peeled a slice of cheddar cheese from the silver serving platter. "Nice try."

"Foiled again." Barbara snapped her fingers. "Clients are asking when she'll have the next collection done."

"This painting is private," Kat said. She'd sworn up and down that no one would see it. "But I'm working on others. A couple at home you haven't seen yet."

"When can I pop by?" Barb asked over her shoulder.

"Any time. You know that."

I was curious to see how the public would take to the drastic change in her style. Most thought Goya mad after viewing his black paintings. I tried to imagine the press releases. Would Charlotte's death and a line about the artist reeling from the loss appear in the first or second paragraph? Of course, I'd wondered the same thing about my next novel, which had been heavily revised after the incident.

Mom and Barbara shared a conspiratorial shrug, and I sensed they'd do everything they could to get to the bottom of the mystery project. I didn't trust them. Not one bit. Secretly, I admired their grit, but I enjoyed trying to stay one step ahead.

"So, Kat tells me Harold has a new woman." Mom sipped her wine and leaned against the edge of the island. She wore a thick woolen sweater. For as long as I could remember, Roger and Barbara kept the heat low, even on the coldest winter days. Granted, it probably cost a fortune to properly heat their ten-bedroom Colonial revival home built in 1881, which Roger had inherited decades ago. Not that money was an issue. Roger was a business magnate. While he wasn't as wealthy as Warren Buffet, he wasn't too far behind the "Wizard of Omaha" either.

"Yes and no. Harold now has two women. Thanks to you." I gestured to my mother.

"What'd I do?" She put a hand on her chest and wobbled her head about as if she'd been shot.

"Formed your sex book club."

"All we do is read and discuss. Harold's responsible for his own actions," she tutted with a satisfied smirk.

"You can ask him for yourself." Kat deposited her cell into her jeans pocket. "He's on his way over."

"That doesn't sound good. What's up?"

She shrugged. "You know Harold."

I did.

"Is it Simone?" Mom steered back to her favorite topic: sex.

"Yep. What's up with this chick?" I loved Harold, but a hunch clued me in to the possibility that Simone was up to something. Harold wasn't the kind to attract a beautiful vixen.

Mom and Kat shared a worried glance.

"What?" I asked.

"I'm worried she has the hots for Amber." Kat retrieved ranch, blue cheese, and French dressing from the stainless-steel fridge door and set them next to the bowl on the counter. Every appliance was brand spanking new, giving the kitchen in the century-old home a modern feel. The rest of the house retained late nineteenth-century touches: arched ceilings, crown molding, and an abundance of fireplaces. Most of the furniture had been handed down over generations.

"Why the throuple charade, then?" I tossed my arms in the air.

"Because Amber's never been with a woman." Kat's *duh* look urged me to get with the program.

"And Simone thinks this will convert her permanently to the lesbian side, gradually awaken her lesbianism? Seems far-fetched." I stroked my chin. "Kinda brilliant, though."

Dad and Roger returned from the back deck, shivering. Mom had insisted on steaks for dinner. I wondered whether she'd done that to temporarily evict the men to the deck.

Roger hoisted a platter heaped with steaks, burgers, and my two veggie patties—crisper than crisp—over his head. "Me return from hunt." He grunted and puffed out his chest.

Barbara shook her head and smiled at her foolish husband of forty years. Mom sneered. Most of the time, she thought Roger was as classless and brutish as a caveman. I could tell she was envisioning Roger bashing a young woman over the head with a club and dragging her back to his cave.

My father, Warren Tisdale—who went by Dale—slapped Roger on the back. They'd been best buds since before Dad married Mom.

Out of all of us, Dad was the most disheveled. His Christmas sweater was a bit too snug around his expanding belly, and some of the hair on the back of his head was mussed from his Red Sox beanie.

"Cori, you excited to see the Sugar Bowl game in New Orleans?" Dad asked.

"Been counting down the days." This was another trick in my arsenal to get through the days: counting down to anything coming, a way to keep reminding myself I was still trudging forward.

He nodded. "January first isn't far away."

"It will be nice to have a few days in the sun." Dad casually tossed his hand in the air as if we traveled to college bowl games every year, which we didn't.

I pirouetted to Kat, who was grinning. She had been the one who'd come up with the idea to give me a different event to focus on. Not December twenty-fifth and not the anniversary of the accident.

Dad circled his finger. "The whole fam traveling together —it'll be like the Griswolds."

I laughed. "Let's hope we're nothing like the Griswolds."

"Oh, I don't know. Roger can fly on top of the plane, Aunt Edna style," Mom said with zero irony in her tone.

"But Aunt Edna was dead," I said.

"That could be arranged." Mom laughed. Barbara gave her a menacing stare, and Roger simpered. He was used to my mother's abuse, so hardly anything she or anyone else said stung. I wished I had his thick skin. I had known all my life about his sister and parents dying so many years ago, but I was still processing the bombshell he'd shared on the basketball court.

Kat kissed me and then whispered in my ear, "It's the perfect gift for my favorite jock. Now all you have to do is sleep, or you'll be put on the naughty list."

"Does that involve Kat-style torture?" I quirked one eyebrow at her.

She walloped my arm, but I zeroed in on the desire in her eyes.

"I'll take that as a yes," I said and stroked her cheek.

"Roger, can you throw another steak on the grill, please? Harold's joining us." Barbara smiled sweetly.

"Yes, Roger. Back outside. Be a good boy." Mom shooed him to the door, as if commanding the family dog.

"Of course, my love." His gaze landed on Barb's, ignoring his sister-in-law who stood three feet away. I had to admire his skill at brushing off my mother. Nell Tisdale wasn't easily ignored.

***

Harold arrived right as Roger came inside with his steak. Barb had kept the rest of the food warm in the oven. I met Kat's eyes. Harold had a sixth sense when it came to food, always showing up at the most opportune moments.

"How's it hanging, Harold?" Roger coiled an arm around his shoulders. Harold had become a de facto family member a few years back. During the past year, his presence had become even more frequent.

"To the left," he replied, blushing as he swiped his dishwater brown hair out of his eyes.

Mom hefted an eyebrow, and Kat laughed into her hand, initiating a belly laugh from Roger.

"I got us a new after-dinner drink." Roger poked his elbow into Harold's side.

Harold's pallor turned slightly green. Roger, a whiskey man, had been trying to broaden Harold's drinking choices. Lately, Harold had been on a Smirnoff Ice kick, a beverage I was certain my uncle had never sampled until Harold brought a six-pack in watermelon flavor two weekends ago. To his credit, my manly uncle drank one without complaint.

My mind doubled back to my conversation with Roger earlier—the four miscarriages. Was that why he'd always acted like a parent to me, to Kat, and now to Harold? Was it a need that had gone unfulfilled for so many years? So many heartbreaks? Perhaps that was also the source of his countless infidelities, filling a hole that never could be filled. Did Barb understand that? Was that why she'd turned a blind eye for almost four decades of marriage?

Kat leaned her head on my shoulder. "A penny for your thoughts."

"Later."

Her finger snaked down the side of my face. "Oooh. I won't forget to cash in."

I ringed her waist with my arm and walked us into the dining room. A place had already been set for Harold.

Everyone took a seat, immediately passing all the side dishes and salad bowl.

"How have you been, Harold?" Barbara dipped an artichoke leaf into a creamy Parmesan sauce.

He shifted in his seat. "Good. You?"

"Uh-oh. Out with it." I motioned with a hand to lay it out on the table.

"Now?" He eyed his fillet.

"Cori!" Barbara admonished. "No business during dinner. Let the man enjoy his steak."

I groaned. "Is it business related?" I leveled my eyes on Harold, who nodded. "Pass the broccoli, please."

Mom handed me the bowl with a taunting smile. I stuck my tongue out at her. Barbara cleared her throat. "Children."

Harold grinned triumphantly.

"Enjoy your last meal," I mumbled into my napkin. His eyes widened, and he rotated to Barbara, who luckily didn't hear. Score one for me!

"Where's Amber tonight?" Roger bit into a burger, and a trickle of grease dribbled down his chin.

I loved that my family sat in the formal dining room with China plates, silver cutlery, a fancy tablecloth, and a centerpiece befitting George Washington, to enjoy all meals, including hamburgers.

"Out with the girls." Harold puffed out his chest.

"Girls?" Kat pushed.

"Simone and some of her coworkers from the library."

"Why didn't you go out with them?" Kat tapped her newly manicured fingernails on the base of her wineglass.

He pointed his steak knife at my chest with disappointed eyes.

"I ruined your night out with the girls?" I placed a hand on my chest.

"You ruined my week. This may take days to clean up."

"Geez, just tell me. Put me out of my misery."

"Candace Sams."

"What about her?"

Mom's eyes narrowed. "You didn't!"

Harold nodded vigorously.

"Didn't what?" I tossed my napkin onto my half-eaten veggie burger.

"You got into an online battle with a troll," he said, slicing off another chunk of sirloin.

I blinked. Had Harold finally lost his mind and disappeared into a Neil Gaiman fantasy novel?

Kat cleared her throat. "Can someone fill me in on Candace Sams?"

"She was an author who responded to a one-star review on Amazon, posing as another reviewer, not the author of the book. When she was discovered, she claimed she'd reported all the haters to the FBI, as if disparaging a book was a federal crime." Mom shook her head. "Every author knows never ever to respond to a bad review or a troll."

I nodded in agreement.

Her eyes narrowed further, cat-like. "Then why'd you pull a Candace Sams?"

"I didn't." I rapped my spoon on the tablecloth.

Harold ran from the room and returned with his iPad. "Then who is Finndale? Seriously, didn't you read the blog post by Gaiman about Sams years ago?"

"How do you fit Gaiman into every conversation? But to answer your question, I have absolutely no idea about Finndale."

"It's a mash-up of our last names." Kat's voice contained a hint of accusation.

"Still doesn't mean I did it. Besides, don't ya think if I was trying to con the world, I'd come up with a better identity? I'm not a full-fledged moron."

"So you didn't belittle this person on Twitter who attacked your mom's latest book?"

"Me? Who attacked me?" Mom signaled for the tablet. Her jaw dropped, and then she read aloud: *"When a subpar author decides to write serious fiction, it falls flat and is a complete waste of space in all libraries and on bookshelves."* She tsked. "Who wrote this?"

"G-Dawg," Harold said.

"G-Dawg! I'm supposed to take criticism from someone named G-Dawg seriously?" She adjusted in her seat.

Roger coughed into his napkin.

Harold shrugged. "I always advise clients to avoid getting into pissing contests on social media."

"Clients," I scoffed. "All of your clients are at this table."

"I signed another author last week," he crowed.

"Really? Who?"

"Lucy."

I laughed. "Basically still in the family."

"Neither here nor there." His brows met in the middle.

"Cori, focus." Mom turned to Barb. "What should we do?"

"Can we ignore it?" Barb asked Harold.

"A couple of book bloggers have latched onto the story. One is a buddy of mine, and she reached out for comment before publication. Some Twitter users have weighed in, but not any heavy hitters. The conversation has spiraled and claims Cori got a publishing contract because of Nell."

"But I thought G-Dawg said I was subpar? Doesn't make sense." Mom closed one eye.

"There's one bright spot, though." Harold met my eyes. "A book blogger—granted one unknown to me and who only has a handful of views—has rushed to Cori's defense, claiming Cori would never be so stupid to concoct such an obvious nom de plume."

"At least someone is on my side."

"Unfortunately, the haters think this blogger, In the Shadows, may also be Cori. The blogger is a super fan. She claims literature didn't fully exist until Cori penned her first novel. However, some argue In the Shadows refers to how Cori feels about being eclipsed by Nell."

"Man, I just can't catch a break. The one person who comes to my aid is nuttier than fruitcake and I won't even respond to the bogus shadows comments." Ever since high school people had been saying this about me.

"In the Shadows, G-Dawg, and Finndale—people are hiding behind fictitious names. For all we know, it's one puppet master fucking with Cori." Roger shifted in his seat.

"Are you suggesting an angry ex?" Barb asked.

"I was the one who was usually dumped for being too independent or busy with activities, especially in school. Kat's been with me most of my adult life."

"And I thought you were way too independent, at first. Luckily I tamed that aspect." She winked.

"Psychoanalyzing Cori could take years. Right now, let's focus on this problem." Barb made eye contact with Roger.

"I think we should zero in on the pot-stirrer G-Dawg," Roger said.

"I'm with Barb. Can't we ignore it? Sounds like blogger-Dawg isn't a big fish in the social media pond, since the story hasn't caught fire," I said.

Harold released a frustrated sigh over my social media disdain. "So far, it hasn't, but my fear is that it'll become a garden-variety social media lynching unless we jump in front of the story to stop it from becoming anything memorable. The last thing you want is for this controversy to appear on your Wiki page and in all upcoming media interviews and spotlights."

"How bad has it gotten so far?" Barbara motioned for Harold to fill us in completely.

He remained quiet.

"Come on. I can take it."

Every pair of eyes at the table focused on me and then on Harold.

"I haven't finished my steak yet." Harold fashioned his cutlery in his hand as if expecting a frontal assault.

"Wise man," Barbara bellowed. "After you finish, can you reach out to your blogger buddy? Find out if she'd like an exclusive on the Finndale scandal? Get in front of the social media train, as you say?"

Harold nodded.

"Would it be wise to reach out to the other blogger, In the Shadows? Cori's new super fan?" Kat posed the question to Barb. "Maybe this person isn't completely crazy."

"Might be wise to make tentative overtures, but not a full-court press." Barb paused for a sip of wine, or was her problem-solving mind whirring faster than the speed of social media feeds. "I need to check out the site—see if it's a true fan or some wacko. Recruiting a crazy won't help our cause in the long run. Harold, can you send me the link to the blog?"

He thumped his iPad several times. "Done."

"I need to call Floyd. See what he can dig up about G-Dawg and this fake Finndale account." Roger exited the room.

"What's for dessert?" Mom asked. "Cori's humble pie?"

"You've been sitting on that for some time, haven't you?" I downed the rest of my beer in three long swallows.

"I'm sure it'll all blow over soon. Roger's right. Floyd and Harold can help us cut it off before it gets overblown. Finish your dinner." Barbara motioned to my half-eaten burger, dismissing the conversation for the evening.

Roger returned with a tray holding a liquor bottle and seven shot glasses. "Got the pros on the matter at hand. Let's have some shots to forget the unpleasant business."

"Shots?" Harold's shoulders drooped.

Roger twisted the bottle's cap off. "Do you like black jelly beans?"

"They're my favorite." He perked up in his seat.

"Mine too. But last year I didn't get one. I think you were the reason." He waggled a finger. "Every time you came over, all of them disappeared." Roger poured from the bottle.

"Drink this, and tell me what you think." Roger circumnavigated the table, giving everyone a shot glass.

My glass had measurements ticked on the side according to four Ivy League colleges, ranking from Princeton to Dartmouth to Yale to Harvard at the top. Roger had filled mine to Princeton, the bottom rung.

"Roger, you, of all people, should know I graduated from Harvard. How many of my games did you attend?"

"Every single one." He grinned. "But until your name is cleared, you only get Princeton servings." His phone bleeped, and he turned his attention briefly to the text message.

"I'm not Finndale!"

"We only have your word, dear. And it wouldn't be the first time you'd flown off the handle. Hopefully, this episode won't amount to a hill of beans, but it'll be a good lesson." Barbara hoisted her shot glass. "To Harold, who saved the day once again!"

"Here, here," added my father.

I tossed back the Sambuca. "Jesus, that's sweet."

"Just like Harold." Kat strolled around the table and placed a sloppy kiss on Harold's cheek, earning herself an *aw shucks* grin.

"Another round?" Roger asked, shaking the bottle.

Chapter Three

Sam texted first thing Monday morning, suggesting we meet at a popular pizza joint in Cleveland Circle for lunch. It was at least a twenty-minute subway ride from the financial district, smack dab in the middle of the day, but I suspected she'd chosen it for my benefit. I rode the subway to the university and back, but when I could, I preferred getting places on my own trusty two feet. Kat, however, preferred public transportation now. I was sure her memory of that horrific day was lodged deep in a recess of her brain, hopefully never to resurface.

Cleveland Circle was a fifteen-minute walk from our home, although I ducked out an hour early and stopped off at Chestnut Hill Reservoir. I sat on a three-day old newspaper on a bench and watched a gang of geese hiss and spit at all the walkers and runners. My intention had been to read a book I'd promised to blurb for my publisher, but I failed to crack it open. I stared absently at Boston College's football stadium across the water. Scattered beer bottles poked through last night's six inches of snow. The wood was slightly damp, hence the newspaper that had been left by a previous bench-sitter. How many others had claimed this lonely spot by the side of the water on a frosty December day to contemplate this thing called life?

Most runners in sight wore long sleeves and jogging pants, except for the occasional crazy or brave one dressed only in shorts and a T-shirt. Vapor expelled from my mouth with each breath, generating a temporary trail, yet the cold hadn't set into my bones. Sometimes I toyed with the idea that the accident had left me impervious to unimportant things, like frigid temperatures. I shared this thought with Kat, who now insisted I wear a long black winter coat, beanie, scarf, and gloves—another reason I didn't bother opening the book. Gloves and turning pages didn't mesh.

It wasn't that she didn't understand. She did. Years ago, Kat had a shopping addiction that nearly brought us to financial collapse. Since the accident, she hadn't stepped foot into a store. Weeks after coming home from the hospital, I'd discovered her tossing out clothes that still had price tags attached. Roger had hauled three overstuffed thirty-gallon garbage bags off to Goodwill.

The beeping on my iPhone alerted me I had five minutes before my lunch date. After I had missed several appointments with friends and family, including a meeting with the dean of the English department, lost in my own world, Kat purchased the phone and encouraged me to maintain the calendar. She must have plugged in today's event for me, knowing I'd forget. It was another way she took care of me.

Part of me smoldered with shame that Kat insisted on babysitting me, a woman in her thirties. The other part loved her for understanding. We both needed help since that horrific day. I squeezed the bridge of my nose, willing the tears away.

With a sigh, I rose from the security of the isolated bench and ventured across the street to Cleveland Circle. My eyes wandered along the wires draped over the subway tracks and intersection. This particular juncture provided several challenges, with trains pulling in and out of the depot. Motorists heading toward the reservoir had three lanes on one side of the intersection, but only one lane on the other side, forcing assertive Bostonian drivers into a survival-of-the-fittest mentality.

I flinched when a train on the C-line screeched to a halt outside the restaurant.

Sam sat in a plastic yellow booth on the far side of the pizza joint. The place was deserted, except for two men who were frantically prepping and boxing pizzas for delivery. It was only a matter of days 'til Christmas, and the bleak weather outside kept most indoors.

"Goodness, your cheeks look like radishes. How long were you outside in this?" She motioned to the low-hanging clouds that threatened more snow.

I smiled weakly and shrugged.

"I ordered a large cheese pizza."

"Large, huh? Is it that bad?" I slipped into the seat opposite Sam, set the unread book off to the side, and shed my coat, scarf, and gloves. Compared to my lunch companion, I was severely underdressed in jeans and a ratty Harvard sweatshirt from my college days. Sam wore a brilliant white blouse and perfectly pressed navy blazer. Her blonde hair was swept neatly back into a stern ponytail, and her makeup was flawless.

"Before we discuss my mess, how are you? Harold stopped by late last night to discuss a book event with Lucy and he mentioned G-Dawg and Finndale. Everything okay?"

I shrugged. "Harold and Floyd are on it."

"Floyd?" Sam blinked.

"One of Roger's guys who steps in when things get weird. He's worked with my uncle since his politician days."

"Was he the big black guy that used to escort Roger to some of your games in high school?"

"That's him."

"Shit. I wouldn't mess with him."

"That's his purpose." I winked.

"Why would anyone believe you're Finndale? It's so obvious as to be obvious."

"Got me. Honestly, I try to stay out of the public eye. Remember that time I chased the photographer away from Charlotte's grave during one of our weekly visits to leave flowers? Floyd took care of that as well." I drummed my fingers on the tabletop.

"It's crazy. I know you're an author and your mom is super famous, but it's hard to fathom that you have to deal with these kind of invasions."

I shrugged. "Comes with the territory. Roger is also in the spotlight a lot—locally at least." I leaned on my forearms. "So tell me. What's going on?"

"I don't know what to do." She covered her face with both hands, nearly making me laugh. Out of the two of us, I looked like the one whose life was in chaos, not the well-put-together businesswoman across from me.

The shorter Italian behind the register plopped a half-closed box on the counter. Even though we made eye contact and he'd nodded for me to come get it, he slammed his hand down on the bell and yelled, "Order up!" Probably out of habit. No matter whether you ordered to go or dining in, every pizza was served in a flimsy white box.

After I returned with the pizza, two paper plates, and a plastic shaker with pepper flakes, I asked, "Is it as bad as I think?"

"Depends." Sam sprinkled pepper flakes onto a slice until all I could see were circular discs of red and yellow. "What do you think is going on?"

"Nope, not falling for that. Either tell me or don't. I'm not guessing." I tore a triangular portion and set the steaming piece on my plate, licking the grease off my semi-burnt thumb and index finger.

Sam bit into a segment, instantly coughing and covering her mouth. After a moment, she clutched a plastic bottle of orange Fanta and tossed it back as if she'd been wandering through the Sahara for days.

I waited for her to recover. "Is this some form of weird punishment? Self-flagellation via pepper flakes?"

"Maybe. I thought I could handle it."

"Famous last words. I'm sure it's not as bad as you're making it out to be. Come on, talk to me." I waggled my eyebrows. "You know you want to."

She grinned. "That was a tad pervy."

"Maybe, but it got you to smile at least." I put a hand on hers. "What's wrong?"

"Everything," Sam whispered.

I nodded and waited patiently. I'd learned when Sam needed to talk there was no stopping her.

"I haven't cheated on Lucy, if that's what you're thinking," she said in a firm tone.

"Wasn't thinking it," I lied before biting into another wedge of pizza that had just a smidgeon of pepper flakes.

"But…" She scraped some of the pepper flakes off the overly burdened slice.

I quirked an eyebrow.

She pinned me with her tawny eyes. Those eyes had captivated me in my teen years. Hell, they'd singlehandedly been the inspiration of many wonderful sexual fantasies that'd make most blush. Yet, today they were jam-packed with angst.

"I have the hots for my teacher," Sam confessed in her gravelly voice.

"Are you singing the Van Halen song, because I don't think you have the lyrics quite right. You used to sing in the choir. Surely you know the right words."

She threw a wadded up paper napkin at my face. "Don't be an ass."

"I'm sorry." I grabbed a clean napkin from the metal dispenser and handed it to her. "What teacher?"

"My tango instructor."

"You're taking tango lessons! Since when?" I chomped into a new slice.

"Last month. Lucy and I are planning a trip to Argentina next summer to visit Iguazu Falls and to explore some of their wine regions. Research for a novel idea, and I don't know… Her idea for the novel is in its infancy, but she mentioned once that the heroine could tango. I thought it would be fun to learn."

"I hear it's a mandatory requirement to acquire a visa."

She wadded up another napkin.

Before she could fire, I put my hands up in mock surrender and said, "Don't shoot."

Sam laughed. "Are you going to take this seriously?"

"I'll try. So you like this guy. When's the last time you've been with a man?"

"None of your business. And the teacher isn't a dude."

"A female tango instructor—how progressive of you."

"Geez, is someone waving a shiny object behind my head or something?" She rubbernecked over her shoulder. "Focus, Cori. I have the hots for my teacher."

"Is your instructor interested?"

"I think so."

"How'd you find a lesbian tango instructor? Is she Argentinean?"

"She is, in fact. It's amazing; lesbians can come from other countries, not just the US."

"Who would have thunk it?" I smiled. "But back to the matter at hand, are you interested in a fling or a full-blown relationship?"

"I don't know. Don't get me wrong; I love Lucy, but…"

"Something's missing?"

"I wouldn't say that. It's just that she can be so detached, logical, and unromantic. And, well…" Her eyes flittered away. "I'm a bit bored. Do you know what we did last Friday night?"

I shook my head.

"A jigsaw puzzle."

"What image?"

"Paris at night."

"That's kinda romantic."

"Going to Paris is romantic. Putting a Paris puzzle together is just... just... lame! And she's already put the puzzle together and has organized all the pieces into plastic baggies. That's totally weird, isn't it?" She waved her Fanta bottle, causing the contents to fizz.

I thought it best not to say anything.

"And the best part, we didn't finish, but the ever-prepared Lucy bought this fancy puzzle mat so we can save our progress and work on it this weekend. Oh, yay." She clapped her hands together and fluttered her lashes.

I laughed. "Looking forward to it, are you?"

Her death glare was pretty clear.

"What did you two use to do for fun?" I sipped the Coke Sam had ordered for me before I arrived.

"See movies, go dancing, hang out with friends—we were never wild and crazy, but puzzles? Are we eighty?" She put a hand on her forehead. "I'm not ready for retirement, and I don't want to act like we're living in an old people's home."

"Okay, let's go back to the original laundry list. Was she always detached?"

"Not necessarily. But romance hasn't been her strong suit —ever. She's in her head too much with her stories."

"Are you looking for more romance from her?"

She gawked over my shoulder and regarded the men making the pizzas. "I don't know. Maybe."

"And your tango instructor probably oozes romance and sex appeal. I mean, just knowing how to tango proves it."

"And other things." Sam's expression turned dreamy.

I sucked in a breath and slouched against the hard plastic booth. "I see."

"Don't say it like that."

"Like what?"

"Like I'm a bad person."

"I don't think that. Not one bit." I sat up straighter in an attempt to convince her I wasn't fibbing. Cheating was such a sensitive subject for me. My aunt and uncle had their agreement, but I witnessed their unguarded moments, and it was obvious it affected them both. I saw the suspicion in Barb's eyes every time Roger checked his phone.

"But?"

"No buts. I will caution you, though. Before you make a decision that could destroy your relationship for good, think about whether your feelings are based on love or simple lust. Lust isn't sustainable over the long term, and it does more damage than it's worth, in my humble opinion." I placed a hand over my heart.

"How do I determine that, though?"

"Got me." I ate another bite and then added, "You lost Lucy once, so remember how much it hurt. She may not be the most romantic—"

"The jigsaw proves that," she interjected.

I put a hand up for her to zip it. "But she loves you. Real love like hers is rare."

Sam sighed and stared at the half-eaten slice on her plate. "Can lust turn into love?"

"I'm sure it happens. Again, though, I have to ask are you willing to take the chance? All couples go through droughts. If relationships were easy, there'd be no need for divorce."

"Okay, Ms. Relationship Expert. The first time you slept with Kat were you in love or lust?"

"On the road to love."

"Yeah, right," she scoffed.

"Listen, I know when most see Kat all they can think of is getting her into bed. It wasn't like that with me. That's why we've lasted."

I ate in silence for a minute or two while Sam shredded a grease-stained napkin. A lone figure passed the front of the restaurant, a periwinkle scarf fluttering in the wind. The color reminded me of a periwinkle Beanie Baby from *Blue's Clues* that I'd purchased for Charlotte the day of Kat's first ultrasound. Charlotte never got the chance to choose a favorite color. Would it have been the color of her first stuffed animal?

Sam brushed aside her paper plate and rested her elbows on the table. "How do you and Kat do it?"

"Do what?" I lobbed a final bit of crust into my mouth. We had managed to devour three-quarters of the pizza. I'd done most of the damage. Good thing I went running every single day, no matter the weather or lack of sleep.

"Stay so much in love?"

"Jigsaw puzzles," I deadpanned.

She slapped my hand.

I laughed and then slouched in my seat. "It's not easy. We've had ups and downs."

Sam blanched. "I know. I wasn't saying that."

I put a hand up. "Don't worry. What I'm trying to say is relationships aren't easy. They take a lot of maintenance. For us, we've learned to talk things through and we've established only one person can have a breakdown at a time—the other has to stay strong."

"Whose turn is it now?"

"To stay strong?"

Sam nodded.

"I think Kat's." I tried to smile, but it fell before it had a chance to take. "Have you considered talking to Lucy? Let her show her strength."

"And say what? I keep having these fantasies about Inez."

That triggered a memory. "Inez Gonzales?"

"You know her?"

I palmed the top of my head. "She was one of my dance instructors years ago. God, I'd forgotten about her completely. I had so many dance instructors in my youth they've all kinda blurred together. I used to see her in dance clubs, but I haven't for years. Thought she moved." I closed my eyes. "She was in her thirties then. She's got to be pushing fifty." I reopened my eyes.

Sam folded her arms over her chest. "She's forty-five."

"I had no idea she was gay."

"Not surprising."

I shrugged off the fact that my gaydar never fully formed. "She was pretty hot back then. Got my teenage imagination going and then some." I whistled.

Sam's eyes flashed from anger to agreement and then back to anger.

"You've got it bad for her, don't you?" I asked.

"I need to get back to work."

"Don't be that way. Don't run off." I squeezed her arm.

Her body relaxed a little. "I'm not. Really, I need to get back. I lied to my assistant and said I was meeting a client for lunch."

So the lying had started. This wasn't a good sign.

"Can we talk later?" she asked.

"Of course. I'll walk you to the Reservoir stop."

After we bundled up and ambled outside, Sam hooked an arm through mine and rested her head against my shoulder. "Promise you don't hate me."

"I could never hate you, Sam. You're my best friend. No matter what." We sloshed across Beacon Street through mushy gray snow.

"But you'd never consider cheating on Kat, would you?" Sam glommed onto the handrail at the T stop as she navigated around ice patches on the concrete stairs.

I didn't answer, hoping the question was rhetorical.

We stood on the platform while the D-line train squealed to a halt. Sam climbed aboard and waved without saying anything more as I waited for it to pull away. A smattering of passengers got off and on, and within a minute, the train departed. I tarried until it was out of sight, looking like a lonely fool. But I secretly hoped I'd gotten my message across to Sam: cheating only led to a long, painful, and drawn-out good-bye.

Chapter Four

"What would you do if you thought I was cheating?" I asked Kat later that night. We were in the back of my aunt's art studio in the workroom, well after closing. Kat, wearing a tight, paint-splotched T-shirt and ripped jeans, was busily applying paint to a canvas while I reclined on a divan, thumbing through a stack of art magazines to keep my brain occupied.

"Are you confessing?" Kat, brush still in hand, peered seductively around the easel and arched a dark eyebrow in the way only she could.

I shivered.

"Sorry, I forgot." She waltzed by the metal desk next to the easel and yanked one of the four drawers all the way open. Tubes of paint, brushes, paper towels, tattered rags, coffee cups, and other odds and ends covered every square inch of the desk's surface. She'd flipped on a space heater. "Can't have my model freeze her tits off."

I rounded back to her accusation. "Come now, you know how I feel about it."

"And I thought you knew how I felt?" She repositioned herself behind the canvas.

"Good point. Rip my toenails off." I tossed a magazine on the hardwood floor and picked up the next in the pile.

"That'd be a start."

"Just a start? Yowsers!"

"Does this have anything to do with your lunch today with Sam?"

"Maybe."

"Lucy or Sam?" she asked.

"Sam. At least Sam told me Lucy suspects. She, of course, asked me to stay mum on the subject."

"Do you think she'll confess?" The easel was set up at an angle from my position, so I could only catch glimpses of Kat's brush flying across the canvas as if the paint directed where it should be placed. Kat's fearless style was doing wonders for my libido. There was something so sexy about a woman who knew what she was doing.

"I don't know. I'm having a hard time believing Sam would do such a thing. I mean, just a few years ago, she fought to get Lucy back after they separated. Why throw it away now?"

"Fought? I don't remember it that way."

"Because you were too busy imagining her chasing after me."

"I lost my head for a bit." She casually hoisted one shoulder as a way of apology.

"That's a nice way of putting it."

"How would you put it?" she asked.

"Guilty by association." I squinted at the page in the catalogue showing one of Kat's Picasso-esque paintings of a woman and a peacock. It was hard to decipher where the woman stopped and the peacock started.

Kat held her brush in midair, biting her lower lip and half closing one eye as she looked at me. If I had my phone out, I'd snap a photo. Some moments, her beauty still knocked the breath out of me.

Without apologizing or defending herself, Kat slowly pivoted her head back to the canvas.

"I can't blame you, really," I continued. "If word about Roger got out, the press would probably hound the family day and night, or at least hungry, desperate bloggers looking for a quick buck and a huge splash would. Shit, I might even be on the chopping block, given that incident at Fenway. Fingers crossed G-Dawg or Finndale—which is the evil one?"

"G-Dawg. Finndale came to your mom's defense when G-Dawg attacked. In the Shadows is your super fan. This is why Harold doesn't let you near your social media accounts—you can't keep all this straight."

"Whatever. Let's hope G-Dawg or whoever doesn't latch onto that."

"They say everyone gets their fifteen minutes of fame, but you already know that." She made no attempt to mask the smile in her voice.

"It wasn't how I imagined mine. I was hoping for something along the lines of winning a Pulitzer."

Kat's hand continued to sail over the canvas, leaving faint traces of color. "Oh, trust me, your fifteen minutes was viewed more than if you had won a literary award. I'm pretty sure SportsCenter wouldn't have aired you receiving an award."

"But getting beaned in the head with a foul ball at Fenway during a Yankees' game gets international coverage for days. And now it'll live forever on YouTube." I angrily flipped a page, nearly tearing it.

"It wasn't just you, darling. You also spilled your beer all over me, and I was wearing a white tank without a bra, if you remember."

I smiled. "Oh, I remember. I've replayed that part a million times on YouTube."

Again, she scouted around the canvas. "Perv."

"Guilty as charged. You have fabulous tits, my dear." I failed miserably to stifle a yawn.

"Goodness. How am I supposed to believe that line when you follow it up with the yawn of the millennium?" The lilt in her voice and her casual glance back at me made it clear she wasn't lacking in confidence.

"Oh, please. You know you do. And I'm more than willing to take you home and prove it. How are you coming along?"

"Just a few more minutes for tonight. You getting cold?"

Kat's new rage was nudes, and she'd enlisted me as one of her models.

"My nipples could cut glass."

"Oooh… we may have to test that. I've been considering performance art."

"Come now, I have enough bad press at the moment. I don't need the world laughing at my pitiful offerings."

"Don't ever say that about your chest. Never ever. I happen to love your itty bitties."

I laughed. "Calling them itty bitties doesn't help my self-esteem."

She manhandled her right tit with her free hand. "These are more trouble than they're worth. Just the backache alone ruins the experience."

"Good point. Of course, I happen to know a thing or two about hot oil massage."

"Hold your horses."

"I'm trying, but holding still isn't my forte. Can I have a basketball to bounce or something?"

She closed an eye, tilting her head to the ceiling. "Maybe."

"How many more sessions will you need?" I asked.

"A painting takes as long as it takes—deadlines don't mean diddly."

"So it could take many more sessions."

"I do like staring at your body."

I rolled my eyes. "Let's get back to the important thing—you warming me up. It is one of your specialties."

"And how do you propose I do that?" The teasing in her tone suggested she'd put her finger on what I desired. "Clementine, maybe?"

"Now that you mention it…" I winked.

After the accident, it took months before we could be intimate. It was as though we would smash the remnants of our souls to smithereens if we gave into our desires. Then, one night Kat had walked into the bathroom right as I stepped out of the shower. Her dark, soulful eyes had roved over my skin, without any indication whether she wanted me or couldn't handle the sight of my nakedness—the vulnerability we'd both pushed down deep. Sex, even with the one you trusted more than you trusted yourself, allowed the other person to see all the fissures under the surface.

Then she had slammed me against the wall, kissing me, unleashing our sexual fetters. That night, instead of shattering the pieces, the act filled the gaps with emotional glue that grew stronger with each touch. It was as if we craved being close to each other as a reminder that we were still alive.

Kat cleared her throat. I hadn't sensed her probing eyes as I drifted into the past. "You okay?"

I nodded. "Yes, indeedy. How are you, beautiful?"

"Done for the night." Kat grabbed the top of her head with one hand while the other cupped her chin, and she cracked her neck to the left and then right. "Let's go home and warm you up."

I popped off the divan and motioned for her to walk ahead.

She tittered. "Aren't you forgetting something?"

"What?"

Her eyes hungrily roamed up and down my body.

I looked down at my stark nakedness. "Oh, yeah. Be right back. I'm surprised you didn't let me wander out into the streets like this."

Kat feigned being hurt. "As if I would ever do such a thing." She followed with an evil laugh, which was both unsettling and settling in equal measure.

"At least not without a recording device." I kissed her cheek.

"You know me too well."

I locked eyes with hers. The trace of sadness was still ensconced there, driving me mad at my inability to eradicate her torment. If I could shoulder all of her hurt, I would in an instant.

Kat placed a palm on my cheek. "I know, baby. I know."

Chapter Five

Friday morning, Harold had called for a powwow. It wasn't unusual for him to request a meeting to coordinate upcoming events, but lately I hadn't been in the mood to discuss business of any type. Kat, sensing this, insisted the meeting convene at our home over breakfast.

By the time I returned from my run, Harold was sitting at the dining room table with his sketchpad, working on an idea for a graphic novel.

He barely glanced up. I kissed Kat on the cheek, but she shoved me away.

"You stink. Not even flowers will earn you a kiss at the moment." She gestured with a stainless steel mixing spoon to the trio of yellow tulips in my hand.

I sniffed my armpit and shrugged. "I wasn't trying to earn a kiss. I found these on the doorstep. One of your secret admirers, perhaps."

"Or yours."

"Please. The last to give me flowers was Vanessa, and that was way back when dinosaurs roamed the planet."

"Pre-Kat?" She grinned.

"Exactly." I plucked a card from the bunch. "Just the initials GH."

Kat frowned. "That's weird." She stroked her chin. "Ah, Gail Henderson. It probably pained the woman to write anything else. I'm not high on her 'good' neighbor list."

"But her husband *loves* you," I teased.

Kat wore a cat-that-ate-the canary smile. "He loves that I mow his lawn in a bikini top and short shorts." She took them from my hand, and I attempted to steal a kiss.

"No." She pushed me away again. "Shower, now. No need to torture Harold with your jogger's stench." Kat set two eggs next to the mixing bowl.

"Fine."

Several moments later, in fresh clothes and dripping hair, I peered over his shoulder to see his artwork. "Not bad, Harold. Have you approached any publishers yet?"

He blushed, hovering over the paper. "Oh, this is just for fun. It relaxes me."

"Can I look?" I pointed to the pad.

At the oven, Kat flipped a pancake over on the iron skillet, curiosity in her eyes. Typically, Harold didn't like to share.

Reluctantly, he coughed it up, and I took a seat at the table. As I leafed through the pages, I said, "Talk me through it."

He laughed nervously.

"I know it's the dreaded question for any author. The sales pitch for a story." I tapped a detailed pencil sketch of a German tank. "World War II?"

"Yes." He nodded. "It's about two book nerds who go behind enemy lines to save the world from Hitler."

"Do either have special powers?"

"Of course!" As Harold filled me in on his story, Kat sauntered over with a platter of chocolate-chip pancakes, fresh fruit, and hash browns. After arranging the table, including placing a vase with the flowers in the center, she casually filched the pad from my grasp.

Our interest ignited Harold's chatty switch. While she dished up his plate, he continued chattering, even mumbling around bites of food while I polished off three pancakes and some fruit.

I put a palm up to interrupt. "Wait. Are you telling me this is the fifth installment?" I motioned to the drawings Kat was absorbed in. She'd completely forgotten to eat.

He nodded, chewing on half a pancake he'd shoveled in when I asked the question.

"Harold! This isn't a hobby." I leaned over in my chair and clapped a hand on his shoulder. "This is your life's work."

Harold pounded his chest and sipped orange juice to force the pancakes down. "But I like this job." He gestured to Kat and me. "I like being your assistant."

"And we love working with you." Kat set the sketchpad to the side. "I don't think Cori is suggesting you stop."

I shook my head.

"But it doesn't mean you can't pursue publishing in your own right. Cori teaches and writes. I work at Barb's studio.

Doing one thing doesn't necessarily mean you can't do something else."

My mom sashayed through the front door. She was the reason the table was set for four. Mom plopped down into the chair across from me. With an evil flourish of her eyebrows, she said, "Nice flowers. Cori, are you stepping up your game?" My mother loved to needle me about my lackluster gift-giving skills.

I grunted. "Any idiot can buy flowers. I prefer to give gifts with more meaning. Besides, one of the tulips has seen better days." I prodded the one with a broken stem at the neck of the petals. Kat had used a toothpick to keep it upright.

"They're from Mrs. Henderson." Kat kicked my shin under the table. "Last week she left a plate of chocolate chip cookies outside on a paper plate, but by the time I found them they were inedible after a snowstorm. A shame, though, she put a lot of work into them."

"The old biddy from across the street? Cori's been outdone by a ninety-year-old woman." Mom scrunched her nose. "Looks like she culled these three out of a bunch she'd received and regifted." She tsked, but I couldn't discern whether she was tsking me or Mrs. Henderson. Not that it mattered. She made a motion for the meeting to commence.

Kat scooted Harold's book over to Mom. "We think Harold should look into publishing his World War II graphic novel series."

Mom slipped on her reading glasses.

Harold wriggled in his seat. He had been reluctant to show us, but compared to Mom's publishing success, Kat and I were small potatoes. Nell Tisdale had publishing contacts coming out the wazoo.

The more she nodded, the redder Harold turned. I made eye contact with Kat, telegraphing my concern: was he still breathing? Kat observed him, and her posture relaxed slightly when his chest rose.

Mom laughed and eagerly flipped a page to continue the story.

Seconds ticked by. Harold's discomfort almost reached 911 levels. And then Mom tucked the pad into her lap and said, "I'm taking this."

"What?" I sputtered.

"I want to show some people."

"Ah." I nodded. "You like it. But that's not the first in the series."

She rotated to Harold. "Can you get me the rest?"

He nodded, his mouth opening and closing like a baby turtle's.

"Good. Now, let's talk about Mother's Day weekend." Mom rested her forearms on the table with her fingers laced.

"Mother's Day! It's not even Christmas." The holiday had been hell last year, and I secretly hoped we wouldn't ever acknowledge another one.

Kat stared down at her plate as if she'd expected that reaction.

"I know, Cori. Before you close down completely, just hear me out." Her voice was soft.

I crossed my arms.

"I've asked Harold to set up a signing for both of us that weekend in celebration of Mother's Day." Mom paused to see whether I'd interrupt before continuing. "I want to donate all of the proceeds from the event to the neonatal intensive care unit." She flicked her head in the general direction of the hospital where they'd tried to save Charlotte. "The organizers of the event want us to sit down for a conversation and then take questions from the audience before the signing. Can you do it?" I saw only concern on her face, no judgment.

"I don't know," I whispered.

Kat glanced up, a faint smile on her lips. "It's for a good cause."

"I don't disagree." I sucked in a ragged breath. "This conversation… will it be about Charlotte?"

"Not necessarily, but she'll probably be mentioned."

I massaged my burning throat. "So ticket prices and book sales will go to the unit?"

"All of my book sales on all channels for the weekend will be donated. I'm coordinating my next release for that weekend."

I whistled.

"You don't have to commit right now." Harold finally found his voice.

All three of them studied me as if anticipating I'd fall to pieces.

"No, it's fine. You can schedule it."

"Are you sure?" Kat pushed.

I nodded. "Yep." I stood. "I need to shower." Wet strands of hair brushed against my cheek as I moved past Kat, reminding me I'd already cleaned up. I added, "Or something."

As I rushed down the hallway, I overheard Mom say, "No, let her have a few minutes."

The woman knew me well. She knew I'd never say no to the event, considering it was in my daughter's honor, but she understood I needed to have a meltdown alone right now. I sat under the shower stream until the hot water ran out, still wearing my T-shirt and jeans.

Chapter Six

"Cori! You're naked!"

My mother's voice didn't contain any disgust. She was just in shock. Complete and total shock. My aunt, with her broad shoulders, towered over my mother's runner's frame as both stared down at me on the divan in the art studio. Barbara was just as stunned, if not more. I jumped up and threw on a terry cloth robe, securing it tightly at my waist. My face sizzled as hot as the surface of the sun.

They'd had probably never considered Kat and I would be in the private work room in the studio early on a Sunday afternoon when the space was typically shuttered, let alone that I would be in my birthday suit, clearly modeling for Kat. Little did they know I had spent many hours naked on the divan over the past couple of months. Kat's schedule had been jam-packed, preparing for a summer show, so we had to squeeze in sessions whenever we could. She said it helped her relax, working on a project that didn't require much thought. I wasn't sure whether I should be insulted. When she was naked, certain thoughts definitely entered my mind.

Kat stepped out from behind the easel, a palette in one hand and a paintbrush in another. Her eyes glowed with devious amusement.

My mom and aunt, their mouths dangling open, about-faced to Kat for an explanation, correctly surmising I'd hedge.

"I asked Cori to model nude for me, and she agreed." Kat shrugged, as if this was an everyday occurrence in the life of an artist.

"She agreed?" Mom's eyebrows shot up. She wasn't upset I was posing nude—that would never bother Nell Tisdale, who flaunted her sexuality and who believed in freedom of expression on all levels. But she was the first to wise up to my ways. As a youngster, I'd coaxed Uncle Roger to install a deadbolt on my bedroom and bathroom doors. Mom hadn't seen me naked since I was old enough to dress and shower myself. To say I was reserved was putting it mildly.

My aunt smiled. "What'd you promise her?" She folded her arms over her gray boatneck sweater.

I grimaced at the notion I would only pose naked for Kat to get something in return. What was wrong with my wife painting me in the nude?

"A trip to England," Kat said with the same sexy smirk that had persuaded me to pose naked in the first place.

"Oh, that makes sense," Barbara said.

I stepped closer, keeping enough distance to stop my mother from undoing the ties on my robe—something she'd do just to ruffle my reserved feathers. "What do you mean that makes sense?"

I eyed my aunt and then Kat.

Kat held my gaze, but she bit her bottom lip, letting me know I had been conned, even if I hadn't yet put the pieces together to know how.

The hilarity in Aunt Barbara's face quickly transformed into guilt. My mother, though, grinned malevolently. Guilt was not in her personal vocabulary. Oh, she could write about it 'til the end of time, but to be intimately acquainted with remorse? No chance.

"When did you plan on going to London?" I tapped my now slippered foot. "Is it for work?"

"In the summer." Kat lifted one shoulder shyly. "The upcoming show is in London." There was a smidgeon of black paint on her chin.

"You tricked me!" I pointed to the divan.

"Oh, please. You wanted to be tricked. Not once did you ask where the show was taking place." Kat's luscious lips curved up almost magnetically, the way they always did when I caught her in some type of deception. I hated that it turned me on when I wanted to be angry with her.

"I assumed it was here, where all of your shows have been."

"That's what you get for assuming. You make an ass out of you and me. Well, not me. I'm not the one exhibiting my goods for all to see." She clubbed her chest with the hand gripping the brush, smearing more paint on her chin.

"For all to see…" I waggled a finger in her face, unable to complete the thought.

Kat set her supplies on the table.

"Do you care to fill me in about London?" I perched on the desk, careful not to upset the pile of crap threatening to spill onto the floor.

"Oh, now you want to know the details." Kat patted my cheek. "And I've already promised to take you."

"Only if I posed naked."

My mother ignored my childish behavior. "Do you plan to show it?" She motioned to the easel.

"Ah, no. Cori insisted it be just for me." Kat's downcast eyes brimmed with disappointment. Why she would want someone to see—or worse yet, buy—a nude painting of her wife baffled me completely.

Both my aunt and mom analyzed the canvas.

"How'd you get in?" I stepped in front of the canvas to get their attention and to stop their leers. "Kat said she locked the door and you'd never intrude if the door was locked."

My aunt gently pushed me aside. She had morphed into professional mode. Instantly, Aunt Barbara and Kat launched into a discussion about the painting. Kat's vision. They spoke as if they were the only two in the room.

I knitted my brow, demanding an answer from my mom.

"Barb has a key, of course."

"And?"

My aunt respected boundaries more than my mother.

"And I convinced her to use it." Her slack posture indicated it wasn't a big deal.

I rolled my eyes. Of course Mom was the instigator. After they'd failed to get the dirt about Kat's secret project at the family dinner, I should have known Mom would go into high gear to suss it out.

We locked eyes. I kept hoping an ounce of culpability would flash across her face. It didn't. It never would.

"And London. Did you know about that?" I sensed Kat's eyes on me, but I resisted the urge to flip around and give her the evil eye. Listening to her discuss a painting with such ardor was music to my ears, considering all the weeks her paints had lain idle after last Christmas.

"Tell you what, go get dressed and Barbara and I will take the two of you to a late lunch." That was her way of apologizing without admitting guilt.

It worked. I zipped out of the room to change.

Minutes later, I returned wearing jeans and a merino wool V-neck sweater. Kat had already slipped into a cowl-neck fiery red sweater and curvy-fit jeans.

***

Pablo's Café, a Tex-Mex restaurant, was oddly quiet for a Sunday afternoon, aside from the holiday country tunes softly streaming over the speakers. It was almost Christmas, and the weather had been hideous all week. Someone had pinned a Santa hat on the alligator in the Pure Louisiana Molasses ad on the far side of the restaurant.

"Tell me about London." I tossed the request to the group, since I had a nagging sensation everyone at the table was in the know—except me.

"It's the capital city of England. Many famous authors have lived there, including Charles Dickens. You, being a Brit lit teacher, may have heard of him," Mom said over the salted rim of her red-striped margarita glass.

I plunged a tortilla chip into the queso dip, snapping it in half, and leveled a stony gaze at my mother.

Out of the corner of my eye, I observed Kat and Barbara exchange a worried, although slightly amused, look.

"And the queen of England lives there." Mom's cell cheeped, and she glanced at it and then typed away.

I turned back to Barbara and Kat. "Why do I have the feeling I'm the only one who's out in the cold?"

Kat placed a hand on my fist. "We were going to tell you."

"Tell me what?"

"About the show. My international debut."

"That's wonderful." I grinned, but it turned into a grimace. "Why keep that a secret?"

"Like I said, you never asked."

I locked eyes on her and released an exasperated sigh. "Just admit you intentionally kept key information from me."

She crinkled her face and stuck out her tongue.

I waved for her to spill all of it.

"Okay, you win. It's not just a show," Kat explained.

To keep from saying something stupid, I crammed a chip smothered with queso into my mouth before licking my gooey fingers.

"Cori, do you remember Anselm who visited two springs ago?" Aunt Barbara leaned her elbows on the table.

"Your old friend who helped you open your studio years ago?"

She nodded. "Each summer, he invites a couple of artists to work with him in his prestigious London studio for a few months."

"Months." My mouth fell open, and a half-chewed chip tumbled onto my lap.

Kat shook her head and handed me a napkin.

I wiped the queso smear from my chin and tried steadying my breathing. "You're going to London for months? Without me?" I asked Kat.

The three of them stared wide-eyed. Twice in one day for Mom. Surely this was a record.

I tossed my hands in the air in the universal *what gives* motion.

"I figured she would react this way," Mom said to Kat and my aunt, as if I wasn't sitting at the table in the midst of a fit.

My aunt nodded solemnly.

Kat inclined her head, waiting for my next reaction—or overreaction.

I puffed my cheeks and then slowly let out a cleansing breath, or at least tried to.

"Did anyone think to include me in the conversations when deciding if Kat should leave me for eight weeks?"

"It's more like ten." Barbara smiled to take the edge off; it didn't work.

I ground my teeth and shook my head. "No way."

"Who do you think you are? Kat's keeper?" Mom crossed her arms over her Lilly Pulitzer silk floral shirt and cardigan, which didn't suit the weather or the festive season.

I swiveled my head to Kat. "Why are you leaving me?"

Kat smiled and placed a hand on my cheek. "Who said anything about leaving you?"

"Uh, I have a teaching job, remember?"

"Oh, that." Mom waved a hand in the air. "You'll be on sabbatical. The summer semester is so slow anyway. What do you usually have? A handful of students? A dozen at most?"

"Sabbatical? How is that possible when I didn't request one?" For the past three summers, the university had pleaded with me to teach one course.

The three of them smiled like I was a foolish, petulant child. I hated when they did that, because it reinforced that I was, indeed, acting like a fool.

"Really. Why do you always forget I know everyone in the English department at Adams?" The self-satisfied glint in Mom's eyes galled me.

"So my employers at Adams know I'm taking the summer off even before I do. Did anyone consider I might want to be involved in the discussion?"

"We thought it would be a nice surprise. You keep saying you want time to focus solely on writing. When this opportunity came up, we"—Kat circled her finger to include my mom and aunt—"thought this was an excellent opportunity for both of us. If we didn't get the ball rolling, you'd never take time off. Your Puritan ethic is too engrained. And the university wants you to guest lecture a couple of times. A tradeoff, so to speak."

"Puritan ethic, *pfffft!*" I accidentally sprayed the table with spit. She was right, of course, but at that moment I had no desire to admit it. I never did. It was the stubborn Puritan in me. My mind whirred. Lectures in London. An entire summer to write where Dickens lived. The idea wasn't half-baked. *Hold on, Cori. Don't let them off the hook. Not yet.*

"We'll be staying in *Notting Hill*, in case you're wondering," Kat continued, ignoring my childishness. Her shit-eating grin was quite becoming. How did she do it?

"Notting Hill? As in the Hugh Grant film?" I tried to curtail the excitement in my voice, but I couldn't banish all traces of enthusiasm.

"Yes," Kat said with a Genie-like bounce of her head as if granting me a wish—the wish of a lifetime.

We'd watched Notting Hill early on in our relationship, and I couldn't stop talking about it. Not the actual story, but how much I would love to live there in that neighborhood with the private garden.

"Seriously, we're going to stay there for ten weeks?" I blinked.

"Yes," Kat said.

I leaned back in my seat. "I can't believe this."

"Believe it, baby. We're going to London!" Kat kissed my cheek.

"And we plan on visiting." Mom foolishly waved to herself and Barbara, showing her excitement.

"Hey, don't try to burst my bubble." I scowled at my mom. She didn't mind, and soon a smile nibbled at the corners of my mouth.

"You think you're so funny." Mom snapped her fingers, and the bored waitress pounced instantly. "Four more." Mom gestured to our empty glasses.

"Of course."

"London? Really?" I rubbed the top of my head in complete disbelief. This news was huge. It'd take me hours, no days, to process everything. Right now, though, all that mattered was the smile on Kat's face. A genuine and excited smile. A year ago, I promised myself I would do absolutely everything to help Kat heal. If that meant living in London for a summer, hell, why not? I'd travel to Hades if need be.

Chapter Seven

On the night of Sam's party we donned our mandatory Christmas sweaters. Kat's was a tight red number with a slutty woman in a red bikini and Santa hat twirling on a stripper's pole. I had on a blue sweater with white snowflakes. When we'd gone shopping the day before, I refused all sweaters that had any red or green. Holiday colors always reminded me of our loss the year before, although I'd never admitted it. At least the flakes were large and semi-obnoxious.

At thirty-five minutes after eight, I knocked on Lucy's downtown apartment door.

The door swung open and Sam materialized. "Welcome!" The party had started at eight, but it was clear from her flushed cheeks and silly grin that Sam had been in her cups for most of the day. Her sweater had "Jingle Bells" on it and two red fuzzy balls where her nipples would be underneath.

"Love the sweater, Kat." She screwed up her face when she looked at mine. "I guess I should have expected this from you." She rotated a finger in front of my plain sweater.

Christmas music and various snippets of animated conversation from inside filtered into the hallway. "Hey, if it isn't up to muster, I can head home." I feigned turning around, still grasping the bottle of Dom.

Sam grabbed one of my arms, and Kat latched onto the other. "Nice try," Sam said. "But you're coming in, and you're going to have fun."

Lucy appeared in a red sweater with a Christmas tree on it. The lights were actually blinking. Even Lucy had put more effort into her costume than I had.

I shielded my eyes. "Luce, is that you? The lights. I can only see the lights."

She smiled as I thrust the bottle into her arms. "Happy Holidays."

Sam shook her head, jostling her blonde locks. She nabbed a Sam Adams Old Fezziwig Ale from the ice bucket on the table and shoved it into my hands. "Maybe this will help you lighten up." Without asking Kat, Sam poured her a glass of red wine.

Kat sipped it. "Ah, I needed this. Listening to Cori bitch all day would try Mrs. Claus's patience."

"I'm not so sure she was patient. I mean, she kicked Santa out every Christmas Eve to travel the world. Not to mention he probably had to spend 364 days a year prepping for the big night."

Lucy's face curved up as if a lightbulb had gone on over her head. "Maybe she knew the secret to a happy marriage: never seeing your spouse."

"I know the secret to a happy marriage." Harold wore a green sweater with a Gingerbread Man on it and "Eat Me" scrawled in cursive writing. In his left hand, he clutched a Smirnoff Ice Watermelon Mimosa bottle, and I was sure Sam had purchased the drinks solely for Harold. He drank straight from the bottle, probably to try to up the machismo factor. I thought it best not to remark on the pink color.

"Do share this secret," Kat purred, pawing the front of his sweater.

"Have a spare." He laughed.

"So the throuple thing is working for you?" I asked.

"Like a charm," he slurred.

I swilled my beer.

Sam rolled her eyes.

"Where are they then?" I scanned the partygoers.

Harold squinted, following my eyes. "Who?"

"Your harem, of course."

He paled. "Oh, them. They couldn't come tonight," Harold mumbled, before taking the tiniest sip from his bottle, not that he needed to swig; alcohol fumes got him drunk.

I started to ask why, but Kat nudged the back of my leg with her foot, shutting me up. More than likely, the girls wanted alone time. Was it sexy alone time? Was that allowed in throuples?

"That's a shame. There's always next time. So where's the food?" I greedily rubbed my mitts together.

"In the kitchen. There's way too much, so please eat more than you should. My diet starts on January second, and all leftovers have to be gone by then." Sam shooed me toward the kitchen, Kat hot on my heels.

There was a short line at the makeshift buffet. The man in front of me wore a naughty elf sweater. He turned, checked out Kat's sweater, and tendered his hand with a look that suggested he was doing Kat a favor. "I'm Rick."

Kat shook it. "Kat." She jerked her head in my direction. "This is my wife, Cori."

Rick's smile fell briefly, but then he narrowed his eyes. "Oh, I think you were at Mulligan's when the Pats kicked Tennessee's ass." He elevated his hand for a high five, and I happily obliged, already forgiving his leer not because I liked him but because I had grown accustomed to people's reactions to Kat. He followed up with, "Bring on the Super Bowl."

"Here, here. If I remember correctly, you were dressed as a Santa that day. Now you're an elf. Extremely versatile." I smiled.

He put his arms out, dancing a little jig. "I like to go with the flow. Never saw so many Christmas sweaters in one place. It's a riot." He pointed to a woman in line who was wearing a sweater with the Grinch's hands reaching around like he was fondling her breasts.

"Reminds me of the scene in *Bridget Jones's Diary*," I said.

Rick cocked his head the way men did when a chick-flick was mentioned. "Never saw it."

Kat grabbed three disposable plates and separated them with a manicured nail. She handed me a green one and kept a red for herself. The third she handed to Rick, who dipped his head in appreciation. He made eye contact with a woman who had just entered the room. Her Christmas sweater was actually a dress—a very short dress, although I was fairly certain that hadn't been the designer's intention. "I'll see ya on the flipside. Go Pats." He clamped a hand on my shoulder and then went in for the kill.

Kat smiled good-bye and then rolled her eyes when it was safe. "I've never trusted a man whose name rhymes with dick."

I laughed. "Wiener, my dear." I pointed to a bowl of barbequed little smokies. "You know I can't have them, but I'd love to slip you one."

"Just one."

"Honey, you can have as many wieners as you want. Just as long as you go home with me."

I loaded up my plate with peppers stuffed with cream cheese, baked olives with feta, mini crostini with cheese and artichokes, avocado tarts, and fig and blue cheese skewers.

Kat motioned with her head that we should make our way to the window in the main room.

"I'm seeing a trend." Kat surveyed my plate as she speared a little smokie with a toothpick.

"It seems most vegetarian dishes must have some variation of cheese." I winked. "Not that I'm complaining. I'll just go for a longer run tomorrow."

"You've almost completed a year. Gone for a run every day since you started."

"349 days straight."

"You going to run in New Orleans, then?" Harold joined us by the window overlooking Boston Harbor, stroking his chin, which slipped into his neck. A speckling of hair sprouted on his jawline. Was that a result of the throuple? Now he could actually grow a smattering of facial hair?

"Wouldn't miss the chance of running along the Mississippi River."

"You should write a book—like the one by Haruki Murakami," he said.

"What I Talk About When I Talk About Running," Kat supplied the title.

"Yes, that one." Harold stole an olive from my plate.

"But I'm not training for a marathon like he was. I'm just running. And he started running after selling his jazz bar. I started after—"

There was an awkward silence. I'd always been a runner, but since my middle-of-the-night run weeks after Charlotte's death I hadn't missed a day. Sometimes I went more than once, unable to sit inside in the dark like Kat. I had to keep moving. To do something. Because the night Kat and Charlotte needed me, I hadn't been there to do anything.

"Look at the view." Harold waved to the window. Down below were Faneuil Hall and the Custom House Tower. Beyond the buildings, lights shimmered on the water.

"It looks like a tiny Christmas village." Kat handed her plate to Harold and cinched an arm around my shoulder. Harold immediately pilfered two little smokies, keeping his gaze on the twinkling lights outside the window.

"You okay?" Kat whispered in my ear.

"Yeah. I'm sorry." I swabbed a tear from my eye.

"Nothing to be sorry about. Never apologize for missing Lottie."

I bent my neck to rest my chin on the top of her head.

"What are you three doing huddled by the window?" Sam asked. When she laid her eyes on mine, her smile froze. "Can I get anyone anything else to drink?"

Kat and I nodded.

Harold swished his mostly full bottle. "I'm good."

Sam dashed off and a commotion at the front door caught our attention. Slowly, I turned to see a man and woman enter. Their Christmas sweaters were mundane, like mine. The bundle in the woman's arms was causing the stir. She beamed as she bounced a baby on her hip.

Kat zoomed in on the child.

"I hope you don't mind, the sitter had to cancel at the last minute," the woman said with such a triumphant smile I doubted she ever scheduled a sitter. Who could blame her? I wouldn't want to be without my child, either.

We'd attended a few parties at Lucy's, and not once had anyone brought a child. Yes, some of the guests were parents, but with Sam as cohost the booze would be flowing as freely as the Charles River, so it wasn't wise to bring a baby. The invitation had included a warning: "The raunchier the sweater the better. This isn't your parents' Christmas soiree, folks."

"Not at all." Sam approached and put her arms out for the bundle of joy, who was happy to be passed around like a football. Almost every woman in the room swarmed Sam and the baby.

"How old?" asked one.

"Ten months. She was our Valentine's Day gift last year." The mother tugged her daughter's shoeless foot.

My heart clenched, and I thought I was going to vomit.

More questions were followed with lots of oohs and aahs. The only two women not part of the group were the two of us. Harold studied Kat's unmoving face, which bore a terrified smile. It reminded me of a bad actress in a horror flick, who just couldn't nail the scared emotion and ended up looking like a befuddled Cruella Deville.

I steadied my breathing. "Do you want to go?"

Kat shook her head, the peculiar smile still in place.

"Would you like to go back to the kitchen? Refill our plates?" Both of our plates were full, but I didn't know what else to suggest. The bathroom was another possibility.

Again, she shook her head. The pained smile had eased, but not enough for my liking. For the past few months, Kat had been the strongest of the two of us, but right now she was crumbling inside.

"Look at that!" Harold gesticulated out the window. "I just love fireworks." He clapped his hands together, trying to gain Kat's attention. It was a valiant effort, if only it had worked.

The gaggle of women worked their way over to the window. A woman in a naughty Mrs. Claus sweater now held the child. "Look at the pretty lights."

The toddler cooed and clapped her hands in that cute, soundless baby way that pulled the heartstrings of even the most hard-hearted Grinch.

I'd never heard Charlotte coo.

The inside of my nose started to burn, a surefire sign I was about to lose my shit and bawl in front of a bunch of strangers dressed in ridiculous Christmas sweaters.

Kat crept closer. Harold's boggled eyes focused on mine, and I could sense he was wondering whether he should trigger the fire alarm or something. Gotta love a man dressed in a gingerbread man sweater, drinking a girly drink, and ready to make an even bigger ass of himself for my sake.

I didn't know the answer, though.

Instead of taking any action, I stood like a statue as each second of Kat extending her arms out to hold the baby ticked by in super slo-mo. The baby immediately nestled her head against Kat's shoulder, as if they belonged to each other.

Kat nuzzled the baby's head with her nose. "I love that smell."

"I know. I could just eat her," said the woman closest, completely oblivious to the beauty of the moment. My wife was holding a baby.

My mind flashed back to the moment Kat had kissed Charlotte's cheek before the casket was closed. Turning my head to the side, I flicked away a tear.

In therapy, we'd discussed trying again, but the thought was fleeting and neither of us pushed the subject, not ready to tackle the emotions that would surface.

The mom grinned. "Over and over, women always say that. I used to think it was weird, until I held my own baby."

Harold's face morphed into pure terror. It was like I could see the movie playing in his mind of females tearing apart babies, shouting in shrill zombie-like voices, "I could just eat it."

The women surrounding us chattered like chipmunks, their voices screechy and almost unintelligible. Kat scooted a step away. I joined her. Her dark eyes brimmed with unshed tears.

"Isn't she beautiful?" Kat sagged her upper body so I could see the now-sleeping child's face.

I held her little hand with a finger. "She is."

Kat's smile contained something I couldn't put my finger on.

"Ah, you're a natural." The mother intruded on the moment. "Do you have children of your own?" She put her arms out for her daughter.

My shoulders tensed, but Kat casually said, "Here ya go," without answering the question.

The father joined the group. "Careful, ladies. This is how they trap you—so cute and innocent when they're asleep. But which one of you will volunteer to be there at three in the morning when she starts to cry?"

Out of all the women, everyone laughed except Kat and me. Even Lucy laughed, although the determined way she did so implied she was only being a polite host.

Kat and I locked eyes. The message was clear: we'd wake up seventeen times a night if it meant Charlotte was here, not buried under the frozen ground ten miles away.

The group drifted from the window.

Sam lingered next to Harold, her expression questioning. The contortion of my face, which was the first step to eyestrain, probably wasn't comforting.

Kat linked arms with me. "Shall we call it a night, sweetheart?" she asked as sweetly and confidently as she could muster.

I nodded.

"Are you sure, Kat? We haven't voted for the best sweater yet, and you're in the running." Sam pointed to Kat's sweater with an obligatory smile she probably hoped looked easygoing.

"There's always next year. Maybe I'll convince Cori to actually wear a risqué one."

"In your dreams." Sam walked us to the door, fully aware she'd never convince us to stay now. Harold shadowed us, placing our plates on a table to the side. "You leaving too, Harold?"

"Someone needs to escort these lovely ladies home." He bowed like a knight, handing Sam his half-finished watermelon concoction.

Sam patted his cheek.

"Please tell Lucy thank you." Kat kissed Sam's cheek. "Such a lovely party." Kat looped an arm through mine and then Harold's.

Harold swooped our jackets into his free arm, readying for a fast break to the elevator.

When the elevator doors closed, Kat's sobs released.

I wrapped her in my arms. "It's okay. Let it go."

Mercifully, the elevator didn't stop once as we descended from the twelfth floor.

"I could go for cheesecake." Harold was a pro when it came to perking Kat up.

She sniffled into my chest. "Yes. Salted caramel cheesecake."

"The apple chimi cheesecake is calling my name," I responded with a kiss on the top of her head.

Harold staggered on the balls of his feet. "I'm thinking the Hershey's chocolate bar or red velvet or banana cream or dulce de leche caramel—"

All of us practically had The Cheesecake Factory menu memorized.

"Yes! I forgot the dulce de leche caramel one." Kat squealed to the best of her ability, dabbing her eyes with the collar of her sweater.

"No limits tonight, team. I'm buying all the cheesecake until you pop." I put my hand out like I used to do with my basketball team. Kat and Harold each placed a palm on top. "On three, people. One, two, cheesecake!" We stepped off the elevator. "Harold, can you—?"

He cut me off, mauling his phone with clumsy hands. "Already got the uber. T minus five minutes."

"I'll text Barbara. The place is around the corner from her." Kat fished out her cell.

"Might as well call Mom, if she isn't already with Barb," I offered. A night like tonight called for reinforcements to keep Kat and me from losing our fricking minds.

"Good idea. I'll send a group text." Kat kissed my cheek.

***

"Did someone say cheesecake?" Roger's booming voice matched his confident smile.

Kat, Harold, and I huddled in the corner of the entrance, waiting for a table to open at The Cheesecake Factory in Chestnut Hill on Boylston Street.

Mom and Barb brought their own reinforcements: their husbands.

"Roger." Harold shook my uncle's hand, which he did every time he greeted him. "Dale." He extended his pale, scrawny hand out for my dad to shake too.

My dad and uncle liked having a de facto son around. Both stuck their chests out a bit more than usual when Harold was present.

It was ten p.m. on the Saturday before Christmas, but my family had dropped everything as soon as they got the group text. Whenever cheesecake was mentioned, it was a given Kat was struggling. Not that anyone would bring it up, unless Kat indicated she wanted to talk about it; most of the time she didn't—only in therapy. But cheesecake became code for "Kat needs a pick-me-up."

Kat made the rounds and hugged everyone.

"Love the sweater." Roger nudged her arm. Kat responded by resting her head against his broad shoulder. He held her as if she were his own daughter. We made eye contact over her head, and Roger's eyes conveyed such compassion and understanding I nearly lost it right then and there. God, he would have made a wonderful father. How did he cope with so much loss?

Not now, Cori.

Mom bopped my back. "Next year, I'm taking you shopping for Sam's cheesy Christmas sweater contest. Snowflakes." She shook her head at my lame-ass sweater. "It's an embarrassment. What happened to my competitive daughter who had more trophies and ribbons than shelf space? Look at Kat and Harold. They tried. Really tried."

Dad ruffled Harold's soft brown hair, much to Harold's delight. Harold's father had died years ago, and even though he'd never mentioned it, the way he ate up attention from Dad and Roger was testament he was in dire need of a fatherly figure.

Mom continued with her harangue, shaking her head and muttering, "Disgrace."

Harold nodded his agreement.

Leave it to my mom to sense my waterworks were about to turn on and to alleviate the situation by berating me. Only she would stoop to that level—the level I needed.

I gave her a tender embrace and whispered, "Thank you."

She responded, "Anytime," so only I could hear.

Roger placed a meaty hand on Harold's shoulder. "What's the news on your throuple? I'm expecting a full report."

Harold's cheeks burned with manly pride.

"Are you ready?" The hostess, armed with seven menus, smiled. Her drooped shoulders suggested she'd rather we'd never shown up.

"Lead the way," Barbara instructed, looping her arm through Kat's.

The Cheesecake Factory hostess led us to a round table that comfortably sat the seven of us, with three chairs to spare.

"Now, Cori. Last time you only had one slice. I expect better from you tonight." Roger rapped the menu, which showcased all the options. "No one goes home until they can't possibly eat another morsel without puking. Not that puking to make more room is out of the hat, either."

"Hey now. The slices are the size of my head," I defended.

"You have a tiny head. That means nothing." He waved me off.

Barbara and Mom shared an eye roll. Dad's eyes widened. Harold was too busy pondering the choices, taking Roger's challenge to heart. Kat, wedged between Barb and Mom, slanted her head to see into my eyes.

I mouthed, "I love you."

Her smile mirrored my sentiment.

Operation Cheesecake had begun, and it was working.

Chapter Eight

The day after Christmas we invited Sam, Lucy, and Harold over to watch some bowl games. There were six games scheduled, not that the goal was to endure all of them—probably not even half of them—but we'd purchased enough food to power us 'til dawn. Kat had been doing her best to show an interest in college football this season—partly, I assumed, because she was excited about the upcoming trip to New Orleans, which she and my family had been preparing for months, and wanted to cram some knowledge in about the sport.

"How are we going to break the London news to Harold?" I asked while prepping the vegetarian lasagna, the one meal I could cook with relative success. Earlier, Kat had prepared one with meat.

"Why will Harold be upset about London?" Kat peeled carrots for the veggie platter, which already had celery, cucumber, broccoli, cauliflower, bell peppers, and ranch dip. The guests weren't due for another hour, and with the heat emanating from the two ovens, we were roasting. A slice of carrot shot off the cutting board, and Kat bent down to retrieve it. She was wearing just a top and an apron, and I eyed her naked ass.

Kat grinned over her shoulder. "Getting a good look, my dear?"

"Hmmm… not bad, but I think you dropped something over there." I bucked my chin to the spotless corner of the granite-tiled floor.

She stood. "If you want to see me naked, just ask."

"I want to see you naked." I haphazardly tossed the slimy noodles onto the pan and started to remove my apron.

"Not now," she teased. "Our guests will be here soon."

"I'd be more than happy to cancel." I whipped my cell phone out of my shorts pocket.

"Don't worry. I'll make up for it later. I promise." Her arms encircled my waist and she kissed me passionately, letting me know I wouldn't regret the wait.

"Okay, fine. I'll try to behave." I retied the apron around my waist.

"Help me a second, will ya?" She motioned to the veggie and cheese platters. I picked them up and followed her to the dining area. The floor plan of the house was open in the front, so from our dining room table we could view the television in the family area. We set everything up buffet-style, allowing guests to wander freely to the couches and kitchen. On the back deck, a cooler, minus ice, housed all the beer and

Harold's pink drinks. We worried about the bottles freezing in the subzero temperature.

Kat dumped tortilla chips into a bowl and set the homemade salsa next to it.

"How much time until you put the lasagna in the oven?" Kat asked.

"Not long. Why?"

"Fancy a dip in the hot tub?"

I was already perspiring like I was walking on the surface of the sun, but I would never turn down hopping in the tub with Kat, who usually skinny-dipped, day or night. Thank God for her confidence and for tall fences.

Ten minutes later, we both eased into the water. Since we were expecting guests, Kat had insisted we put our suits on.

She rested her head against the lip of the tub. "Ah, just what I needed."

Since the accident, Kat experienced aches and pains in her lower back and neck she said were minor, but I suspected she wasn't being completely upfront.

"Do you hurt?" I asked.

"Not much. How's your back?"

"Never better."

"You're such a bad liar."

She splashed water at me.

"Take that back!" I sloshed water back at her.

"Or what?"

I floated over to her. "Or this." I swept her into my arms and kissed her forcefully; she met my passion, quickly upping the heat factor.

"Whoa, you two! What'll the neighbors think?" I didn't have to take a look-see over my shoulder to confirm it was

Sam. I'd know her authoritative voice from a million miles away.

"Showtime," Kat whispered in my ear and then nibbled on the lobe. "Perfect timing, you two. Cori just said she was starving." Kat stood on the bench, getting ready to hop out.

"Yeah, and I know for what."

I caught Samantha ogling Kat's wet body. Lucy was as well, which made me chuckle.

Sam put up a hand. "Don't get out. We're coming in."

Kat pivoted to get back into the water, and I glimpsed the C-section scar along the top of her bikini bottoms, a reminder of Dr. Wicks' words that my wife's womb would never house another baby. I cupped some water into my hands and rinsed my face so Kat wouldn't see the lone tear.

Harold unintentionally aided my ruse by bumbling through the kitchen door, holding a book at eye level and pummeling Sam to the ground.

"Now that's what I call perfect timing and justice," I said, feigning a menacing look at Sam, the ogler.

Lucy and Kat laughed.

"Sam, I'm so sorry. Did I hurt you?" Harold picked up the book from the snow, instead of the woman he'd knocked to the ground. Gotta love a dedicated book nerd.

"Actually, I think you saved my hide." She perched on a mound of snow I'd shoveled earlier to make a path to the hot tub.

Harold cocked his head with a confused but brazen smile on his face. That smile used to drive me bonkers when I was first getting to know him; now I found it endearing. It was just so Harold, our clueless but utterly loyal friend.

Lucy proffered her hand to Sam, yanked her up, and proceeded to dust off her ass. They seemed on better terms today, and I wondered whether Sam had talked to her about the Inez situation. I hoped they'd had a heart-to-heart on some level.

"We'll be right back. I think we're a tad overdressed." Sam tweaked the fringe of her black and purple scarf.

The girls joined us first in the hot tub.

"Harold should be out soon. He couldn't find his swim trunks." Lucy shrugged.

We always kept their spare swimwear in a drawer in the laundry room.

I quirked a brow at Sam.

"I only hid it a bit. It won't take him too long."

"Why do you torment him so?"

"Maybe because I was an only child. He's like the annoying baby brother I never had."

I licked my lips, and Lucy's face crumbled. We had made it clear we intended to have more than one child.

Sam, realizing her error, veered away from the topic. "Sorry we came early. I wanted to have a bit of a soak before the football and eating extravaganza." Sam scrunched down in the water, up to her chin. "Damn, Luce, we need to get one."

"You're welcome here anytime," Kat said, meaning every word.

"Shhh… we'll never get rid of them," I said in an effort to keep the conversation away from the danger zone.

Sam filled her mouth with water and squirted it at me, nailing me right in the eye.

I simulated a boxing jab, which didn't intimidate her at all.

Harold stepped outside in his Marvel Comic swim trunks, which featured dozens of characters. He was still clutching the book and I'd bet twenty bucks he wanted to keep reading but feared Sam and I would rough house and ruin the hardcover.

Sam eyed the spine on the ledge. "*Neverwhere*. How many times can you read the same book?"

Harold swiveled away from Sam and locked eyes on Kat, terrified.

Sam studied him and then Kat. Lucy was too busy popping the top off a beer. Lucy pushed her glasses up her nose and took a healthy swig, especially considering it wasn't even noon. Why hadn't I thought of fetching a beer before getting in? Out of the five of us, Lucy was the more practical one.

Then I put two and two together. "Harold knew!" I bellowed.

Kat patted my cheek. "Of course he did. Who do you think has been handling all the details? He's our assistant, remember?"

Harold fit into our professional and personal lives so seamlessly I couldn't imagine him being kept in the dark. Yet, I still was vexed he'd known before I did.

"Oh, you told her about London." Sam motioned for Lucy to pass the Sam Adams' White Christmas bottle.

"Sam knew!"

Everyone shrugged and then ignored me completely.

I stewed for a minute, until Kat's foot found its way into my lap. She massaged my magic spot, and no one in the tub was wise to what was happening under the surface of the bubbling steam. It didn't last long. Kat started to giggle, and heat invaded my face. I'd been had on several levels. She jacked up an eyebrow, and I beckoned with a finger. Sam cheered and Harold's eyes boggled as Kat and I kissed.

"I'll get even, Kat," I grumbled.

"Please do. Maybe plan a secret trip to Paris or something." Her brash smile made my heart flutter and jumpstarted my libido. Kat sat on my lap and leaned into my embrace. "That would really teach me a lesson."

Harold snapped his fingers. "Oh, Cori, before I forget, I scheduled your podcast with my blogging buddy. The end of January. It'll be the kickoff to your tour."

"Podcast? When did you get with the twenty-first century?" Sam hoisted herself out of the water and sat on the lip of the tub, splashing her feet.

"Oh, it wasn't by choice. Somehow Cori got embroiled in a social media spat and now she has to make nice." Kat repositioned, allowing a jet to blast her lower back and letting out a sigh.

"Embroiled! Someone created a fake account, pretending to be me. I'm not making nice because I didn't do anything wrong."

"That's right. The G-Dawg thing." Sam slipped back into the water. "Are you sure it wasn't really you?" The grooves in her brow made it clear she wanted to get a rise out of me.

"How could I? Harold and Kat locked me out of all my social media accounts."

"You invited all your fans to an orgy." Kat mopped steam off her forehead with a towel.

"I did not. I just mentioned I would be signing books at Moggies—a bookstore. My phone autocorrected to orgies."

Sam biffed the back of my head. "Didn't you proofread?"

"I have editors for that." I rubbed my head. "Jesus, have you been working out?"

She flexed her bicep.

"Now I take care of all her tweets and blog posts." Harold thwacked his scrawny fish-belly white chest as if he just harpooned a white whale.

"We wouldn't be able to survive without you." Kat's glare silenced my comeback.

"Harold, where are the women?" Sam asked.

The question piqued my attention.

"Returning Christmas gifts and buying new ones." His smirk didn't have the same confidence as earlier.

"I'm starting to feel dissed." Sam wasn't teasing.

Harold swatted the idea away. "Not true. They're just busy all the time."

Without you.

From the looks on the other three faces, I wasn't the only one thinking it.

"Do they spend a lot of time alone?" Sam asked.

I sensed Lucy had kicked her shin, but with the noise of the jets and all the bubbles, it was hard to determine. However, Sam shot Lucy a look that meant *Do that again and I'll coldcock you.*

"They like their girl time, and neither is into football," he said in his most self-assured tone, but his eyes shone with reservations.

"I wasn't aware you liked football." The words slipped out of my mouth. Kat elbowed me in the gut.

"Is the game on yet?" Sam asked, a little too quickly.

"We'll check. And we need to put your robes in the dryer." Kat stood and put a hand out for me. Her sheepish smile indicated she wanted to talk to me alone.

I shivered as my feet hit the tiled floor of the laundry room, and then I reached into the dryer and handed Kat a toasty robe before slipping into mine. Kat pulled three clean robes off wall pegs, each marked with a Kat rendition of the owner, and tossed them into the dryer, setting the timer for ten minutes.

"Let's put the lasagnas in," she commanded.

I dutifully followed her and waited as she placed casserole dishes on the top and bottom racks of the ovens. Without turning around, she said, "Yes, you were the last to know."

"How long has everyone known?" I slouched against the far counter and tightened the robe.

"Several weeks now. Harold longer." She extracted a bottle of cava from the freezer and placed it in the fridge.

I snorted. "Why?"

"I wanted to know it was a sure thing. I didn't want to get your hopes up." Sadness slumped her shoulders. "We've had a tough year."

That was an understatement. When we'd decided to get pregnant, it was hard to pinpoint who was more excited, my family or Kat and me. Even Uncle Roger couldn't stop talking about it. We had used my egg. The first two attempts didn't take; the third did. And then the accident happened.

Now we weren't sure if we'd ever have a family. A living one.

"Come here." I spread my arms out and Kat buried her head in my chest.

"I'm okay, really. We have guests." She didn't budge from my arms.

"Don't worry. They're good at entertaining themselves. Sam has probably tied Harold to a post and is ripping pages out of his book and tossing them into the tub."

Kat laughed and wiped her eyes on my robe. "They've been wonderful friends since…"

"That they have. And I'm sure we can convince them to visit."

Kat drew back. "I think you need to know something else."

"About London?"

"Yes. Harold's coming with us." Her eyes never left mine.

A smile burst onto my face. "Of course he is! No wonder he's rereading *Neverwhere*. He's probably memorizing every page and plans to ferry us through London's Underground, recreating the story. Not to mention wandering through London streets will help with his World War II series. I really hope Mom can come through for him."

"You aren't mad?"

"I could never be mad at you." I flicked a tear off her cheek and cradled her chin. "I love you, and I'm so proud of you for scoring this opportunity. You remember how many times you talked me off the ledge when I couldn't finish my first novel. You've always supported and believed in me. And I support and believe in you. We make a great team, and we're going to love London. Hell, I'd move to Zimbabwe if you asked me."

"Zimbabwe! Not sure I can outrun a leopard." Frivolity replaced some of the sadness in her eyes. "I'm betting I'm faster than Harold, though."

"That's the spirit."

"I checked. Paris is only a two-hour train ride away." Kat cupped her ear. "Do you hear that? The Louvre is calling my name."

I groaned playfully. "How many museums are you going to drag me through?"

"None with that attitude."

"I'm not easy to shake and you're easy to spot in a crowd. I just have to keep an eye on all the heads turning at whiplash speed." I jutted my head to the patio door. "You ready to go back out?"

"I think we should get dressed first. I don't want Harold to have a coronary, and I think Sam's in enough hot water these days." She led me to our bedroom, where I changed into jeans and a lightweight sweater. Kat's skinny jeans and scoop neck, long-sleeved shirt were anything but tame.

I whistled. "Not sure that's much better."

"Should I change?"

"Never. Promise me you'll never change."

"This outfit or my style?"

"At the moment, I'm voting for both." I winked. "Come on, or they'll turn into prunes." I grabbed the robes from the dryer.

***

"About time. I thought for sure you two were having a quickie in the laundry room." Sam raised her beer.

"Really?" Harold squeaked.

I helped each one out while Kat wrapped them up in robes.

Inside, after changing into dry clothes, everyone reported to their battle stations. Sam and Harold reconnoitered in the front room to get the TV on the right channel. Not sure it took two people, but Harold was pretty much useless in the kitchen and Sam anointed herself Mrs. Technology.

"All right, give me the meat." Lucy held her palms out. She manned the grill ever since I'd gotten so distracted by a Sox game two summers ago that I'd burned all of the burgers and brats beyond recognition.

"Wow. Never thought I'd hear you say that, Luce." Kat's mischievous grin returned.

"Oh, she says it to me all the time." Sam scooted by and snatched a beer from the cooler on the back deck. "And, oh boy, do I—"

I nudged Sam with an elbow. "Mind the children please."

Harold's mouth dangled open like a German shepherd's waiting for a raw steak. "Do what?"

"I'll fill you in later, Harold, when Mom goes to bed." Sam jerked her thumb in my direction.

"Don't mind Cori. She's a prude and assumes everyone else is. Totally different story when we're alone." Kat pinched my cheek before opening the fridge to pull out the hot dogs and burgers. Even though we had lasagnas in the oven, Kat's idea, it wasn't natural to watch college ball without proper tailgate food.

"What's the score?" I leaned over the counter, facing the dining/front room, giving all of them my best side. Sam nodded for me to join her on the couch.

When the coast was clear, Sam whispered, "Is Kat okay? Your text was brief."

"Isn't that the purpose of texts?" I rubbernecked over my shoulder. Kat and Harold were deep in conversation in the kitchen. "She's doing better. We executed an Operation Cheesecake," I whispered.

Sam squeezed my thigh. "Damn, I missed it. I'm so so so sorry. I had no idea Carol and Steve would bring Abby."

Abby. I never even thought to ask the girl's name.

I puckered my lips to hold my emotions in check. "There's nothing to apologize for."

We remained silent, neither of us watching the game, just pretending to.

"Can you meet me after work tomorrow?" Sam asked.

"Briefly. We have an early flight the next morning. What's up?"

Sam stealthily peeked into the kitchen, where only Kat and Harold stood. Lucy was still outside, but the glass door was ajar. "Nothing really, it's just…" She shrugged as a way to postpone the conversation until tomorrow.

"Gotcha. Near your work? I have to pop into my office tomorrow anyway." I didn't, but I felt bad about making her schlep out to Brighton after a grueling day in the office. Sam's finance job was full-on, ten to twelve hours five days a week.

"Yeah, is Revere's okay?"

"What are you two whispering about?" Kat parked herself on the arm of the couch.

"Not S-E-X." Sam forced a giggle.

I stared at the television. With one look at my face, Kat would smell a rat and hound me to spill the beans, even if I didn't have any beans to spill. Not yet, at least.

"Right. I'll leave you to it." Kat kissed the top of my head.

"Quick, give me a cover story for when she asks later."

Sam whipped her head around. "Aren't you the writer? You make up stories for a living."

"Trust me, Kat has some kind of voodoo magic. She knows when I'm making up shit and not leveling with her."

"Tell her I'm thinking of getting a puppy."

"A puppy… you're never home!" I shook my head. "Horrible idea!"

Sam blinked and shook her head. "I'm not actually getting one, ya moron!" She whacked my leg. "That's the cover story."

"Oh, right. It's weak, but that may make it better." I stared at the ceiling. "I can work with that."

"You're weak," she teased.

"Really? Care to make a friendly wager?"

"Yeah, let's arm wrestle. Loser has to convince Harold to bring Amber and Simone to a dinner party. I'm not buying that they always have plans."

"Bring it." I pushed myself off the couch.

We marched to the dining room table behind the couch and cleared some of the platters to the hutch along the back wall.

"What are you two up to now?" Lucy demanded. She stood in the kitchen, with the barbeque tongs under her arm, rubbing her hands for warmth near the ovens.

Neither of us answered. Sam made a show of stretching her arms before placing her elbow on the table, game face firmly fixed, ready to battle.

"Arm wrestling? Seriously?" Kat's countenance was amused and annoyed.

Harold took charge, placing his palm over our clasped hands. "On my mark." He eyed Sam and then me. "Go!"

Our muscles tightened and strained.

"You aren't in high school anymore, Sam," Lucy called before heading back outside to the grill. She left the door open to observe, though. The grill was just off to the side of the door, so Lucy wouldn't freeze to death.

Kat huffed. "As a former cheerleader and basketball jock, we should have known these two would never grow up. Not completely." She leaned against the counter, arms crossed, engrossed in our dual.

Sam's arm started to make headway. I groaned and put all my might into pulling my arm away from the table.

"Nice manicure, princess," I said.

"Not going to work. You aren't getting into my head." Sam's face tensed, but the determination in her glare intimidated me. "P90X, baby."

"Buying workout DVDs doesn't actually build muscle."

"I don't just own them. I live by them. Can't you tell?" Her bicep tightened.

Harold clasped his hands and rocked on his feet. "Come on, Sam. You almost have her."

"Never going to happen." With a surge of energy, I wrenched our arms back to the starting point.

"Maybe you should hit the gym again. Not just run. Or you could borrow my DVDs," Sam taunted.

"Please. I do fifty push-ups before you're even out of bed."

I could sense Kat's eye roll. She never understood my competitiveness, but she had never competed in anything—not even tee-ball. How un-American. Kat sauntered over, leaned down, and whispered in my ear, "Save your strength for later."

Sam sensed her moment and slammed my arm all the way down. "Winner!" She threw her arms up in the air.

Harold cupped his mouth, announcing, "And the 2015 arm-wrestling champion is Samantha Clarke!" He made crowd noises.

Lucy and Kat laughed.

"Cheater." I pouted.

"Such a sore loser." Sam strutted to Lucy, who was still standing in the open door, for a victory kiss.

Kat took pity on me and kissed me.

"What about me?" Harold whined. Both Sam and Lucy pounced and pecked a cheek, which made him blush.

"Dogs are ready, in case anyone is interested." Lucy plucked the plump franks off the grill and held one aloft with tongs. "Just the right amount of char, don't ya think, Cori?"

"You are the grill master." I bowed.

Everyone laughed, putting the arm wrestling fiasco behind us. I locked eyes on Kat, who flashed a smile. This last year would have been miserable without the support of each and every one of them.

Kat poured cava into crystal flutes with pale purple stems. "Come, everyone. I want to make a toast."

Lucy came inside and leaned against Sam.

Kat handed out the drinks, raised her glass, and simply said, "To friends."

***

When I waltzed into the spacious master bedroom later that night, after all the guests had beat it, I found Kat sprawled naked on the king-sized bed, waiting for me.

I skidded to a stop in the middle of the room and palmed my head. "Holy fuck, I've died and gone to heaven." I was at least four feet from the bed, and the only light came from the candles flickering around the room. Despite that, Kat's goodies were plain as day.

"You like?" she purred, spreading her legs to show me the money spot.

"Yes, me like very much." I didn't move, enjoying the view.

"Sometimes it's hard to believe you're an English teacher." She sniggered.

"What can I say? Your beauty knocks proper English right out of my head."

"Ah, you say the sweetest things. You going to just stand there?"

"Give me a sec. I'm doing my best to permanently etch this vision into my memory bank." I tapped the side of my noggin.

"Is that so?"

I nodded, feasting on her nakedness. Kat watched with a curious grin. Then she decided to play along. With both hands, she kneaded her breasts, and my sharp intake of breath only encouraged her. She played with one of her nipples until it hardened, all the while still massaging the other breast.

One hand trailed down her toned stomach and across her mound of pubic hair. She lazily raked her fingers through it.

I was fairly certain my eyes were boggling more than Harold's had earlier in the evening when Kat had leaned down to pick up a dropped tortilla chip and her tits made a brief, albeit memorable, appearance.

"You enjoying the show, sweetheart?" Kat lifted an impish eyebrow.

Like a teenage geek who'd never seen a naked woman, I could only nod. I was curious to see how far she would take it, and I didn't want to interfere with the magical moment. No one else in the world had front row seats to Kat Finn, artist extraordinaire, pleasuring herself.

I licked my lips.

"Pull up a chair. This could take a while," she instructed.

Without taking my eyes off her roaming hand, I yanked a black antique stool from Kat's makeup table in the corner and placed it at the foot of the bed. The perfect spot for the show.

Kat spread her legs further.

I rubbed my forehead.

"I love the look on your face," she said in a breathy tone. "It's like you've never seen me naked before."

"It feels like that each and every time. God, Kat, how'd I get so lucky?"

She smiled.

Her fingers continued to rake her pubic hair. She knew I wanted more. Oh God, I wanted more. I wanted Kat to full-on fuck herself.

"Tell me how turned on you are," she demanded.

I opened my legs. "I'm surprised you can't see the wetness from there. I'm already gushing, and I haven't even laid a finger on you yet."

"Show me." A finger slid over her clit, and she moaned.

It wasn't difficult to guess where this was going. Excitement pinged through my body.

I stood and shucked my jeans and panties.

"I can't see. The shirt has to go."

That wasn't a problem.

"Go on," Kat said after I tore the powder blue Adam's T-shirt and black satin bra off and tossed the items on top of my Gap jeans on the floor.

Confessions from the Dark

I sat back down on the cream satin cushion and spread my legs for her to take a gander.

"Ah, you *are* turned on. You're glistening," she purred. As my reward, Kat spread her lips with one hand and dipped a finger inside momentarily.

"You keep doing that and I may ruin this." I motioned to the stool.

"What if I do this?" She slid two fingers inside and pumped her wrist, gliding her fingers in and out.

"I may have to reciprocate, but first..." I leaned down and placed my Adam's university shirt over the cushion. "I know how much you love this stool." Her grandmother had given it to her when she was just a kid.

She smiled. "I wonder what Granny Faye would say if she saw you right now."

"Good Lord, she's probably rolling in her grave. Let's not think about her." I'd never met her grandmother, but I'd seen enough photos to know she was the typical Bostonian of her generation: hard, practical, and repressed. "I want to concentrate on this." I ran my fingers over my pussy.

"That's what I was hoping for." Kat continued to penetrate herself, with three fingers now, while her other hand stimulated her clit.

I massaged my clit, too.

"Inside," she pleaded.

My index finger glided into the wetness.

"More."

I added two more fingers.

Kat pumped harder, her hand slickening with each thrust.

She was getting closer. Her excitement spurred on my orgasm. "How do you do this to me?"

"Me? You're taking care of yourself." She winked at me. I could tell she was doing her best to keep her eyes open.

There was no way in hell I'd close mine until she came. I slowed my fingers and then pulled them out. Kat started to protest, until I rubbed them over my torso, creating a shiny trail. When my fingers dried, I dipped inside for more, smearing my nipple with the slippery wetness.

"I'm rubbing off on you," she said in her most seductive tone. "You're creating art." Her back arched as she plunged her fingers deep inside herself. She was no longer teasing. Kat was intent on bringing herself home.

Her face was screwed up in ecstasy, pure and simple, and I couldn't rip my eyes away from the show. I'd seen her masturbate before, but never like this. It was almost primal.

And fucking hot!

Kat's hand moved furiously, her other fingers concentrating on her clit. Part of me wanted to help her climax, but the other part wanted to stay put. Opportunities like this were rare, and every blissful second must be savored.

Her moan quickly transformed into a scream. Kat's body writhed. She panted. But still neither hand slowed, not until she was done. Kat climaxed for what seemed like an hour.

When her body stilled, I realized I'd stopped touching myself completely. An ache developed.

"What are you waiting for?" she asked.

"What do you mean?"

"Come here. I need to make love to you."

"You aren't exhausted after the performance of a lifetime?" I grinned.

"Exhausted? I feel alive. Totally and completely alive. Now get your ass over here." She reclined her head, beckoning.

She didn't have to tell me again.

***

Kat ran fingers, still sticky from our earlier lovemaking, through my hair—not that I minded. "I think we'll use the studio here for the rest of your modeling sessions."

I draped my arm over her abdomen. "The rest? What makes you think I'll continue after the humiliation of having my mom and aunt walk in the last time?"

"Because you can never say no to me." She kissed my forehead.

I rolled my eyes, knowing she was one hundred percent right.

"How are you going to keep them away?"

"Not sure, yet. Your mother loves to embarrass you; that's for sure. And your aunt has critiqued every one of my paintings, so it'll be hard not to ask her advice."

"Has she seen the works in your studio here?"

"Not yet. Why?"

"I was just curious. How do you decide which paintings to work on where? Home or Barb's studio?"

"Not sure. Some are more personal right from the start."

I laughed. "Does that mean the one of me naked isn't personal?"

She slapped my buttocks. "You know what I mean. The ones here—they're different. I don't even know what comes over me when I'm painting them, and at times it scares me."

I adjusted to envelop her in my arms. "I think I understand. The novel I'm working on now, the words just spill out of me and it's the darkest shit I've ever written or thought of."

"Someone once told me you can't have beauty without darkness. Or something like that."

I racked my brain. "*Stars can't shine without darkness.*"

"Yes, that's it. Leave it to you to know the exact quote. Such a nerd." She snuggled closer.

I gave her a quick peck. She responded with gusto, pulling me down on top of her.

"How do you always have so much energy?" I asked, bewildered.

"Can't help myself around you. I could ask the same about you."

I propped myself up on both arms, hovering above her. "Are you kidding? Have you seen your body? A ninety-year-old monk who had never had an impure thought in his life wouldn't be able to keep his hands off you."

Kat squished her eyes shut. "Eww, eww, eww! Why in the world would you put that image in my head?"

"Says the woman who mentioned her grandmother earlier." My finger roved from her neck down to between her legs. "Does that mean when I'm ninety you'll cut me off?" She was still wet, and my finger slithered through her folds.

Kat's eyes remained shut, but the hitch in her breath urged me on.

"I need to taste you."

She nodded fervently.

The moment my tongue flicked her clit, Kat moaned. "God I love you."

I reached for her left hand and intertwined our fingers, enjoying the feel of our wedding bands clinking against each other.

Chapter Nine

"What evil plans do you and Sam have this evening?" Kat poured some OJ into her glass, set the carafe back on the table, and took her seat across from me.

"How'd you know?" I sliced into a blueberry pancake. We made a point to sit down together for breakfast every single morning. And now that I was off for winter break and wasn't in my usual mad dash state, we had time for leisurely meals that didn't consist of just cereal and fresh fruit.

"You two aren't sly." She crossed her legs.

I grinned. "Probably a good thing you know. I'm not good at keeping secrets. As of now, I only know she wants to talk. Pretty sure it has to do with Lucy."

Kat knitted her brow. "And the affair."

"What affair? As far as I know, Sam has a crush. No more." I wolfed down a third of a pancake.

She circled a finger in the air, not appreciating my attempt to stall for time. "Here's to hoping Sam snaps out of it." She smiled coyly. "Just a heads-up, Lucy knows something's going on. And…"

I nodded. "I know. But they seemed to be on better terms yesterday." I sipped some juice. "How 'bout you? What's on your agenda?"

"No drama on my end. Lunch with a friend and then the studio."

I set my knife and fork down on my plate. "I do need your help."

She quirked a sexy eyebrow, a smile in her eyes. "Shall I get on all fours?"

"What? No… I mean, unless you want to." I waved to the floor.

She chuckled. "Sometimes you're worse than a dude. Just the hint of sex and all logic falls out of that jock brain of yours."

I shrugged, not insulted. "That wasn't just a hint, by the way."

"Go on. What mess did you get yourself into this time?" She motioned for me to let the cat out of the bag.

"Last night I lost a bet."

Kat scrunched up her face. "The arm wrestling thing?"

"Yep."

She sighed. "What'd you bet? Last time we had to pay for a weekend for Sam and Lucy at the Cape." She singled out a juicy red grape from the fruit bowl and hurled it into her mouth.

"Nothing so extravagant this time."

123

She crossed her arms, and not in a playful way—in a *confess your sins now* way.

"I need to convince Harold to bring Amber and Simone to a dinner party." I avoided her eyes.

Kat sighed. "A weekend away would have been easier. What makes you think Harold is the one that needs convincing? It's the girls who never come." She let that thought sink in, and then added, "Why do you think I'll help you out of this scrape?"

"Plotting and you go together like baseball and beer."

"Whatever." She held her head proud. "It just doesn't seem right. I don't have high hopes for Harold's new situation."

"You mean the throuple?"

"I'm pretty sure Harold's cruising for heartache, and I'd rather not be involved in playing a trick—"

"Trick? We just want to meet his significant other. The other one. That's not so unusual for friends. Hell, we met Amber on their first date."

"It's more than that, and you know it. Have you noticed how he clams up every time they're mentioned? I fear getting them all in the same room would spell disaster, and I, for one, don't want front row seats to the impending catastrophe. He's our friend, not a sociology experiment."

"Gosh, when you put it that way…" Now my curiosity was beyond piqued, not that I would admit it. "It'd crush him. But maybe it'll give us a chance to size up Simone. Offer some advice. I'm on a roll lately with relationship advice."

Kat enfolded her arms again, angled her head, and stared at the ceiling. "Ever since Simone entered the picture, I've been toying with the idea of introducing him to a woman in my painting class—"

"We should set them up!"

Kat laughed boisterously. "I haven't even told you anything about her."

"Is she a woman?"

"Yes."

"Married?"

"No."

"Breathing?"

"Yes."

"Sounds like a perfectly viable candidate." I cut into my cold pancakes. After swallowing, I said, "Can you fish to see if she'd be interested?"

"I'll have to take it slow. She's really shy. Shyer than shy." Kat perked up in her seat. "She's the one I'm having lunch with today. I can start laying the foundation."

"Fantastic. You're the best when it comes to this." I winked at her. "What's her name?"

"Gertrude."

My lips puckered. "How old is she?"

"Early thirties, I guess."

"Man, school must have been rough on her. Why did her parents name her that?"

"What's wrong with it?"

"Nothing, if you're from a previous century."

"I think it's lovely. Not that I would name our…"

I reached across the table and patted her hand.

Kat glugged her OJ.

We avoided each other's eyes. No matter how hard we tried, we couldn't help walking into the baby trap.

***

Sam scored a booth in the back of the poorly lit and musty sports bar across the street from Boston Common, a stone's throw from Downtown Crossing.

Making my way across the room, I bumped into a dowdy speck of a woman coming from the opposite direction. "So sorry," I mumbled.

"Not a p-problem," she stuttered, scampering off to the bathroom.

"Cori," a woman said off to my side.

I squinted at an attractive brunette in black trousers and Ralph Lauren V-neck sweater. "Vanessa?"

She nodded. "It's been too long."

We hugged. I hadn't seen her in over ten years. Back in school, Vanessa had been my first serious girlfriend. "I thought you lived in New York now."

"I do. Had a client meeting today." Vanessa placed a hand on my shoulder. "I wish I had more time to chat, but I have to catch a plane. Email me." She rushed out the exit before I had the chance to ask for her email address.

It seemed odd that she'd flown in from New York for a client meeting during the frenzy of the holidays but wasn't staying in Boston with her family. Oh well. I wheeled about and continued my trek to the table.

"Almost didn't see ya here." I slid into the dark burgundy booth and hoisted the beer Sam had ordered for me. Wiping my mouth, I said, "I needed that."

"Tell me about it. Work was a bitch today. Most are on vacation, so there were only three of us." Sam's top lip glistened with a foam beer moustache. For some reason, I took much delight in not telling her. Maybe I *was* my mother's daughter.

"I just bumped into Vanessa. Did you see her?"

"Nope. Gosh, I can't remember the last time I saw her. Graduation maybe."

I thought back but couldn't put my finger on an exact date. After another much-needed sip of beer, I asked, "How are things with Lucy? You two seemed cozier at our place."

"Uh, that's why I asked you here." She regarded a table where three men in suits looked battered from a rough day in the office.

"Trouble in paradise?" I sat ramrod straight, bracing for the bad news.

"Not really, I'm just..." Sam's eyes wandered to the TV screen behind my head. Nebraska and BYU were battling in the Foster Farms Bowl.

"You're just what?" I pushed.

"I want to ask her to marry me." Sam leveled her eyes on mine.

"Really? That's wonderful." I pretended to sound thrilled, even though my brain hovered in the what-the-fuck zone. Leave it to lesbians to complicate the hell out of their relationships instead of talking through things.

Her eyes grew big. I turned and watched the replay of a once-in-a-lifetime catch.

"Does this have anything to do with Inez?" I asked once the commotion in the bar settled down.

Sam glanced up and then avoided my eyes as if I'd just said I wanted to fly to Venus to propagate a new race. "I think it'd help."

"What are you talking about? Does Inez only date married women?" I joked to gage her response.

"Of course not! If I were married, I wouldn't cheat. Simple as that."

"I see." I took a cautious sip of my beer to wash down a snarky *yeah right*. "Do you want to get married? For real? Or are you just looking for a way, any way, to stay faithful?"

"I do. I really do." Her eyes darted to the ceiling. She was obviously struggling to hold her feelings in check.

"To get married or stay—?"

"Married." She nodded her head to stress each syllable.

"Because of Inez?" I pushed.

"Pffft!"

The young waiter, who resembled a marine, stood at attention. "Need anything?"

Sam started to say something, but the fire in her eyes urged me to intervene before she uttered something unpleasant and totally unwarranted. "Another round and the app sampler with ranch and blue cheese, please, sir." I didn't need to look at the menu. Sam and I met here at least twice a month, more during baseball season.

When the wannabe marine marched into the kitchen, she said, "Sir?" She laughed. "He's probably not even legal."

"I was afraid he'd tell me to drop and give him fifty if I didn't. Twenty bucks he's about to enlist."

"He does have that look about him." Sam twirled the straw in a water glass she hadn't touched. "What should I do?"

I was praying she wouldn't ask me that. I sucked in my cheeks, buying some time. Maybe if I stopped breathing, she'd let me off the hook. But Sam could be relentless. As soon as the paramedics revived me, she'd demand an answer.

"I really don't know what to tell you. I don't think getting married is the best way to save a relationship." I tried to soften my expression to ease the importance of the words.

Sam propped her elbows on the table and supported her chin with both palms. "How'd you get so lucky? Kat's the perfect woman: a free spirit, intelligent, funny, sweet, successful, and she's almost like a fifties housewife. Except for her risqué outfits."

"Your guess is as good as mine. We sit down for breakfast together every day. She even has a June Cleaver apron."

"Which one? Over the shoulder or waist?"

I gave Sam a *don't be an idiot* look.

"Waist." Sam joggled her head. "Right."

"My wife never misses a chance to show off her ta-tas."

"You really are a lucky bastard." Sam leaned back in her seat.

"Don't I know it." I guzzled my beer to make room on the table for the next round. After the waiter made a hasty retreat, I said, "Don't forget, Kat accused me of cheating once. I nearly lost her. And there was also her shopping addiction. No matter what, couples go through shit." Even though Charlotte was never far from my thoughts, I didn't mention her loss. Anyone who knew me understood how much I suffered. I swallowed. "Do you want to face it head-on or run the risk of being alone? You aren't getting younger, ya know."

She flipped me the bird. "How can I deal with the shit we're going through when I can't even put my finger on the issue?"

"Have you thought about couple's therapy?"

Sam snorted.

"No, I'm serious. Maybe there's a deep-rooted reason causing a rift between you two."

"Did therapy help you two?"

I nodded. "It did. We went for different reasons, obviously. I wasn't sure I'd take to it, but it helped. Kat's not holed up in our bedroom anymore. That was a major plus."

Months after the incident, my aunt and I practically had to carry her to our first therapy appointment. Mom had the car outside ready to go, just in case Kat tried to bolt back into the darkness at the last second.

"It's hard to believe it's been a year," I said. "Kat's doing much better now."

"Any word about the driver? Has the investigation—?"

I shook my head. "Doubt they'll ever find that bastard now. I would love two minutes alone with the asshole."

Sam's face displayed understanding, albeit coupled with a healthy dose of fear. "Are you worried she'll slip away again?"

"Yes. Before… it… I never really paid much heed to kids. But now, it seems no matter where we go, what we say, we can't get away from reminders."

Sam placed a hand on mine. "Do you think you two will try again?"

"Only time will tell. We touched on it once in therapy, but Kat… well she hasn't said it, but I think the guilt is killing her. Or the wondering what if. What if she'd left the house two minutes earlier or later? What if she'd taken a different route?"

"Where was she going?"

I shrugged. "Haven't asked. Her memory of the day is foggy at best."

Sam blinked, cleared her throat, and said, "Would you consider… you know?" She mimed a pregnant belly.

"Being the birth mom?"

She nodded.

"Of course. We talked about it in the beginning. Me carrying a child. But how do I broach that now without making her feel like I'm laying the blame at her feet, or like I'm making a statement about how she can't have kids anymore?"

"What about adoption?"

"I wouldn't hesitate. I think right now we just need time. We're both still young. And with London on the horizon… we need to wait and see what the future holds."

Sam stayed silent.

The waiter arrived with the steaming-hot appetizers. Neither one of us dug in.

"What about you two?" I asked.

"Kids?"

I fanned a fried mozzarella stick and dipped it into the creamy ranch sauce, blowing on it before placing it in my mouth. "Yeah."

"Lucy wants one." She dunked a piece of celery into the blue cheese dip.

"And you?" I gave the fried cheese one last blow before carefully nipping off another small bite.

"Y-yeah, of course… just not right now."

I swallowed. "That wasn't convincing. Not one bit."

She slapped a palm over her mouth and spoke through her fingers. "I know. That's part of our problem. Lucy wants to start a family. Like now. And right now, we don't even live together. Not officially at least."

"Maybe that's the first step. Get a place together or move in with her. Jesus, her apartment has the most amazing views."

Sam lurched upright in her seat. "That's not a bad idea. Let us get used to the idea of domesticity."

"You want one of Kat's June Cleaver aprons?" I winked.

"That's an idea. But I'd wear it with nothing else." Sam slathered a buffalo wing in blue cheese. She always used her own sauce, since I didn't eat meat. Not that I was that much of a diehard veggie. It was Sam's style.

"Do you think June ever seduced Ward that way?"

Sam chortled. "Now that's an image I wish I didn't have in my head." Her eyes lit up. "Oh my God, let's throw a Halloween party next year and everyone has to dress up as their favorite black-and-white TV show character."

The unassuming woman I'd collided with earlier walked by, and I nodded in her direction. She stumbled into an empty table. *Accident-prone much*?

I focused on Sam. "I'm still recovering from the Christmas sweater thing."

"Don't be a spoilsport," she chided.

"Okay, I call Marilyn Munster."

"But she was normal." Her face screwed up.

"Exactly."

"Gosh, Cori. You can be such a buzzkill when you really put your mind to it."

I flicked my hand to brush off the insult. "I'm trying to imagine Harold as Eddie Munster."

"Do you think we can sway him? That'd be a hoot." She clasped her hands like a child begging for cotton candy.

"Kat can."

"Speaking of, how's the Simone project coming along?"

"Oh, I put my specialist on it, but her heart's not in it. Kat's worried Harold will be a single man soon."

"Really?" The excitement whooshed out of her shoulders.

"The theory is Simone has a thing for Amber and only Amber, and this throuple bit is a way of pushing Harold out of the picture completely."

Sam bobbled her head. "I can see that. And it explains why she's avoiding us and keeping Amber to herself all the time."

"Really? Who has time to think of shit like that?" I crunched into a carrot stick.

"This is a whole new world. Everyone is coming out as this and that. It's wonderful, but it also opens the door to a lot more creative solutions for conniving bitches like Simone."

"Hey now. We haven't met the conniving bitch yet. Maybe we should reserve judgment." I smiled.

She laughed. "Fair enough."

"Kat has a painting buddy who she thinks would be perfect for Harold—if we need to go down that road in the future. Goodness knows the man doesn't know how to find women on his own."

Sam's broad smile knocked the sadness out of her eyes. "Kat should open a matchmaking business. Do you think she'd talk to Lucy for me?"

"The marriage gambit?"

"It's not a gambit."

"If you say so, but if I looped her in, she'd be talking to you. And once Kat senses trouble, she can be relentless. If you want me to open that can of worms, I will. But I'm warning you, she can make your life hell, in a well-meaning way of course."

"Maybe that's what I need."

I thought she needed a swift kick to the ass. Cheating! Never an option. Never. "Are you giving me the green light to fill her in on our talks?"

Sam stared blank faced.

"That's what I thought. I'll try to keep it quiet, but she has a way of getting things out of me."

"That's because you're like a dude."

"That's the second time I've been told that today. And don't think I haven't noticed the way you look at Kat. People in glass houses…"

Sam's face went up in flames.

"Need ice?" I pointed to her water glass.

"Don't be an ass." She sipped the water.

"Yeah, I'm the ass for noticing you leering at my wife. Of course, everyone does." I munched a tater tot, grinning as I chewed.

Chapter Ten

I had my arm around Kat's shoulder. Mom and Dad were hand in hand, and Roger and Barbara huddled with their heads together, peering at a shop window on Bourbon Street. Each of us held a foot-long plastic neon-green cup containing the special New Orleans brew called Hurricane. Within the French Quarter, drinking on the street was permissible and encouraged, with several places selling booze to go.

"Where are we heading?" Dad asked, teetering a bit. We'd been drinking since noon, and the clock had just ticked past seven.

"Just a bit further," I said.

It was the day before New Year's Eve and most everyone we encountered on the streets was in a festive mood. Many of the buildings had Christmas lights and wreaths, even though the temperature was a balmy sixty-one, almost the equivalent of walking on the sun for us Bostonians. Christmas jazz drifted out on the street from most of the shops, restaurants, and bars. The French Quarter had a charm of its own. A mix of old and new. Sophistication and drunkenness. High society and strip clubs. American, French, Creole, and African influences. What really stuck out was how many of the old buildings had garish neon advertisements. Barely Legal Club. Tropical Isle. Daiquiris. Big Daddy's. Voodoo. Temptations. Big Easy. Red Rhino. On and on.

Kat wore a loose skirt and a lightweight long-sleeved top. I'd casually suggested earlier that she wear a tank top underneath, since my plans involved her working up a sweat before the night was over.

Outside Bourbon Street on the corner of St. Peter Street, I waved an arm and said, "Ta-da!"

Kat eyed the building. "This is the special place you insisted on dragging all of us to?"

"Yes! From what I hear, it's one of the best places to dance."

Mom, Barbara, and Kat eyeballed the squat white building with numerous mint-colored shutters on both levels. Their expressions said, *thanks but no thanks*. I went into sales-pitch mode.

"It's called the best karaoke bar in the world."

Roger cupped a hand to his ear. "Did you say karaoke?"

"I did," I drunkenly chirped.

Roger rubbed his hands together. It was no secret my fun-loving uncle was nutty about karaoke, but I was the only family member who would join him. Even Kat wouldn't get up on the stage. When I had learned about this place, I couldn't let my uncle leave the Big Easy without us singing one song together.

"Many famous people have graced the stage here, including Smashing Pumpkins, Depeche Mode, and N'Sync, but Roger," I placed a hand on his shoulder, "there's one name I know you'll really love. Charles Barkley."

"Who's Charles Barkley?" Kat furrowed her brow, unimpressed.

"You don't know Sir Charles?" Roger puffed out his chest. "That's like me asking you who Miro is."

"Oh please, you can't compare the two." Mom waved a dismissive hand and turned to Kat. "Barkley is the basketball player who spit on a young girl during a game." She adjusted her Diane von Furstenberg silk chain-link scarf over her spaghetti-strap gown.

"That was one incident!" I defended him, which only made Kat scowl even more. "He didn't mean to spit on the kid. He was aiming at a fan who had been shouting racial slurs throughout the game."

Kat and Mom rolled their eyes.

Roger protected me from their glares. "Don't mind the haters, Cori. You and I have a singing date."

I looked over my shoulder and smiled as my father gallantly put an arm out for my mom and aunt to escort them inside. When tipsy, he was quite playful but still the perfect gentleman.

Roger and I marched to the bar and discovered that a three-for-one happy hour special was in full swing.

"Three-for-one!" Roger's eyes gleamed like a child in Willy Wonka's factory.

Kat sidled up behind me and twined her arms around me. Her breasts pressed against my back.

"Hello, beautiful. What's your poison?" I asked.

"Something strong as fuck. I need some liquid courage." She licked my earlobe.

"I've never known you to need courage. What's up?"

"I'm going to sing," she crowed.

Kat was an exhibitionist in almost all areas except for one: singing in public. In the shower, she belted out lyrics like a pro. In public—no chance in hell.

"Get out." I enthusiastically pounded Roger's shoulder. "We got a live one."

Roger scrunched his face.

I jerked my thumb over my shoulder and shouted over the music and wall-to-wall tourists. "Kat wants to sing."

Roger gave a thumbs-up and beamed. An overeager man in a Hawaiian shirt bulldozed past a woman clutching three beers in her hands, causing her to sideswipe Roger, spilling beer all over his polo and khakis. He laughed it off, patting the woman on the shoulder as if to say, "Thanks for the initiation into the club."

Kat tightened her arms around my waist. "Only if you'll sing with me."

"Anything for you, Kit Kat." I swiveled my neck to kiss her cheek. "Do you have a song in mind?"

"'Hot Blooded.'"

"Ooooh… I've never sung that one."

She slapped my arm. "Yes, you have! You sing it in the shower all the time."

"I meant in front of a crowd. Sheesh. You're always trying to bust me for something." I flashed my *I'm innocent* grin.

She squeezed her arms around me tighter. "I know. I'm soooo hard on you."

"I'm sensing sarcasm."

She craned her neck so I could see her quirked eyebrow. "You think?"

I about-faced and gave Kat a quick peck on the cheek. "Go easy on me. Remember, I'm just a dumb jock."

"With two Harvard degrees. Nice try."

Roger motioned for everyone to gather around so he could divvy out shots. Barbara and Mom inspected the cloudy liquid, but then each shrugged. We were on vacation, after all.

Roger's method for a toast was more like a coach rallying his team to kick some ass. "One, two, three! Take no prisoners!" He tossed his drink back with gusto.

I drank mine in one swallow, regretting it instantly. "Shit. What was in that?" I rubbed my tongue on the roof of my mouth and shook my head, trying to dislodge the foul taste.

He grinned. "Don't be a wimp. Here's another."

"Wimp? Just try to keep up, old man." I shot another round of nastiness. Why were shots always revolting yet such a mainstay to having a night on the town? Probably because people, me especially, hated being called a wimp or party pooper.

The screen of Roger's cell phone lit up in his khakis. He'd been talking on the phone and texting more than usual. I prayed it was work bugging him during our family vacation, not some bimbo. Kat nodded, and she quickly pointed to something across the room to steer Barb's attention.

Roger tweaked my pink Red Sox tee. "It's time to sing!"

Kat waved good-bye. Barbara playfully shook her head. Roger's mania for making an ass out of himself in public was beyond her reserved east coast mantra.

While Roger negotiated with the dude in charge, I studied our party from afar. My father whispered something in Mom's ear, and she whacked his arm with a wicked *I'll show you later* grin on her face, making me cringe. Barbara and Kat had their heads together, deep in conversation. They related to each other like mother and daughter, so I imagined they were getting along just fine even though it was loud as shit.

Roger tapped my shoulder and thrust a microphone into my hand.

"What are we singing?"

He twitched his silver eyebrows. "It's a surprise."

I had a pretty good idea.

Three minutes later, the host introduced us, squiring us to the colorful stage in front of the obnoxiously large pink and green neon sign. "Come on people!" said the man in a black T-shirt and jeans. "Make some noise for our special guests, Cori and Roger!"

The stage was the most jovial I'd ever performed on. Red paw prints were spattered over the yellow walls. Two pianos, one pink and black, the other green and yellow, were shoved against the wall. Festive colored balloons were tied on an arch. Some strategically placed guitars added to the orderly chaos.

Roger wore his karaoke game face.

Still clueless, I waited for the music to start. The unmistakable beat of "Sweet Caroline" got the crowd's attention. I saluted Roger, and he flicked his fingers in an *aw shucks* way.

The song was not only a Neil Diamond classic; it was also sung at every Red Sox game. For diehard fans like Roger and me, it was holier than a hymn. My uncle once told me he wanted it played at his funeral.

Kat put two fingers in her mouth and belted out an impressive whistle. She pumped her arm in the air, shouting, "Whoop! Whoop!" She could do that, but not sing?

Dad clapped as if he was enjoying a St. Paddy's day parade.

The crowd cheered, screamed, and after Roger egged them on, joined in singing. A group of Sox fans, evident by their baseball caps, howled with encouragement.

By the time we were nearly done, everyone in the place held their drinks aloft, swaying back and forth, like we were in Germany during Oktoberfest. Roger spread his arms out wide, soaking in the adulation.

The host appeared on the side of the stage and shouted into his mike, "That's what I'm talking about. Ladies and gentlemen, give it up for Roger and Cori!"

Everyone went berserk.

We jostled our way through the crowd back to the group, and Kat's eyes were wide as if a flying saucer hovered overhead.

"Scared, Kit Kat?" I teased.

She slammed her lips shut and shook her head, giving zero illusion she wasn't freaking out. I found it fascinating that someone who was usually so comfortable in her own skin had such a fear of singing in front of well beyond inebriated people whose only goal was to have fun.

"Don't worry. Most of the people here tonight won't remember a thing tomorrow. Hell, they probably won't remember what happened after another hour." I yanked her hand and led her to the courtyard outside for a much needed breath of fresh air.

"You and Roger were amazing." She wrapped her hands around my neck and moved in for a kiss.

I was more than willing to oblige.

There was a smattering of people outside, and some hooted encouragingly as we kissed. Kat deepened it, much to the tawdry crowd's delight. Two women kissing in public usually pleased crowds.

"You can do that, but you won't sing."

She ran a finger down the front of my shirt. "The thought scares the crap out of me."

"Don't worry. I won't make you."

She smiled. "I know. But I'm making myself. When you think about it, it's silly really." She leaned in and whispered, "I mean, I've gone down on you in a movie theater."

I tossed my head back and crackled with laughter. "Yes, you have. More than once, I might add."

"I love the sense of danger." Her chocolate eyes gleamed with excitement.

"Maybe that's the problem. When singing, there's no sense of danger, just fear."

She crinkled her nose. "So I need more oomph to get me going?"

"I think so."

"Well, how can we add that?"

"I could go down on you while you're singing." I tilted my head, waiting for her to thump my arm or something.

"Not with Barbara present!" she shrieked.

"So if I sent them back to the hotel, you'd let me?" I asked out of curiosity. I'd never do such a thing. At least I didn't think I would. But in the past, Kat had talked me into doing many things way outside my comfort zone—like letting her eat me out while we watched *The King's Speech*. I still had no idea how that movie ended. Did he actually speak?

Amazingly, she mulled it over for a brief moment. "No, but I have an idea." She ensnared my arm and tilt-a-whirled me around. Holding my hand over her shoulder, she led us back into the smoldering, singing jungle. I wasn't afraid. Not completely.

Kat conferred with the host while my pulse skittered. I had a feeling this karaoke experience would top all of my other performances; however, I wasn't entirely certain that was a good thing. Or whether I was up to the task.

Luckily, my family slipped out into the courtyard, unaware Kat and I were about to grace the stage. That provided some solace.

We were ushered onto the stage and even before the music started, men and women cheered for my knockout of a wife. Kat fed on their energy and practically dripped with sexual appeal.

She whispered in my ear, "Follow my lead."

I mouthed, "Yes, ma'am," while tapping the mike to my forehead.

We started singing "Hot Blooded" and I was relieved. Kat stood in one spot, clutching the mike, singing quietly, shell-shocked, but still words were coming out of her mouth. I kicked my singing into a higher gear to give the crowd something to cheer, which they acknowledged with an encouraging shout.

But then something flipped inside Kat's head. Oh boy, did she put me to shame. She started strutting around the stage in a porn-star style that would have made Miley Cyrus blush. I nearly forgot the lyrics to the song, which I could sing in my sleep. Kat noticed and glanced over her shoulder. One flick of her head beckoned me to dance with her.

If my wife wanted me to grind with her while singing one of my favorite songs, I was happy to accommodate her wish. We put a show on for the crowd that I think exceeded most people's expectations. Our singing wasn't stellar, but our moves spurred several others to jump on stage and perform with us. Kat welcomed them like a seasoned performer in front of a sold-out crowd at Madison Square Garden.

The experience ended much too soon, but the crowd went bananas. Kat curtsied like a coquettish virgin, which the men gobbled up. I flashed my *rein it in a tad* look so Roger and I wouldn't have to fight off the sex-crazed tourists. Kat laughed, slinked across the stage, and planted a kiss on my lips that stated she was with me and me only.

Much to my surprise, the crowd cheered. One guy shouted, "Take it off." I assumed he meant our clothes. The host politely escorted us off the stage. Four twenty-something girls were prepping for their act off to the side. Kat said, "We warmed them up for you girls." She swayed her hips, making a beeline for the courtyard.

Once outside, her confidence waned. With the color draining from her face, she said, "I can't believe I did that."

Roger sidled up. "Kat! Cori! You two sounded incredible!"

My parents, aunt, and uncle swarmed around us. "You saw that?" I squeaked.

"No. We could only hear it. The crowd wouldn't let us inside. Seriously, you two rocked the house." Roger patted both of us on the back as if we had just singlehandedly won the World Series.

Kat slipped her hand into mine and winked.

"Anyone hungry?" Barbara asked.

That was the cue it was time to leave. We'd had our karaoke fun, but it was time to be grown-ups again. Drunk grown-ups.

***

Later that night, Kat and I were ensconced in complimentary terry-cloth robes after we'd luxuriated in a bubble bath together. Snuggled on a plush hotel couch, we stared out of the eleventh-floor window at the majestic Mississippi River on the horizon.

I nuzzled my nose against Kat's cheek. "Penny for your thoughts."

"Just a penny?" she crooned into my ear.

"How about my undying love?" I was putty in her hands.

"I already have that." She poked my side. "I was imagining what it was like during Mark Twain's days—riding a steamboat up and down the Mississippi."

"Ah, I should have known. After the game we can take the ferry to the other side, have a mini-experience. And we're having dinner on a steamboat our last night."

"A ferry? Steamboat?" She turned and peered into my eyes with such a look of child-like innocence it was hard to imagine she'd just brazenly strutted across the stage, performing an X-rated version of "Hot Blooded" that would put all other performances of the song to shame. I loved that I was the only person who witnessed Kat like this: simple, pure, and with the biggest heart.

I tightened my arms around her. "Of course. I'll take you anywhere you want to go."

"I know you will. You're the first person I've known that I completely trust. Most times, when people spout stuff like that, it doesn't mean anything. With you—it means everything." She melted into my embrace. "I manage to fall in love with you more each day."

"I'm the luckiest bastard alive to have your love and trust."

"You got that right."

We shared a tender kiss. Since returning to the room, we hadn't fooled around, yet I felt closer to Kat now than if we were in the midst of making love.

We enjoyed the view in comfortable silence.

"Singing tonight was a good step for me," she said.

"Yeah. How so?"

She shrugged. "It just was. Conquering one of my fears, and boy did it feel good."

"I'm glad I was there to witness it."

"I couldn't have done it without you." She laced her fingers through mine, keeping her eyes trained on the river, childlike.

When she yawned, I asked. "Shall we go to bed, sweetheart?"

"A few more moments," she murmured into her hand, smothering another yawn. "I don't want this to end."

Kat fell asleep in my arms, and I let her rest for a while as I continued to soak in the dark river snaking along the edge of the city. As a child, she'd never had an opportunity to travel—

even school field trips were out of bounds. We'd gone on a few trips together, but I made a silent vow, as the murky water oozed below, to travel the world with my sweet Kat.

Chapter Eleven

My phone vibrated on the podium in front of the classroom while I sat perched on the edge of a table in mid-lecture, and I had to quash the urge to answer. Ever since the night of the accident I never turned my phone off. Now I always carried a backup phone, just in case I was needed. In most areas of my life, I was responsible, but cell phones caused me more trouble than they were worth. Either I was losing, dropping, or crushing the infernal devices. This surprised me a little, since I'd been known for my sure hands when I played basketball. Kat loved to joke that I needed a mobile the size of a basketball to keep track of it.

I glanced casually at the screen. Sam's face appeared on the display. Surely she wouldn't be the first to call if something had happened, unless Kat was with Sam or Lucy. Damn.

Luckily I had only seven minutes left of class before I could dismiss the students.

Would the ringing of my phone ever cease to instill instant panic and painful memories in me?

Once outside, I texted Sam to say I'd finished lecturing.

The phone rang immediately. "I'm so sorry. I didn't know you had class tonight. I didn't mean to..." She left the rest unsaid.

She didn't mean to propel me into full-fledged panic mode. I steadied myself and said in an *everything's normal* tone, "Yeah, the university switched my schedule this semester. No biggie. What's up?" I waited at the red light to cross Commonwealth Avenue.

"What are you doing Friday night?" Sam sounded like she had something up her sleeve. Something I wouldn't approve of.

"Not sure. Have to check with Kat." I stomped my feet on the ice-cold ground to stay warm.

Sam ignored my attempt to casually brush her off. "Do you remember that arm-wrestling bet?"

"You don't really expect me to finagle a meeting with Simone this Friday, do you?" The walk signal flickered, and I joined a throng of half-frozen students in the middle of the road on the subway platform. If it hadn't been two degrees with a wind chill making it seem like fifty below, I would have schlepped to the D-line. The B-line along Comm Ave was murderously slow during rush hour, with stops every few feet, plus too many red lights and car traffic.

"Don't worry about that. I did the heavy lifting for you." Her arrogance drifted down the line.

The brakes of the T caught my attention, and I positioned myself near the door. I didn't want to miss the train and freeze for another five minutes until the next. "Can I call you back? The train's arriving."

"Don't bother. I'll text where we're meeting Friday." There was blissful silence in my ear.

Right after the T doors jacked open, I pushed my way onto the crowded train, wishing I had stripped off my black pea coat and beanie before stepping aboard. Everyone was crammed in like sardines, not leaving enough wiggle room to ease the jacket off without getting overly fresh with surrounding passengers. Heat blasted through the train's vents, and with all the bodies, it didn't take long for a bead of sweat to form on my brow and snake down the side of my face. I longed for nice weather, when I could walk back and forth to campus and avoid the stale stench of too many bodies in one place. *One word, people: deodorant*. Many of them could have used mouthwash too.

By the time we cruised past Allston, I was able to procure a seat and checked my phone for Sam's text. Apparently, she'd figured out a way to get Harold and his chicks to go dancing, which made me smile. Harold and dancing were as incongruous as pickle juice and milk. Kat and I had tried teaching him some moves, but he couldn't manage to move his upper body and lower body at the same time. Either he wiggled his ass or he flapped his arms like a baby bird, but he never could handle both moves simultaneously.

I hopped off the train at the Boston College stop. From here, I only had a fifteen-minute walk home. By the time I reached the front door of our house, the warmth of the train had worn off and I was shivering in my gray slush-caked L.L. Bean snow boots.

Kat greeted me with a kiss on the cheek. "Let's get those wet boots off." She pushed me down onto the bench and kneeled to help me yank off the snow-splattered boots. Her cardigan slipped off her right shoulder, exposing her milky skin. If I wasn't completely numb from the cold, I would have taken advantage of the situation.

"You poor thing. You're half frozen. Good thing I prepared." She wandered into the kitchen and returned with a hot chocolate sans marshmallows, shoving it into my hands before guiding me by the hand to the couch in front of the fireplace.

"I miss New Orleans," I sputtered through chattering teeth. I eased my icicle feet into fleece-lined slippers Kat had warming on the tile in front of the fire.

She nodded dreamily. The brief break from the harsh New England winter had been far too short.

We curled up on the couch under a plaid quilt her mother made. Kat rubbed my arms and hands to get the circulation going again. "Why didn't you wear your gloves?"

"Lost them." I hitched up one shoulder in my *I'm hopeless when it comes to gloves* way.

She rolled her eyes. "You've never paid a bill late, always remember to set aside money in our savings, never take a sick day, and you're the first one up to shovel our sidewalk and old man Henderson's. But cell phones, gloves, and wallets—you can't handle that kind of responsibility."

"It's part of my charm. Besides, you can't blame me completely. I swear someone keeps stealing my stuff. How can I lose seven cell phones in a little over two years?"

She huffed, completely dismissing my rampant pickpocket theory for the umpteenth time.

I smiled to ease her frown. It didn't work, so I changed the conversation. "Do we have plans on Friday?" I asked through chattering teeth.

"This Friday? Yes. Why?" She cocked her head.

"Oh, good." I rested my head against the back of the couch. "Sam's up to something and wanted us to go dancing."

"I know. That's what our plans are. She called half an hour ago. You love dancing, so why the scowl?"

"I think Harold's in for a rough night."

Kat stopped rubbing my hand. "Because of Sam or dancing?"

"Both, I suspect. Sam is desperate to see this Simone chick, and Harold will feel extra pressure to be Kool, with a capital K. I don't know… I don't see it ending well."

"Ah, Sam didn't mention Harold and his harem would be joining us." Kat shook her head, looking like my third-grade teacher after catching the boys sneaking into the girls' bathroom. "You've really grown up." She squeezed my leg. "I remember when you used to join in and mock Harold along with Sam."

"I regret that now. Harold's a great guy—he's just, well… the only word that describes Harold is Harold."

Kat kissed my cheek, and we both sat back and put our feet up on the coffee table. I hoisted my mug. "Thank you. This is helping."

"I had a feeling you'd be a Popsicle tonight."

"What flavor?" I joked.

"Cherry."

"Maybe later when sensation returns to my fingers and toes, you can pop me."

"I knew you'd go there." Kat jammed an elbow into my side, nearly causing me to spill.

I steadied my cup. "Careful. Let's not add couches to my list of casualties."

"What's Sam's fascination with Simone and Harold's throuple?" she asked.

"I think she's focusing on Harold's relationship because she doesn't want to admit hers is in trouble."

"How serious?" Kat held my free hand with both of her warm ones.

"TBD." I hadn't been all that tight-lipped about the whole Inez aspect, but I hadn't supplied the crucial details either. Not yet.

"She hasn't admitted to stepping out of the relationship?" Kat strove not to look judgmental, hopelessly failing.

"Nope."

"Is she planning on it, though?"

"I think she feels guilty about a harmless crush. The last I heard, Sam wants to ask Lucy to marry her." I neglected to tell Kat the reasoning behind Sam's plan. It was difficult for me to see Sam actually succumbing if she was married, but then again… Roger would walk through a spray of bullets to save Barbara, and that didn't stop him from cheating.

"Poor Lucy." She rested her head against my shoulder. "Why do people cheat?"

I shook my head. "Who knows? It seems our good friends are intent on destroying their relationships. Harold and his Simone problem and Sam's roving eye. It's funny. Most people probably would have bet money that we'd be in worse shape, considering." I wrapped an arm around her shoulder, and Kat slipped a hand under my shirt and squeezed my side. "Let's hope for the best. Every relationship has to steer through troubled waters."

Kat laughed. "When did you become the relationship Buddha?"

"Over the top?" I grinned.

"No, I like it. Just not used to it." She moved her hand to my chest. "But I know the jock is still there, hibernating."

"Not sure I can help that. Given the right conditions, it kicks into high gear. Maybe this Friday."

"Let's hope not. We need to do our best to protect Harold without wounding his fragile male ego. It'll be a fine line."

"I'll try, but if Super Jock needs to come to Harold's rescue, she will. There's no keeping her locked up."

"Does Super Jock wear a cape made of jock straps and smelly gym socks?"

"You know it! The sight and smell make mere mortals crumble at my feet," I said in a superhero cartoon voice.

"Gross!" She pinched her eyes shut. "Are you warmed up?"

"I have an idea that'll get me there and beyond."

"I'm sure you do. But I have something else in mind."

I gulped down the rest of my hot chocolate. "Hit me with it."

"A modeling session. I have the heat cranked in the studio."

"And then my version of warming up?"

"Only if you're good." She flattened my nose with a finger.

"So no whining about holding still. Gotcha. Anything else?"

"Of course, but it's a secret."

"Sounds promising." I jiggled my eyebrows at her.

"Come on, Super Jock. Let's get you naked."

Chapter Twelve

The club was fuller than I expected, considering the arctic temperature outside. Inside, though, it felt like a summer day, minus the sticky-hot humidity, a major plus. Kat and I shed our winter layers and handed the pile over to the skinny lesbian in a wife beater and jeans in charge of the coat check. Skinny gave Kat an approving once-over and whistled when Kat wheeled about in her four-inch heels and short, skintight red dress, which strained against her curves.

Kat managed to hear the whistle over the din, either that or she had a sixth sense when people ogled her. She blew a kiss over her shoulder at Skinny, who mimed catching it and placing it on her heart. Skinny patted my shoulder as we both watched my wife sashay into the club, the shiny, red fabric accentuating the curves of her ass. Kat added more twist than usual.

"Jesus," Skinny whispered.

I put a hand on the coat check's shoulder. "That twist was all for you."

She grinned. "Made my night."

I tailed after my wife at a distance to take in more of the show. Kat stopped at the edge of the dance floor, covered her eyes, and scoped the joint for our posse.

Several women sat on black lacquered barstools at the bar, and a handful of other tables were scattered around the perimeter of the octagonal dance floor. Rainbow beads, flags, stuffed animals, and other oddities dangled from the ceiling.

I sidled up to her. "They here yet?"

Kat shook her silky dark locks and gripped my hand. "Let's get drinks while we wait."

Two tables off to the side were free. "Nab a table, sweetheart. Drinks are on me." I jabbed a thumb at my chest, caveman style. We both used this line, even though all of our finances had been intermingled for years. Kat didn't understand anything with numbers—except bra sizes—and left the finances to me and Dad, our accountant.

"Get me something sexy." She kissed my cheek.

"Nothing can be sexier than you," I called after her. She rounded, and flashed me a bawdy grin that suggested my compliment would be repaid later in the evening.

Smiling, I headed for the bar, slipping in line behind a metrosexual dude who looked like a cleaned-up version of Ryan Gosling, along with a beefy bodyguard type a step behind, canvassing the crowd. One quick glance assured me the man was not the actor. He may have been famous though, I suspected, or he wanted people to think that.

Meghan Trainor's "All About That Bass" boomed over the speakers and the gay boys on the dance floor squealed. I snooped over my shoulder, and sure enough, Kat was wiggling her ass in a seat, arms overhead—she'd been blasting this song in the house lately. Right then, Sam and Lucy appeared at the entrance. I waved to them and pointed to where Kat was seated. Lucy headed in Kat's direction while Sam joined me in line.

"Jesus, it's fucking cold out." She blew into her cupped hands.

"Hey, no complaining." I stabbed her shoulder with a finger. "This was all your idea. I had other things in mind for this evening."

Sam's eyes grazed over Kat's outfit. "No doubt." Then she looked me up and down and shook her head. "Jeans and a T-shirt when your wife dresses like that."

"Hey, she knew what she was getting into when she married me. At least I ironed my shirt. Besides, you're wearing jeans and a T-shirt."

"You ironed it?" She folded her arms across her chest and leaned to meet my eyes.

"I set up the board and plugged the iron in."

"That's what I thought. And, I'd like to point out, Lucy is also in jeans and a T-shirt."

I shrugged. "I doubt Lucy owns a dress like Kat's."

"Ha. I think the number of women who can pull off Kat's look is less than one percent."

"What can I get you?" asked the burly bartender. He looked more like a cast member from *Sons of Anarchy* than a man pouring drinks in a gay bar.

"What's your sexiest drink?" I asked.

He stroked his beard. "Not sure about the sexy factor, but I can fix you A Piece of Ass."

I put my hands on the edge of the sleek black bar and hunched over to hear. "What's in it?"

"Amaretto, Southern Comfort, and sour mix."

I nodded. "One of those and three beers."

"Actually two Pieces of Ass and two beers," Sam corrected.

Burly politely bobbed his head and mixed the drinks.

"Is the Ass for you or Lucy?"

"Lucy."

I kinked my eyebrows up. "Damage control?"

"You could call it that."

I inched closer. "How's the Inez situation?"

Sam's attention was elsewhere, and I followed her gaze to Harold, who had one arm flung around Amber and the other around Simone. I'd yet to meet the infamous Simone, but the confidence dripping off Harold made her identity clear. Harold, dressed in a black zoot suit and a black porkpie hat with a white band cocked to the side, surveyed the room like a 1940s Harlem gangster. Where in the world did he find that outfit? A costume shop?

Simone's fierce look suggested she wouldn't be relegated to costar status. Her plunging black dress was the very definition of risqué. She was the blond version of Elvira, minus the heavy makeup.

"Jesus. Her dress doesn't leave much to the imagination." Sam's eyes boggled.

"That it doesn't."

Amber, surprisingly, wasn't in her typical baggy sweater and flowing skirt. Her form-fitting, mid-thigh regal purple dress suited her, but compared to Simone she was the equivalent of a boiled potato next to potato au gratin.

"Is Amber wearing contacts?" I asked.

Sam squinted. "Either that or she got Lasik."

Harold whispered something in Elvira's—or rather Simone's ear. He may have thought he was in charge, but Simone apprized the crowd like royalty surrounded by doting servants.

Kat inserted two fingers in her mouth and whistled. Harold nodded, cool as Mr. Kool, and escorted the women to the table, drawing bewildered stares from half the people in the club.

I paid for the drinks, and Sam grabbed the girlie drinks, leaving me with the beers.

We set them on the table. "How are you?" I asked, hugging Harold dude-style.

"You have no idea. No idea." His voice was deeper, but the façade more than likely wouldn't last and the Harold I'd learned to love and respect would make an appearance before the end of the night. "I'd like you to meet Simone." He waved his arm like a game show host.

The blonde she-devil shook hands with everyone, except for Kat, who was already acquainted with her from The Smut Patrol club. Simone nodded dispassionately at Kat, who did a slight curtsy that made me laugh.

"What's your poison?" I clapped my hands together.

Simone gestured to the drink Kat was sipping. "What's that?"

"A Piece of Ass."

"Cori, is that what you call me in public?" Kat smugly chided.

"In public, never. In bed, yes." Kat rewarded me with a smooch on the cheek, and she slung her arms around my neck. Was Kat marking her territory?

Simone wasn't amused. From her perpetually pursed lips, I gathered she was extremely hard to please. Poor Harold.

"A cosmo, then." She shook her head like a movie starlet in front of photographers. I swear his woman was ticking every box of stuck-up bitch.

"Amber?" I spun to Harold's girlfriend and gave her shoulder a one-armed squeeze.

Amber smiled wickedly. "A Piece of Ass."

"Thatta girl." Lucy raised her glass.

Harold pinched Amber's ass, and they shared a giggle. When he put his hand behind Simone, she pirouetted and ended up behind me. All of us pretended not to notice—even Sam. I wondered whether she was feeling like a jerk yet for her role in the Simone spectacle. I could practically see letters spelling S.O.S in neon lights over Harold's head.

"And for the master of the house?" I bowed to Harold as if he were a knight returning from battle.

"Uh, surprise me." Harold wasn't much of a drinker.

Sam and I returned to the bar.

"She's a piece of work," Sam said as soon as we were out of earshot.

"Seems that way. Promise me you won't go above and beyond to humiliate Harold tonight." I pinned her with a determined look.

Her eyes shone with guilt. "I won't now." She stood closer. "Simone scares me."

"And Harold's our friend. Remember?"

She saluted me. "Yes, boss."

I gave Burly our order, and Sam and I stepped to the side.

"So, Inez?" I entered the fray once again.

"Totally over." Sam pretended like she was squashing a bug on the bar.

"And?"

"And what?"

"How far"—I moved my mouth to her ear—"did you take it?"

"Coffee after class," Sam whispered into my ear. "It was weird."

"How so?"

"It was like a date—a very boring date. The kind your mom sets you up on. Turns out we have nothing in common." She shrugged.

"That's good though, right? Crisis averted."

Sam bolted ramrod straight. "Absolutely. Now I just need to figure out a way to confess to Lucy and find a romantic way to propose."

Burly got my attention, and Sam and I whisked the drinks to the throuple before I got a chance to probe her statement. Did she plan on confessing and proposing all at once? How unromantic and idiotic. I was all for honesty, but... did having coffee with a crush equate to cheating?

Harold suspiciously eyed the glass I'd handed him full of clear, bubbly liquid with a slice of cucumber floating at the top. "What is this?"

"Gin and tonic. If you're going to London, you better start drinking one of their staples." I raised my beer and he tapped his G&T against my pint glass.

"London." Harold put a hand on my shoulder. "Oh, I can't wait!" he squealed. That was more like Harold.

"Can't wait to see how our travels affect your series? Mom reported the meeting with her publisher went well."

He nodded, too excited to speak.

I maneuvered closer. "London won't cause problems, will it?" I motioned to Amber and Simone, whispering to each other off to the side.

"No way!" His eyes didn't mirror his exuberance.

"You sure. We can set you up remotely."

"Don't you want me to go?" His voice was shrill.

"Of course I do—"

He knifed the air with a palm. "Good because I'd never miss the chance. Never."

Kat yanked me to the floor by my hand.

I barely had time to thrust my drink into his hand. "Hold that thought, Harold," I shouted over my shoulder.

"Need to dance, my dear?" I twirled Kat as we reached the middle of the floor.

"Needed to get away. Simone is unbearable. She hasn't said a word to anyone and won't let Amber out of her grip." She ground against my ass and all verbal communication stopped.

Kat and I had always loved to dance, and dammit, we looked good together when we did. David Guetta's "Bang My Head" was playing, and Kat shimmied with her hands in the air.

Sam and Lucy joined us. Sam's dancing lessons had paid off, and the extra ass wiggle proved her desire to show off some new moves. Lucy—God bless her—was about as rigid as Herman Munster, but I gave the uptight novelist credit for hitting the floor with her partner, the former cheerleader.

The four of us danced as a group, and Lucy cunningly moved into the center, shielding herself from catty gay men who loved to supply a running commentary on anything and everything under the sun. Most of the time, they didn't have to speak; their expressions and finger pointing spoke volumes.

Sam suddenly swung around, away from the group, and it took a couple of seconds for my eyes to adjust to the dim lights and strobe flashes. Through the rainbow-tinted haze, I spied Inez. She was wearing skinny jeans, a plain white T-shirt, and red suede heels, and she was gyrating with Sam. *Over my ass*, I thought. Had Sam picked this club knowing Inez would make an appearance?

Kat questioned me with a glance, and I tossed my hands up, gesturing *I don't know*. She studied my face through narrowed eyes, clueing me in that she smelled a rat. We closed ranks around Lucy and did the only thing we could do: danced our butts off.

The next song started, and someone latched onto my hand and promenaded me around.

Inez.

She leaned close and shouted into my right ear, "Cori Tisdale!"

I responded with, "Inez Gonzales."

She hugged me. Kat watched intently on the periphery of the dance floor. It wasn't often that I had my arms wrapped around a woman who was the spitting image of Sofía Vergara. To make matters worse, Inez had her arms wrapped around me, too, and she was kissing both of my cheeks. Of course I reciprocated. It'd be rude not to.

"Shall we show them how it's done? You were my best student," she said.

"By all means!"

We squared off on opposite sides of the floor. Inez clapped her hands, and the deejay nodded. Within a minute, tango music streamed overhead. Everyone on the floor, including Kat, parted. Inez smiled like Moses separating the Red Sea. She hadn't changed one bit. Back when I was a teen, the dance instructor had exuded confidence, fun, and oooh-fucking-la-la.

The tango was one of the few types of dance the self-taught Kat didn't know, so I hadn't done it in years, but it came back to me in a rush. Truth be told, Inez was an excellent partner. We whirled, spun, and stomped back and forth, our bodies pressed against each other. At one point, while Inez ran a hand down my front, I glided my leg up to her midsection. It was nearly impossible to tango without looking like you were making love to your dance partner.

Halfway through, I caught Kat's eye and winked. She seemed entranced—in a good way, which was a relief.

At the end, Inez dipped me, and I did my best to bend myself in half. The crowd whooped. Kat applauded. This time, I shepherded Inez off the floor.

"I thought you'd moved," I said.

"Went to New York for a few years, but I'm back now." Her face glistened.

Kat slipped her hand in mine.

"Inez, I'd like you to meet my beautiful wife, Kat."

They shook hands.

"Kat, this is one of my dance instructors from when I was in high school."

"So I have you to thank." Kat leaned forward and whispered something into Inez's ear.

The eyebrows on my former teacher shot up before she burst into a loud guffaw. "If that's true, Cori is my greatest success story," she said in a thick Spanish accent, slapping me on the back.

"How do you know Sam?" Kat asked.

Luckily, Sam had hustled Lucy back onto the dance floor for a slow number as soon as Inez and I finished.

Inez covered her mouth and said, "Top secret." She was trying to be sly, but Kat's frown screamed her displeasure.

"Sam's been taking tango lessons to surprise Lucy for their trip to Argentina," I said in an attempt to bury my guilt for not telling Kat everything.

Kat placed a hand on my lower back and gave me a pinch under my shirt. Just in case I didn't get her message, she whispered in my ear, "I thought you said it was an innocent crush." Kat could ferret out a stab of dishonesty with one glance. I'd learned my lesson years ago about the dangers of keeping things hush-hush around Kat, and I had a feeling I was in for a lecture to refresh my memory.

"Ah, you know about that?" Inez eyed Sam and Lucy on the floor.

Sam had kicked into Operation Save Relationship, so she was kissing Lucy passionately. Inez smiled, no traces of jealousy or displeasure. Maybe their flirtation had been merely that—on Inez's end, at least.

Harold bumped my elbow. "Wow, Cori. That was awesome."

He was alone, and I followed his forlorn eyes. Amber and Simone were slow dancing, looking like they didn't want Harold to intrude in any way. Simone laughed and brushed some hair off Amber's cheek with a tenderness I didn't think the she-devil possessed. I'd hoped Simone hadn't entered the throuple merely to gain Amber's affection and steal her away from Mr. Zoot Suit. But seeing her with Amber annihilated any glimmer of that hope to smithereens. Did Harold suspect he'd been conned? His sagging shoulders said yes.

Noticing his pitiful expression, Kat bustled him off to the dance floor.

"I have a feeling he's in love with someone who doesn't love him back," Inez said, following my stare.

"It's a tad more complicated. You see those two." I jutted my chin toward Simone and Amber. "The mousier one is Harold's girlfriend. The vixen moved in and convinced everyone to… share, I guess. Except no one is really sharing with Harold."

"Poor Harold." She studied the two women.

"Poor Harold, indeed."

"The blonde is very attractive." Inez seemed captivated by Simone.

"And conniving," I said through clenched teeth. "Harold's my friend."

"Ah, I see." She clasped my shoulder. "So, you want this Simone to leave?" She bobbed her head as if calculating a chess move.

The slow song ended.

"That would be a start."

Inez winked seductively. "Let's see what I can do." She marched toward Simone and started dancing with her—not an innocent dance at all. An *I want to fuck you* dance. Simone responded, which I found odd. Inez was the exact opposite of bookish Amber, but she was Inez: a dancing goddess who could tempt even the most committed. Sam was proof of that.

I'd bet she could get a church-going soccer mom of five to jump into her bed.

Sam and Lucy joined me on the sidelines.

"Holy shit, that woman can move," Lucy said.

"Tell me about it," Sam and I said in unison.

Sam's eyes overflowed with panic, but Lucy was transfixed on Inez, and I didn't think she'd paid heed to Sam's dreamy tone.

"I need to pee." Lucy tottered off toward the back.

After studying Inez dancing with Simone for an entire song, Sam muttered under her breath, "I can't believe it."

"What?"

"She dances like that with everyone." Sam's cheeks burned.

"Do I detect jealousy?"

"More like anger. She's a tease. A dangerous tease."

"Always has been. Back in the day I think everyone I knew who had lessons with her thought she was in love with them. And I'm pretty sure Inez likes it that way. Probably helps business. And her confidence."

"But it's not nice to toy with people's emotions like that." Sam cracked all her knuckles on her left hand.

"Hey now. She poured on the charm—you're practically married, or want to be." I waggled a finger in her face. "You didn't have to fall for her act. You wanted to."

She put a palm up. "I know. I know."

"Know what?" Lucy threaded an arm around Sam's shoulder. Lucy was trying, really trying to show more affection. Did Sam notice?

Sam gave her a peck on the cheek as an answer. This wouldn't have worked on Kat, but Lucy accepted it. Or maybe she was the type to pounce later in private.

Kat returned with a round of drinks. I'd been so focused on Sam and Simone, I'd missed Kat getting Harold and Amber to dance. They looked happy, but if I were Harold, I'd be questioning Amber's dedication right about now.

"Guess who I bumped into."

I took the last pint off Kat's tray, and she set it on the table. "Who?"

"My painting buddy."

"Gertrude?"

She nodded. "She was on her way out or I would have introduced you."

"Does that mean she's not an option for Harold if need be?"

Our eyes skated toward our hapless friend on the dance floor.

"I'm pretty sure she likes both." Kat sipped a purplish concoction through a cocktail straw.

"What are you drinking now, sweetheart?"

"Tango whore." Kat wiggled her eyebrows over the brim of the glass as she took a sip; that was her sign I wasn't in deep doo-doo but I wasn't in the clear, either. Like she had anything to worry about.

"Haven't heard of that one," I teased.

"Just discovered it."

"Does that mean you don't want me to dance with Inez again?"

"*You* can never dance with her again." Kat set her drink down and wrapped her arms around my neck. "*Me*, I'm signing up for lessons."

Sam had a *you're in for it now* grin on her face. Did she think Inez would cast a tango-spell on Kat?

"By all means." I raised my glass. "I love to tango, and you, gorgeous, would be the perfect partner, on and off the floor."

"I know you do," Kat murmured in my ear.

Sam frantically tugged the back of my shirt. I shooed her away. Kat was many things, but never a cheater.

I lassoed Kat's waist with a free arm and whispered in her ear, "How about a naked tango later?"

"That's in the cards, for sure. I knew you could move, but shit, I almost came all over myself," she whispered in my ear.

"Ha! You rarely see me dance with anyone else. And you got turned on. I'll have to keep that in my back pocket."

"Was that your motive for pouring on the dance charm? Part of your seduction plan?"

"Partly."

Kat cast a thoughtful glimpse in Sam's direction. "Tell me more later."

"Of course." I sealed my promise with a peck on her cheek.

Harold and Amber sidled up. "I think we're heading out," Harold said. They held hands, but it didn't take Sherlock to detect ripples of unease in their eyes.

Kat gave each a hug. "Have a great night, you two."

I raised a hand in good-bye, and Harold nodded.

"So glad I'm not in Amber's shoes." Lucy took a half step away from Sam.

I was glad I wasn't in anyone's shoes but my own this evening.

Moments after Harold and Amber made their retreat, Simone and Inez hit the bricks together, laughing and conversing like long-lost lovers.

Was the throuple dead?

"Anyone hungry?" Sam asked. I wondered whether she'd done that to

delay Lucy from asking how she knew Inez.

"Famished." Kat sucked down the rest of her drink.

Sam and I slammed our beers, and I pretended to toss the empty pint glass over my shoulder, making Kat laugh.

Sam feigned slugging me in the stomach. "I almost followed suit, you idiot."

"Crowd behavior is astonishing," I said in my professor tone, motioning for the ladies to walk ahead of me.

Kat patted my cheek as she moseyed by. "Always so polite."

Next door was a trendy college hangout with low ceilings and walls smeared with signed BU basketball jerseys, pennants, photos, and posters. Fortunately, right when we walked in, a group vamoosed and Kat claimed the table before a staff member had a chance to clear the dishes.

A waitress appeared, stacked five empty pint glasses, and swabbed the table with a wet rag. "What can I git ya?" She was quite perky, given that it was close to midnight.

"The appetizer sampler and grilled cheese with fries," Kat piped up first.

I turned my head to Kat. "Are you sharing?"

"Only if you're nice." Her smile wasn't reassuring.

"Two appetizer samplers and two grilled cheeses. And a Sam Adams." I motioned for Sam and Lucy to order.

"Sam Adams for me." Sam looked expectantly at Lucy.

Lucy queried Kat with boosted brows. "What shall we try now?"

I was liking this side of Lucy—the adventurous side. And I caught a glimpse of Sam running her hand down Lucy's thigh, obviously enjoying Lucy coming out of her shell. Maybe it would help for Sam to talk to Lucy. Really, all she'd done was fantasize about a hot chick. I mean seriously, who hadn't done that? Of course, going to coffee with said hot chick may rub Luce the wrong way, but the author was many things, including practical. Would she toss Sam aside for such a minor infraction?

Kat eyed the drink chalkboard over the bar. "Oooh, the Bailey's shake will hit the spot." She widened her eyes at Lucy who nodded. "Two, please."

The waitress skedaddled and quickly returned with the beers and iced waters for four. We probably reeked of the dance club, and the waitress didn't want four obnoxious drunk lesbians on her hands. You couldn't pay me enough money to work in a bar in downtown Boston on a Friday night. Of course, I could probably get some great material for a novel.

Sam and I swiveled our necks to watch SportsCenter on the TV hanging over the bar.

"So, Sam, how do you know that woman you danced with?" Lucy tapped the top of the straw in her water glass, causing it to jig up and down.

Sam didn't move a muscle. I tried to telepathically explain the best option at the moment was to confess she'd been taking lessons to surprise Lucy in Argentina.

I could tell by her frozen expression she wasn't receiving the message.

Somehow, Kat intercepted my mental wavelengths. "Inez was one of Cori's dance instructors from the dinosaur age."

"Hey now, I'm only a few years older than you." I squared my shoulders.

"But you'll always reach all the milestones before me." Kat smirked.

"And I'll always have a younger wife." I pinched her side.

"So you think." Kat fluttered her lashes at me. "Did Inez work at the school you and Sam attended? Is that how you met her?" She directed the last question to Sam. I couldn't tell if her question was innocent or if she was throwing Sam a bone.

"In a roundabout way," Sam stammered.

The waitress arrived with the shakes. I dipped my finger into the whipped cream and licked it off. Kat shifted in her seat to cross her legs. I imagined her legs wrapped around me in T minus ninety minutes if I played my cards right.

"How many wet dreams have you had about Inez?" Kat pivoted her head and met my gaze.

The color drained from Sam's face, even though Kat had directed the question to me.

"Ha! You want me to share about those memories in front of an audience?" I rushed to Sam's rescue and then sipped my beer to stall for time. "Not going to happen."

"How did I fall in love with such a prude?" Kat squeezed my leg.

"Dumb luck."

"Yours or mine?"

"Remains to be seen."

"What about you, Sam?" Lucy asked. "Any dreams about Inez?"

Sam still hadn't recovered from earlier, and now she was deathly white.

Lucy offered Sam the cherry from her shake. Sam shook her head.

"I'll take it," I said. Lucy nodded and I popped it into my mouth.

"Well?" Lucy focused on Sam's answer.

"Did you see her?" Sam rooted out an ounce of bravado. "Who wouldn't?"

"Shit, I may be thinking of her later," Kat confessed.

"Ouch!" I feigned being hurt.

"Would that bother you?" Lucy was on a roll with uncomfortable questions.

"From now on, only beer for you." I pointed my fork playfully at her. "To answer your question, no it wouldn't. We all have fantasies. Anyone who says they don't is a liar."

"Do you fantasize about men?" Lucy sat up straighter to meet my eyes.

Did she suspect Sam was having an affair with a man? Was she asking the group these questions to gage Sam's body language?

I rested an elbow on the table, cupping my chin. "Not that I can recall." I scooted my butt farther back on the bench. "I mean, I find some men attractive, but I never think about them in a sexual way."

Lucy nodded. Her relaxed shoulders and serene face didn't lend any insight into what was running through her mind.

"And you?" she asked Kat.

Kat tapped her bottom teeth with a finger. "In high school there was this one boy who I wanted to sleep with. I wonder how many times I scribbled Kat with his last name on my notebooks. Hundreds, maybe."

I turned my head. "Really? You never told me that."

"Hadn't thought about him much since then." She shrugged.

"What was his name?"

"Budziszewski."

I squished my nose. "Kudos for learning how to spell that one."

"It wasn't easy," she said in all seriousness.

"Shit, after learning how to spell that name, I'm surprised you didn't marry him. That's a commitment all in itself."

"What happened to him?" Sam swigged the last third of her beer.

Kat tossed two hands in the air. "Who knows?"

The food arrived. Kat snatched half of a grilled cheese before the plate hit the table.

"Excuse her," I said to the server. "We only let her out of the house once a week."

The waitress laughed and pointed to the empty glasses. "Another round?"

Sam and I nodded. Lucy declined and Kat ordered a gin and tonic. I found that endearing because she never drank gin and tonic. Had she overheard my earlier comment to Harold?

"What about you, Luce? Any male fantasies?"

Lucy ripped an onion ring in half. "Quite a few."

My jaw dropped. She devoured half of her onion ring and then primly pushed her glasses into place.

"When was the last time?" Sam rested her chin on laced fingers. Her eyes had that drunk, glassy shimmer.

"I had the most vivid dream last week about a man I saw at one of my book signings a few weeks ago. I kid you not—this guy was ripped. He looked like he belonged on a cover of a romance novel, but not as cheesy." She flexed her arm to indicate bulging biceps. "Except that he was black. Not sure there are many black models on swashbuckling romance covers."

"Tell us more." Color was slipping back into Sam's face.

Lucy's cheeks tinged crimson, but she whispered, "He bent me over my desk and took me from behind."

Kat slapped the table. "Wow! That's what I call a fantasy. Have you ever been with a man?"

"No, but I feel like I have now after that dream." Lucy sucked up the dregs of her shake through a straw.

"Is it true? Once you go black, you never go back? Even in dreamland?" Kat swirled a fry in the blue cheese.

Lucy regarded the dingy ceiling. "Haven't had a sex dream since then. I'll have to get back to you."

"Why didn't you tell me about this dream before?" Sam shook her head.

"Does it bother you?" Lucy asked.

"No, not really. I'm just surprised; that's all."

"Why? I can tell when you're having a sex dream. You moan in your sleep. Sometimes you make kissing noises and you grind against my ass." Lucy pretended to hug a person and kissed the air.

"Cori does that!" Kat brandished a half-eaten cheese stick at me.

"I do not!" I put a hand over my heart as if testifying before God.

Kat bobbed her head. "Oh, yes you do. Just last month you woke me up from one of your dreams and attacked me."

I smiled, remembering that incident and dream.

"It's okay to have erotic dreams. Acting on sexual desires outside of our relationship would make you a douchebag." Kat's evil grin was oddly comforting.

"Duly noted, but you have nothing to worry about." I kissed her cheek.

"Could you forgive Cori if she did cheat?" Lucy was a dog with a bone tonight.

Kat leaned back with a pensive frown. "I don't know if I could. What kind of cheating?"

"What do you mean what kind?" My voice trilled.

"Was it just a fuck or did you have an emotional and physical connection? I may be able to get over something that meant nothing—but an emotional connection, I think that'd hurt more."

"I agree," Lucy said.

"Wait? You don't mean friendships, do you?" I clarified.

"Of course not. I mean, if you had a connection with someone else that was like ours, that'd cut me to the bone." Her voice hardened.

"Ah," I said, finally wrapping my head around the thought. "Yeah, that would hurt." I peeked at Sam, who seemed to be digesting every comment.

"So what about the Harold situation?" I asked.

"Come again?" Kat glared at me.

"If we had an agreement, would we survive if the throuple ended?"

She snorted. "If you don't know that I wouldn't agree in the first place, then we need to have a chat."

"Of course I know. Hypothetically." I patted her hand. "I wouldn't either, just to be clear."

"How could we survive? There'd always be that doubt that I wasn't enough. That you needed more. Or vice versa," she said with a sneer.

"Ouch!"

Kat's phone chimed. "That's odd. Who'd be texting me at this hour?"

I had a hunch.

"Oh dear." Kat put a hand over her mouth. "Harold and Amber broke up."

I leaned over to read the text message.

"That surprises me," Lucy said. "Nerdy guys and confrontation don't usually go hand in hand."

"It was Amber who broke it off." Kat displayed her phone on the table for everyone to read.

Amber left me. Said she likes women now.

"Invite him here. He shouldn't be alone." Sam picked up Kat's phone to punch in the message.

A second later, he responded. "He says he'd rather be alone." Sam handed the phone back to Kat. "Poor guy. This will crush him."

"It was only a matter of time." Kat drummed her nails on the table.

Sam nodded, avoiding my eyes. Maybe the demise of Harold's relationship was hitting her almost as hard.

By the time Kat and I made it home, it was well after two in the morning.

We stood in the bathroom, brushing our teeth. Kat withdrew her toothbrush from her mouth. "So, Inez?"

I spat out a gob of toothpaste and took a sip of water to rinse. "Me or Sam?"

She continued brushing, staring intently at my reflection in the mirror. "Do I need to know anything about you and Inez?" The flourish of her hip punctuated the question.

"Only that she taught me how to tango years ago. Well before I met you, I should add."

"Stop hedging. You mentioned Sam had an innocent crush. From what I saw tonight it's more than that." Kat leaned over and spat into the basin.

I snapped off some floss, debating whether I had the energy, until images of gum disease ran through my mind. With clumsy fingers in my mouth, I slurred. "I'm not so sure what she feels."

Kat rested against the countertop with her arms crossed. It was hard to concentrate with the way her tits poked out of the top of her tank.

I gargled Listerine, the original yellow kind that burned. Mint was for sissies. Kat pinned me with her *tell me everything* eyes.

"Let's go to bed. I'll fill you in there."

She waggled a finger in my face. "I want to be very clear, no hanky-panky until you spill."

"Hanky-panky? I'm beat!" I slouched against the wall.

She pressed her breasts against me and kissed me. Not surprisingly, I responded with vigor.

"That's what I thought." She took my hand and walked us to the master bedroom. Neither of us glanced through the half-open nursery door.

We slipped under the bed covers, and I smooshed two pillows behind me. Kat rested her head in the crook of my arm.

"I don't have much to tell, really. Sam mentioned she had the hots for Inez and vice versa. They went for coffee and Sam said it was horrible, like a blind date your mother sets up. No chemistry."

Kat's hand slid under my T-shirt and she teased a nipple. "Do you think she's telling you the whole truth?"

"I did… until tonight." I closed my eyes as Kat squeezed my nipple between her thumb and forefinger. "If I knew my interrogation would involve this type of torture, I would have skipped brushing my teeth."

She squeezed harder. "What changed your mind?"

A moan escaped my lips. Kat applied more pressure. Clearly the interrogation wasn't over.

"The way Inez spun her away from Lucy, like she was staking her claim," I answered. "She just grabbed her by the hand. At least she asked me to dance."

"Which you were more than willing to do." Kat raked her nails across my stomach, causing a hitch in my breath.

"Can you blame me? She's an incredible dancer."

"You two looked good together." Kat nipped my earlobe. "Once I learn, we'll look better."

"Of that I have no doubt."

"Back to Sam. What else is bugging you?"

"That Sam was so upset seeing Inez dance with Simone. Recently she said she wanted to marry Lucy, but then she gets jealous about Inez and Simone. Things aren't adding up in my head. I don't think they're adding up in hers, either." I cocked my head and noticed Kat nodding with me.

"I hope she figures it out soon, before it's too late."

"Me too. I know she loves Lucy. Maybe she's getting cold feet just thinking of marriage." I paused to enjoy Kat's skin against mine, and to forget about Sam and Lucy for the moment. "You really going to take lessons from Inez?" It was hard to get the question out because Kat had her tongue in my ear.

"Absolutely. God it was hot watching you two on the dance floor. That leg thing you did! Of course, I'll be the one doing that since you're taller." Kat climbed on top and straddled me. I sat up and helped her remove her tank top, which was losing the battle to constrain her breasts. "I thought you were tired," she teased.

"Second wind." I nuzzled my face into her naked breasts.

Kat tossed her head back.

My teeth clamped down on her nipple and I sucked it into my mouth.

"Harder," she commanded. I alternated between biting and sucking. "God, that feels good. Yes, harder."

In the beginning, I'd worried I might hurt her, but over the years I learned just how much pressure Kat liked applied to her nipples. More than I could imagine enjoying, but I was more than willing to appease her need.

Kat's back was arched almost all the way back, allowing my tongue to skate over her taut stomach. How was she so flexible? She credited Pilates. My mind was soon consumed with other thoughts—fucking.

I wanted to fuck Kat. Make her come alive. Feel alive myself.

Her head snapped up and her dark eyes penetrated my soul. "Take me there. The place for just you and me. Take me there now." She guided my lips to hers.

"There" had become our code word. Kat had muttered it the first time we made love after the accident. She didn't have to explain for me to understand—the act took her away from the pain, the memories, and the guilt.

Kat fisted my hair, her excitement escalating tenfold by the second. She ripped my shirt off.

I tossed her onto her back and disposed of her panties in the blink of an eye. Mine disappeared, too, and I separated her thighs with a hip and let her grind against me. She was wet. So fucking wet.

I wanted to take her there, but I didn't want to rush things. Well, not too much. My hands and tongue explored her body. Each touch felt as if the sexual current zinging through her body also pulsed through mine.

Her pelvic thrusting took on more urgency, and I moved up to stake my claim on her mouth. Her tongue met mine with an all-consuming hunger. To ease her desire, I gyrated against her hot zone, making her moan. It made me kiss her even harder. More passionately. Desperate to connect on a level that was only reserved for us. No one but Kat ever made me feel this good, and Kat often told me I was the only one who could connect with her in this way.

Fucking wasn't just sexual, nor physical. It was the only way I could show my wife just how much I loved her, no matter what. It was the surefire way to communicate that my life would be nothing if she were gone.

Kat pulled away and sank her head into a pillow. I could tell she was close to explosion.

My mouth made the beautiful trek down. I raked her hair with my teeth, gently pulling. She smelled absolutely wonderful. Kat's juices were like no scent I'd ever experienced before. It got me from zero to sixty in seconds.

I smothered my face in her slick, warm pussy, grinning as she let out a satisfied yelp. Licking her lips, I parted them with a finger, and entered. Kat's hands clenched the sheet. From my vantage point, I marveled over her wondrous breasts heaving up and down.

When I inserted three fingers, Kat's knuckles went white where she clutched the fabric. The first stroke of my tongue on her clit made her right leg kick. The second elicited another moan, even more primal.

She didn't want to be teased anymore. She wanted it.

My fingers hammered deep inside her as my tongue concentrated on the sweet spot. My mouth swam with the taste of her slickness, and I greedily consumed the goodness.

Her back arched further as I dove in deep, tripling the efforts of my mouth. Hands cradling my head, Kat jolted upright. I could no longer see her face, but if history was any indication, her head was lolling back, her mouth open ready to belt out a primitive scream that would heal both of our souls.

Four more brushes of my tongue and another lunge inside brought her there. I stilled my mouth.

"No, don't stop!"

Her wish was my command. If I could spend every waking moment between her legs, I would. Right then, she was the only thing that mattered in my life.

Kat's entire body convulsed and another holler left her luscious lips.

After the fourth cry, she collapsed onto the bed. It was then I realized every fiber of my body was exhausted, but it still thrummed with desire.

"That was amazing," Kat said, her arm draped over the lower half of her face. Clearly she was too spent to adjust to a more comfortable repose.

"You are amazing." I slithered up her body to lie on top of her, hearing her breath coming sharp, like she'd just finished a marathon.

She tapped my head. "Don't even think about falling asleep."

"What?" I asked, groggy.

"It's your turn."

Before I could respond, she tossed me onto my back and sprawled over me to yank out the sex treasure chest from under the bed.

"Goodness. I'm not a machine." Despite my protestations, I couldn't quash the shit-eating grin from my face.

"True." She sat up. "But this is." She flipped on the seven-inch purple vibrator she lovingly called, "My darling Clementine." She never explained, but I was certain the name had something to do with the mining song.

"You aren't messing around tonight." I swept loose strands of hair off her cheek and leaned in for a kiss.

My wife repositioned on the bed, legs over the edge, feet dangling. "Sit on my lap."

I did, hearing the steady, dull hum as Kat restarted the beast and brushed the tip against my swollen bud. I nearly shot off her lap onto the ceiling. "Easy," I said.

She grinned and then kissed me, one hand holding my face in place while Clementine, on the lowest speed, entered me below. Lately, Kat loved to smooch while I came. She said it was the closest way she could connect with my heart and soul from the inside.

My fingers fisted her dark hair as she pushed Clementine in and out of me. I'd been rearing to go from fucking Kat before we even started. Now, sitting in her lap with Clementine penetrating full blast deep inside of me and my wife kissing me with unreserved passion, it didn't take long. My legs, wrapped around Kat's waist, began to quiver.

Sensing it would be only a matter of seconds, Kat drew her lips away and stared deeply into my eyes. "Come for me. Oh God, come for me." She cradled my cheek with a hand.

My eyes started to close, and a rocket flashed behind my lids. A jolt of electricity pinged to all of my nerve endings. Kat held me close as the tremor built throughout my body. And finally, when the tempest cleared, Kat pulled me down on top of her, rubbing my back.

"I love it when you come like that."

"Like what?" I rested my head on her breasts and peered up into her lovely, dark eyes.

"Like a tidal wave of bliss is slamming every fiber of your being. It hits you so hard I swear it brings me one step closer to you."

"A tidal wave of bliss…" I left the rest unsaid.

"Don't mock me, especially not now. I want to feel the thrum of your heartbeat with mine."

I closed my eyes, and we both drifted off to sleep. An hour later, Kat stirred under me. I scooted to the side and wrapped her in my arms. She didn't wake, whispering our baby's name over and over in her sleep.

Chapter Thirteen

The sun had barely peeked over the horizon when my eyelids flung open for the day. There was no use fighting my brain's urge to be awake. Kat rolled onto her side, clasping a pillow in her arms. I sat on the side of the bed and stroked her back, watching as a slight smile appeared on her lips even though she was still sound asleep.

I leaned down, kissed her cheek, and wandered to the bathroom to change into running gear.

By the time I ventured outside, my phone read 6:45 and twenty-three degrees. I fired up iTunes after completing a minimal amount of stretches to avoid injury. My thermal running pants and jacket didn't do much to combat the cold; only movement would keep blood circulating to warm me. I activated the Runmeter GPS app on my phone and took a few stutter steps to test my footing. Not too icy. We hadn't experienced a blizzard yet this winter, but I'd already determined I'd run in it, not to miss the opportunity.

The path along the water's edge was mostly clear of snow, but from past experience it was wise to stay vigilant. One slick patch of ice could ruin the day.

Only a handful of joggers braved Chestnut Hill Reservoir on such a frigid Saturday morning. I recognized two of them and acknowledged them with a nod when they cruised by, grateful that neither ever stopped to chat. I'd been running here for years now, but I still managed to keep most regulars at bay. Not that any of them were dying to become buds. Running was a solitary exercise—something to be cherished and honored. Occasionally, I encountered a different breed of runner: the ones who chatted the whole time, clogging the trail with their perfume.

A layer of fog hung low to the ground, making it nearly impossible to see the houses across the water on Beacon Street. The only one I could make out was the simple pale yellow colonial that always appealed to me for some reason. It was the type of house a child would draw: rectangular with an equal number of windows on either side of the door.

I shook my arms, rolled my neck, and took off. Each step elicited an intrusive crunching sound as my shoe pulverized frozen mud. I grimaced at the sacrilege of breaking the silence of such a beautiful morning in an eerily horror-like way.

By my second lap around the water, roughly a mile and a half loop, the fog was burning off and a reddish-gold sun hung over the eastern horizon, painting the remaining patches of cloud with vibrant colors that'd make most hearts sing. Even mine felt a momentary blip on the "I'm alive!" meter.

Three laps around the water were all my sleep-deprived body could handle. According to the running app, this was my slowest run of the week, maybe ever, with twelve-minute miles.

I sighed and mopped my brow with my sleeve. The fifteen-minute walk back to the house would provide a decent amount of time to cool off.

When I got back, Kat, dressed in a short turquoise cotton-knit robe, was camped in front of the coffeemaker with a mug. Her hair was disheveled and when her eyes landed on me, she gave a sleepy nod.

"Why are you up so early?" I extracted a water bottle from the fridge and downed a third of it.

"Breakfast with Harold." Kat's eyes were puffy and red.

"Why so early?" I leaned against the far counter, arms crossed.

She didn't answer, but the disappointed look in her eye was enough of a reminder.

"That's right. Amber left." I swigged more water.

Kat reached for the coffee pot. "You want some?"

"Please. I'm starting to cool off." I peeled my wet shirt away from my stomach.

Her eyes softened. "Change out of your sweaty clothes. I'll make you some breakfast."

"No need to cook for one. I can have cereal." I tried to sound like that wasn't the worst possible scenario on a Saturday.

"Don't waffles sound better?"

"Tons better than soggy Cheerios." I kissed her cheek, careful not to brush my stinky body against her.

"Scram!" She swatted my bum.

By the time I toweled off, I could smell Belgian waffles and veggie sausage cooking.

Kat was pouring a second cup of coffee for herself. The table was set for two.

"You eating with me?" I asked.

"Fruit. For some reason, I'm exhausted today. Need some natural energy." She winked at me.

"Blame Clementine." I slipped into my seat and dished cut oranges and bananas into a bowl.

"I noticed your ginger gait to the bathroom." Kat placed a steaming cup of joe by a glass of soy milk. She was obsessed with my calcium intake recently. "How was your run?"

"Not enjoyable. It's nearly snot-freezing weather."

"And you do love to shoot snot rockets when you run."

"It's not that I enjoy it. I have to most days or I can't breathe. It's not my fault you can't do it without it smearing all over your face."

She crinkled her nose. "Another reason not to run."

"One day you'll come around."

"I'll stick to the elliptical at the gym. Much more civilized." She rested both elbows on the table.

"Civilized? I've gone to the gym with you. All the dudes turn into Neanderthals with their tongues lolling to the side, drooling. Maybe you should wear more than a sports bra and shorts." I scowled. "You prefer that over seeing me shoot a snot rocket?"

"They aren't that bad. Just last week one spotted me on the bench press and helped with the weights."

I laughed. "I'm sure he did. It was probably the highlight of his week."

"Do I detect jealousy?" Kat held her mug under her nose with both hands as if inhaling caffeine fumes would energize her.

"Not in the least. It seems we're the only couple out of our friends who's rock solid."

It was true and odd, considering.

Kat sat quietly as I munched on waffles and sausage. "What are we going to do about Sam and Lucy?"

I swallowed a bite of waffle. "Uh, what *can* we do?"

"What's the issue, you think?"

"Boredom. Too many jigsaw puzzles."

Kat was pensive, not the reaction I was expecting. Maybe she was still half asleep. "I've noticed Lucy stepping out of her shell lately."

"True, she has been."

Kat tapped her nails against her coffee mug.

"What time are you meeting Harold?" I asked.

"9:30."

"You want me to go with?"

Kat let out a bark of laughter and followed it with, "No."

"Why not?" I shoveled in a slice of banana.

"I love you, but you can be an ass when it comes to this stuff."

"What stuff?"

"Broken hearts."

"That's not true. Sam comes to me when she wants to talk."

"She's not sensitive like most. You two are so much alike it's freaky. And look how it turned out when Sam talked to you."

"Hey. You can't blame me for Sam thinking of stepping out on Lucy."

"Did you categorically tell her not to?" Kat set her mug down.

"Of course not. I can't tell her what she can and can't do."

"Why?"

"She's a grown woman."

"Do you agree with cheating?"

"Absolutely not. Never." I sliced a hand through the air.

"What about Roger and Barbara?"

"I never understood. I'm starting to wonder whether Roger seeks attention because of everything he's been through. The loss of his parents, sister, and the miscarriages. Still, it's hard to justify."

Kat huffed. She loved Roger, but his affairs tested her loyalty. "What if I was disabled and unable to perform?"

"Is Clementine out of batteries?" I teased.

"I'm serious."

"Sex is one part of a relationship."

Kat's eyebrow formed an upside down V.

"Hold on." I put a hand up. "It's one of the most delightful parts of our relationship, but it's not the most important." I reached across the table and put my palm on her hand. "I love you, and nothing—and I mean *nothing*—will ever change that."

"For better or worse?"

"For better or worse."

"What are the disagreeable parts to our relationship?" The tension in her face was slowly melting.

"These conversations." I pulled my hand away before she had a chance to slap it.

"Such a wisenheimer." She waggled a finger.

"Don't shake that at me."

"What do you want me to do with it?" Her voice oozed sex appeal.

"Is that a trick question, considering our conversation?"

"Ha! Maybe you aren't just a dumb jock after all."

"Whew!" I wiped imaginary sweat off my brow. "Saved this time." I sipped my juice. "How bad is it with Harold?"

She tucked a dark lock behind an ear. "What do you mean?"

"Will he recover?"

"Does anyone ever really get over their first love?"

"I'm not pining away after Vanessa," I defended.

"You were fifteen, and you two dated for what, three months?"

"More like seven. And she took my virginity."

She rolled her eyes. "This is different. You've been with other girls since Vanessa. Harold didn't fall in love and pop his cherry until his late twenties. This won't be easy. Besides, you might not be pining after Vanessa, but I'm willing to bet the hurt still resides deep inside, not that you'd ever admit it."

I sucked in some air, not wanting to venture down the slippery slope. Just the other night, Vanessa had been in one of my sex dreams, and not for the first time.

To deflect, I stood and carried my dishes to the sink. Kat followed with the fruit bowl, which she promptly covered with Saran wrap and placed in the fridge. I rinsed the dishes and put them into the dishwasher.

"I'm going to shower. Want to hop in again?" She wrapped one hand across my breasts, cupping my pussy with the other.

"Is this another test?"

"Absolutely."

"Yes, I want to hop in." I peered over my shoulder. "Did I pass?"

She patted my crotch. "What do you think?"

"Easy. Clementine, remember?"

"I'll be gentle." She led me by the hand to the bathroom.

***

Around two in the afternoon, Kat still wasn't home. Not overly surprised, I decided to lie down on the couch, hoping to catch an hour or two of Zs.

Right when I started to drift into la-la land, my phone buzzed. A text from Sam. I groaned, shook my fist at the ceiling, and then read: *Help! We're working on the jigsaw again. She won't consider doing anything else. Come over now before I lose my mind.*

My gut reaction was to ignore the text, but then I remembered Kat chiding me this morning that I hadn't done enough to steer Sam through her relationship crisis.

Heading over. Hold tight, I replied.

The sun shone overhead, but vapor spewed out of my mouth with each breath. I trudged to the Reservoir stop, not wanting to endure all the stops on the B-Line.

Twenty-five minutes later, I rapped my knuckles on Lucy's apartment.

Sam opened the door, a fake grin on her face. "Cori! What brings you over?"

Lucy peered around Sam, a mystified expression on her face.

"Uh, I was just in the neighborhood." Kat was right. I was a horrible liar.

Sam looped an arm through mine. "Would you like a beer?"

"Yes, please." I gritted my teeth.

Sam patted my arm and whispered, "Thank you."

We settled on the couch, each with a beer, not saying a word. So far, my dashing to Sam's rescue was crashing and burning.

"What have you two been up to?" I asked, tweaking the corner of The Long Thaw Harpoon label.

"Putting a jigsaw puzzle together." Sam tried to sound like that was the most exciting thing to do on a Saturday with your girlfriend.

"Really. I love putting puzzles together." I swallowed a significant amount of beer to force a giggle back into the pit of my stomach. I couldn't resist.

Sam glared as if she was envisioning ripping my toe nails off one by one and force feeding them to me. But then her face softened. "I didn't know that. Would you like to help us?" Sam jolted off the couch, not giving me a chance to decline.

"Sam, I'm sure Cori would prefer relaxing." Lucy motioned for Sam to retake her seat.

"Come on." Sam tugged on Lucy's arm. "It'll be fun!" The former cheerleader was laying it on thick. "I can't wait to see the final product."

Yeah right. Sam wanted my help to end her jigsaw puzzle misery.

"Bring it!" I played along.

The three of us sat at the table by the window. I whistled at the view. "I could sit here all day." The ocean seemed endless, and boats of all sizes bobbed in the harbor.

Lucy straightened in her chair.

Sam snapped her fingers in my face. "I thought you were the jigsaw queen."

"Just you wait. I'll have this baby done in no time." I swooped up a piece and hunted for its place. My phone chimed. "After I get that," I said.

Sam sucked in air.

"Can Kat and Harold come over and help?" I asked after reading a text from my wife wondering where I'd disappeared to.

"Yes." Sam practically bounced in her seat. "The more the merrier. Right, Luce?"

Lucy stiffened, but nodded.

"Great. They'll be here in twenty." I snapped a piece into its rightful place. "Told ya!" I crowed.

"Great work!" Sam scooted over a handful of pieces.

"Should I order food?" Lucy asked.

Sam nodded. How was she not exhausted from putting on such a show? "Chinese. We can make a party of it."

With slumped shoulders, Lucy shuffled to the kitchen.

I whispered, "Are you sure this is a good idea? It's obvious Lucy doesn't want any puzzle helpers."

"That's not true," Sam brazenly lied to my face.

I punctured the air with a finger.

She pantomimed raising a white flag. "Okay, okay. But please don't go. If we don't finish this puzzle today, I'm going to flip my lid."

I bent over the table. "What happens if she buys another one?"

"I'll burn it." She jerked her head to the fireplace.

Lucy sauntered back into the room before I had a chance to ask Sam why she didn't burn this one. Sam and I plastered our happy faces on. "Food will be here in thirty," Lucy said. "I'm going on a beer run."

"Do you want me to go?" Sam stood.

"Nah. Keep Cori company." Lucy gave a half wave.

When the door closed, Sam and I eyed each other.

"This is going splendidly," I said.

"Shut up and keep working." Sam quaffed her beer.

I snapped another piece in place. "Really, how is this much different from watching a game on TV?"

"It just is," Sam said through clenched teeth.

"I think you want it to be."

"What does that mean?"

"Maybe the fault isn't with Lucy. Kat and I have noticed she's really trying lately. Showing more affection. Telling us about her fantasies." I pointed a puzzle piece at Sam. "Why aren't you trying harder?"

"I'm doing the puzzle, aren't I?" Her tone lost its forcefulness.

"And inviting the world to help to get it over with." I gestured to the plastic baggies filled with puzzle pieces. "She's obviously gone to a lot of trouble. Why?"

Sam scrunched her forehead. "Good question."

"For someone who wants to marry Lucy, you might want to open up with her more."

"Are you suggesting I don't want to get married? That I'm self-sabotaging?" She crossed her arms.

It was hard not to shout, "Glad you noticed." Instead, I said, "Nope. Just pointing out you suck in the communication department." I smiled sweetly.

She pretended to be engrossed with the puzzle, but I could tell she was deep in thought.

Ten minutes later, the doorbell rang.

"The reinforcements are here." Sam hopped up and skipped to the door, ever the cheerleader, as if my speech and her pondering had no effect. Maybe it was time to bring out the big gun: Kat.

Kat held up a six-pack of Harpoon Leviathan. Its alcohol content was ten percent.

"Now that's thinking. Let's get Lucy stinking drunk so she forgets about your jigsaw-puzzle sabotage." I rose from my seat and kissed Kat on the cheek before whirling around to give Harold a hug. He clung on, instead of his usual dude hug. "You okay?" I asked him.

He nodded, but avoided my eyes. Harold was many things at the moment, but he wasn't okay.

"Would you like a beer?"

He shook his head. "Got any gin?" He looked to Sam.

"Of course. Come with me." Sam led him to the kitchen.

"How bad?" I asked Kat.

"Bad. Here?"

"Horrendous. Not sure how I walked into the middle of this."

Kat studied the nearly finished puzzle. "This isn't good. Not one bit."

Before I had a chance to probe, Lucy strolled in with beer and the Chinese. "Hi, Kat."

Kat gave her a *chin up* smile. Lucy responded with an *I'm trying* shrug. I realized they'd been having conversations without cluing me in. While I'd been coaching Sam, Kat had been working with Lucy. And from the looks of it, Kat possessed way more intel than I did.

"Shall we get to it?" Lucy half-heartedly gestured to the puzzle.

"Are you sure? We don't want to finish what you *two* started," Kat said.

Lucy's resigned dip of her head didn't ease the awkwardness. "Might as well. We don't have that much left."

All that was missing was the Eiffel Tower set against a pink-purple sky at dusk, the center of the puzzle.

Sam and Harold joined us.

"I haven't done a puzzle in years. Mom and I used to work on them." Harold set his gin and tonic on a coaster and squinted at a piece. He deftly locked it into place. Less than sixty seconds later, he had found the home for two more pieces.

"Looks like we have a new puzzle champion." Sam patted Harold on the back.

Harold cruised through the remaining pieces on the table while the rest of us chowed down on Chinese. Lucy, maybe in an effort to keep her mind off Sam's sabotage, bussed the plates and leftovers to the kitchen.

"Babe, where are the rest?" Sam rifled through empty bags.

Kat and Lucy exchanged a worried glance, but then Lucy shrugged and retrieved a Ziplock bag out of the cabinet drawer next to the couch. "These are the final pieces."

"Are you sure you want our help? You're so close to finishing now." Kat stared at Lucy.

"Hell yes, we want help." Sam was overly enthusiastic. "I wouldn't want to deny Harold any happiness today," she said, her tone softening.

The deep-set crease in Kat's forehead was an irrefutable sign I was missing something, something so obvious I'd be kicking myself for weeks to come.

Harold sifted through the pieces. "There's writing on these." He held up a piece, comparing it to the box. "But there isn't any writing on here. Weird."

Kat nudged my foot under the table.

"Any veggie spring rolls?" I asked.

Kat narrowed her eyes. Clearly she didn't want me to stall for time. She wanted me to fix the problem, but how could I fix it without understanding the problem?

"In the kitchen." Sam held a piece. With the end in sight, she focused on the matter at hand. Her face wore a *deer in headlights* look, as if she sensed she should be doing something different but she couldn't change course.

I stood and stretched my back. "Anyone want anything?"

Everyone but Kat declined. "I'll come with you."

I tendered my hand, which she squeezed the life out of. When we were in the confines of the kitchen, I wormed my hand free. "Jesus. What was that for?"

"You need to stop it. You need to stop it *now!*" Kat paced the five steps from the counter to the fridge, and then about-faced and retraced her steps.

"Stop what?" I dipped a spring roll into soy sauce.

Kat knocked it out of my hand. "Go in there and stop Harold, the puzzle machine."

"But why? Sam wants it done, and Lucy seems resigned to it now." I scooped the splattered spring roll into my palm and then dumped it into the trash can. "Such a waste."

Kat gripped my arms with both hands. "Who gives a fuck about the spring roll? Lucy is about to pop the question!"

"Propose?"

"The jigsaw puzzle."

"The jigsaw puzzle," I repeated, hoping some clarity would emerge.

Kat shook my upper body. "Lucy and I put the puzzle together weeks ago and she used a marker to write, 'Will you marry me?' on it."

"Wait. She's using the puzzle to ask Sam to marry her?"

"Yes!"

"That's kinda sweet. Odd, but sweet."

Kat groaned. "Focus. We need to stop Harold."

"Right." I slapped my forehead with my palm. "Stop, Harold." I eyed Kat for guidance.

Kat shoved me through the swinging door.

The three of them glanced up from the puzzle.

"Uh, Harold, I need you."

"Can it wait? I'm almost done." He waved to the puzzle and took another sip of his drink.

"Nope. Can't wait. Come here," I barked.

Harold threw down a puzzle piece and glowered.

"Please. It's a Twitter thing," I added.

I dragged the reluctant man through the door.

"What's going on?" he demanded. "Is G-Dawg or Finndale back?"

Kat put a finger to her lips. "Lucy is going to propose."

"What? How do you know?" Harold tried to snoop through the door, but Kat slapped his hand. "Ouch!"

"Shush!" we both said.

Silence filled the front room—the type of silence that comes right before a storm. And then Sam shouted, "Fuck!"

Kat's mouth formed an O.

"That doesn't sound good."

Then there was a squeal.

"Is that a happy or sad squeal?" I asked.

Kat placed her ear to the door. "Happy, I think." She pressed harder. "I think I hear kissing." Without another word, she forced the door open.

Sam and Lucy were embracing.

"Shall I get some champagne?" I asked.

"In the fridge." Lucy didn't let go of her fiancée.

"I can't believe you!" Sam said.

Lucy swiped blonde strands off Sam's cheek. "I was thinking Paris for our honeymoon. What do you say?"

"Hell yes." Sam peered at the puzzle. "You must think I'm such an ass."

Lucy laughed. "Next time I come up with a plan to propose to a girl, I'll think of a faster way."

Sam punched her shoulder. "Next time? You're only getting married once. And I was trying to come up with a way to ask you. Wasn't I, Cori?"

I nodded. "She was." I didn't have to lie. *Thank the fucking gods*. And for the first time in weeks, Sam seemed completely at ease. Maybe thinking of a way to propose was too much pressure for her.

"Cori, are you forgetting something?" Kat jerked her head toward the kitchen.

"Uh—"

"The bubbly." Kat smiled.

"Right! I'm on it. Harold, help me get the glasses."

He hastened into the kitchen, grinning.

I put a hand on his shoulder. "Are you okay?"

"I couldn't be happier." His beaming face attested he was telling the truth.

"You're a good man, Harold. One of the best. I have no doubt you'll find someone to settle down with. Until then, you'll always have Kat and me to keep you company. And in London, no less. Ooooh, maybe you'll meet an English lass." I tapped my fingertips together.

He looked to his feet. "I do like a girl with an English accent."

I swatted away a rude thought about his inability to find girls with a pulse, let alone ones with an accent. Now wasn't the time. Instead, I hefted the bottle. "Let's help our friends celebrate."

Chapter Fourteen

April arrived almost as fast as a wink of the eye. It was Sunday, and all of us were at Barbara's for the weekly family dinner. Everyone was present and accounted for, except uncle Roger, who would soon return from playing tennis.

The cerulean sky, sixty-degree weather, and chirping birds called the five of us to sit on the back deck while we waited for the last family member to arrive. Dad and I had the Sox game on the TV, which Barbara had installed outside because she hated baseball, and Roger, in her opinion, watched too much.

My aunt looked at her watch and tsked. "I don't know what's keeping him. He's never late."

"I can man the grill for you," my father offered. He was the guy you wanted to do your taxes, not to cook a fifty-dollar steak.

Barbara lightly pinched him on the cheek before handing the tongs to Kat. My father shrugged it off. Sidling up to Kat, he asked, "Are you excited about London?"

My mom and I exchanged a glance. Dad was your typical guy. He didn't talk much, but ever since the accident, he, like everyone else in the family, went the extra mile to help Kat and me through the painful ordeal by keeping us focused on the future.

"Excited and scared." Kat scraped the barbeque rack with a metal brush.

"Scared?"

"What if I fail?" Kat kept her eye on the grill, twisting the knobs to spark the flame.

"Not possible. You're the best artist I know." He puffed his chest out and placed a supportive hand on her shoulder.

The doorbell rang.

Everyone exchanged questioning looks. It wasn't the type of community where salespeople or religious nuts came a-knocking, and Barbara and Roger didn't entertain much anymore.

I laughed. "We're like bad actors in a murder-mystery game. I'll go see who's at the door."

"Thank you, Cori," Barbara said.

Two police officers stood on the front porch.

"Hello," I said, unsure what to think.

"Is this the home of Roger Ginnetti?"

"Yes, he's my uncle." I was about to ask whether something was wrong, but my vocal cords seized up.

"Is his wife home?"

I nodded, ushering them inside the foyer.

"Cori, who's at the door?" My aunt shouted from the kitchen.

Not answering, I eyed the police officers. The gray-haired one was more imposing than the other, who must have been a rookie. He couldn't have been older than twenty. He stepped from side to side, his duty belt creaking hideously in the deathly quiet.

My mind flashed back to that terrible night. Had police officers shown up at my house while I was drinking at the bar?

"Cori—" My aunt turned the corner. "Oh. Can I help you, officers?"

"Are you Barbara Ginnetti?" The older cop asked, his tone low and soft.

"Yes." My aunt blotted her wet hands on a dish towel and then put her hand out to shake.

"Ma'am, is there some place private where we can talk?"

"Of course." Her voice wavered. She motioned for them to enter the office to the right of the entrance. "Cori, please go tell your mother to join me."

My feet refused to budge.

She nudged me. "Please." Her eyes implored me to act.

Somehow I managed to make it to the deck. Kat and my parents turned to me.

"Goodness, you look like you've seen a ghost." Kat's smile slipped off her face once she peered into my eyes.

"I…"

Kat rushed to my side. "What's wrong?"

"Where's Barbara?" Mom demanded.

"With the cops in her office."

"What cops?" Mom didn't wait for a reply.

Kat rubbed my back. "Did they say anything?"

"They asked if this was Roger's house and whether Barbara was home."

My father chased after my mom. If I didn't fear the worst, I would have laughed—my father, the overweight accountant stuffed into chinos and a navy Polo, never chased anything in his life.

"Do you think…?" Kat left the rest unsaid.

I nodded.

"Oh God." Kat collapsed onto the arm of the wicker sofa, covering her mouth with a trembling hand.

Tears slithered down my cheeks.

Dad returned and wrapped his arms around me, pulling Kat into the embrace.

And that was when I knew for certain Uncle Roger was dead.

Chapter Fifteen

Kat found me outside in our backyard, shooting hoops. It was well after midnight, but she didn't admonish me. She positioned herself near the hoop and tossed the ball back to me wordlessly after each swish. We continued this for at least twenty minutes.

"Would you like a cup of tea?"

I shook my head.

"A whiskey?"

I was about to say no, but then I thought better. "Sure. Roger would like that."

We sat at our kitchen table with the lights off. A sliver of moonlight danced on the wall behind Kat's head.

"What are you thinking about?" Kat asked, yanking me out of my fog.

"The first time I tasted whiskey. It was after winning State during my freshman year. We had a big family celebration, and Roger whisked me outside to shoot hoops. No one questioned him. Instead of handing me a basketball, like he'd done so many times in years past, he placed a tumbler in my hand. 'Well done, Cori. Well done.' I can still picture the pride on his face. The game came down to a foul in the final seconds."

"And?" Kat leaned her forearms on the table.

I laughed, spraying snot. After wiping my nose and dabbing my eyes with my shirt, I said, "I sank both. Nothing but net, baby." My vision blurred. "When I was on the line, I kept hearing Uncle Roger's voice saying, 'You got this.' He always believed in me." I sucked on my quivering lip and lifted the whiskey to my mouth with a shaky hand.

"He still does." Kat squatted in front of my chair and patted my knees. "He'll always be with you." She placed her hand over my heart and then rested it on my forehead.

I blinked away a tear.

"Hey, it's okay. Let it out." She pulled me into her arms, unleashing the flood.

"I can't believe he's gone. He was a second father to me. Always there. Roger was the one I called when my car broke down or when I got busted for drinking when I was sixteen. He never told a soul about that."

Kat clutched me tighter.

"And Barbara… they've been best friends for forty years and now she's—" A sob rendered me speechless.

***

"The other driver was drunk." Kat's muffled voice from the hallway drifted into the bedroom.

I'd asked her to cancel our Sunday barbeque with the gang. She was either on the phone with Harold or Sam.

It was a hair past nine, but it seemed like I'd been up for hours, if not days. Maybe I had drifted off to sleep for an hour or two, but what rest I got was fitful. For the first time in over a year, I'd skipped my run.

"Hey, you," Kat said when she sat on the edge of the bed, causing it to lurch to the right.

"Thanks for calling everyone."

She waved. "Everyone wants you to know if you need anything, just ask."

The phone rang, and Kat flinched.

I sat up and looked at the caller ID on my cell. "Morning, Dad."

"How are you, sweetie?"

It made me smile. I'm not sure he'd ever called me *sweetie* before.

"How's Mom?"

"She's at your aunt's. I'm calling to tell you the driver died."

A rush of relief whooshed through my mind, quickly followed by a twinge of guilt. It was a relief to know my aunt wouldn't have to endure a trial and all the sensationalism that would bring. Roger's family was wealthier than ours, and the press had jumped on the story quickly on a slow news day in a desperate ploy to garner more viewers. Until the news broke, the biggest story had been about a stray cat that had moved into the governor's mansion.

"I see," I said.

Kat slanted her head, seeming disturbed by the roiling emotions that must have flashed over my face.

"Do we need to bring anything?" I asked Dad.

"No, that's been taken care of. I'll see you when you get there. I'm heading over now."

Before I had a chance to end the call, Kat asked what was going on.

"The driver died."

Roger had died instantly in the crash. He'd probably never even known what happened, according to the cops. But the drunk driver had been rushed to the hospital.

We learned from the ten o'clock news last night that the driver's twenty-six-year-old son, who'd recently returned from his third tour in Afghanistan, had just committed suicide. The press was desperate to get an exposé and one merciless reporter had even tried to interview the man's wife in the hospital. After seeing it on the television, I vowed to only watch sporting events and nothing else. Ever.

"His poor wife." Kat circled the pad of her thumb on her other palm. "First her son and now her husband."

I pulled her to me, not speaking. Words were of no use in these situations.

We'd lost a child, but we still had each other. I sighed and Kat pressed harder against me.

After we had showered, as Kat buttoned up one of my blue Oxford shirts she usually wore when she was down in the dumps, she asked, "Are you hungry?"

"Not really." I yanked a gray Harvard T-shirt over my head.

"You haven't eaten…" Guilt clouded her eyes.

"I know. You haven't either. Should we stop and pick up something?"

She nodded. "But what?"

"Good question. Nothing sounds good. You could feed me sandpaper and I wouldn't notice."

"I could use a medium regular."

"Dunkin' Donuts it is."

***

We stepped into the Dunkin' Donuts on Beacon Street, near the Reservoir stop. Kat, on a good day, hated making up her mind, but when stressed or upset, she flipped into panic mode. She started to point to everything. "One of those, one of those, one of those…"

"Maybe we should get a dozen. All different, though, and a dozen munchkins," I suggested to alleviate Kat's stress.

The pimpled teen didn't say a word, but her eyes conveyed sadness and understanding.

An antiquated TV, muted, sat on a flimsy shelf in the corner. Roger's accident was still the highlight of the local news, and grisly footage of his mangled car played on a never-ending loop.

I turned my back. Kat grimaced and yanked out a credit card. I grabbed the two bags and a tray of coffees while Kat finagled the rest.

The Uber driver picked us up outside, and no one said a word all the way to Barbara's.

"Goodness, there are more donuts, bagels, muffins, and munchkins than we could ever possibly eat." Mom plucked two coffees from the holder. After handing one to my dad, she sipped her drink. "Hits the spot. Always does."

Earlier in my life, I never realized how much the donut chain was ingrained in New England culture. Then, one of the girls on Harvard's basketball team made a comment that got me thinking. She was from California, and she said the first time she was in New England she got lost and every person she'd asked for directions used Dunkin' Donuts as a reference point. I could still hear her mimicking them in her surfer girl voice, "Turn left at Dunkin' Donuts, when you pass the second, turn right. Dude, there're more Dunkin' Donuts than churches and gas stations in this state."

Kat quirked an eyebrow, and I realized I was smiling.

My father also had an awkward grin on his face. "Do you remember the time we dared Roger to eat a dozen donuts?"

Roger was a donut fanatic—not that you could tell, since he was stick-thin. Weekly tennis matches, golf, and the gym had helped maintain his athletic build.

"Oh, he didn't eat a donut for months after that," Mom said with a smirk.

"But he finished them all," Dad boasted. "Every last one."

"He moaned on the couch for hours, holding his stomach." I took a sip of my coffee and held up a glazed donut. "For Roger." I chomped off half of it in one go.

The four of us slipped into silence.

"Where's Barbara?" Kat asked.

"With her attorney." Mom nibbled on a blueberry muffin.

None of us looked at anyone else. The thoughts racing through my mind made my stomach churn, and from the palpable fear hanging over everyone's heads, I was fairly certain the same ideas were running through their minds. Had

Roger left any money to his mistresses? I never sussed out his pattern. Did he have lots of flings or steady relationships over the years?

"Do you remember the time that seagull pooped in Roger's mouth?" I asked to divert everyone's attention.

Kat's eyes boggled. "Pooped in his mouth? How?"

Mom cackled and my father smiled broadly.

"There was a seagull flying overhead, squawking like mad, and Roger looked up, curious. His mouth was wide open—"

"Oh, no." Kat covered her mouth.

"Oh, yes!" Dad said.

"Roger kept spitting the rest of the day." I took another bite of donut.

We burst into laughter right as my aunt and her attorney came out of the office on the main floor.

Instantly, we snapped our mouths shut like naughty school children who'd been reprimanded during a field trip to the museum.

Barbara's eyes were red but dry. She cocked her head at my mother and then turned to the man, her hand held out. "Thank you, Neil. I'll be in touch."

Neil shook her hand, nodded in our direction, and flew the coop.

"What's going on?" Barbara took the last coffee.

"The seagull," I confessed, more to my shoes than my aunt.

Confusion clouded her eyes, and then it cleared as she remembered. "That was funny." Her face tightened.

None of us reacted or spoke… until she cackled with laughter.

It lasted a good minute before she wiped her eyes and perched on the arm of a leather chair. "I can still see him spitting. Oh, and the cursing. I think he drained an entire bottle of Listerine as soon as we got home."

Barbara wiped away a solitary tear. Kat threw an arm around her shoulder, and my aunt patted her hand.

"It's odd not hearing his voice," Aunt Barbara said. "I woke up late, and I expected him to say something sarcastic like, 'You're burning daylight,' but all that greeted me was silence. Not sure I'll get used to that."

Silence filled the room.

Chapter Sixteen

"Cori, are you ready?" Kat shouted from our front room.

"Yeah, coming."

Kat wore a dark navy skirt and blazer. Her hair was pulled into a librarian bun. It was odd to see her looking so respectable and ordinary. She slipped on a pair of black-framed glasses. Her eyes were beyond bloodshot, making it impossible to wear contacts.

"You look nice," she said.

I glanced down at my black trousers and suit jacket, fidgeting with the house keys in my pocket. "Thanks."

Kat put her hand out. "Here," she commanded.

I handed over the keys, and she dropped them into her purse.

"We can't have you clinking your keys during the service."

I nodded.

She eyed me. "You going to be okay speaking today?"

"I guess so." I shrugged.

"If you don't want to speak at Roger's funeral, it's all right. No one will think less of you."

"I will." With that, I headed outside to wait for the limo Mom had arranged.

It took us less than thirty minutes to arrive. My heart skittered, and my hands were clammier than a clam. I wiped my palms on the seat cushion and plastered on a be strong face. Kat met me in front of the car and slipped her hand into mine, tightly lacing our fingers, our wedding rings rubbing together.

Dad stood outside, and he wrapped me in a bear hug as soon as we exited the car. "Here, you may need this." He shoved a handkerchief into my trouser pocket. My father wore a black suit and a somber gray tie. I tried to remember the last time I'd seen him in a suit, regretting it instantly—the memory of Charlotte's funeral rattled my soul.

A smattering of people were taking their seats inside the church. We were early, but hundreds of people were expected for the service. I did my best to block that out of my mind. The only people that mattered to me at the moment were my aunt and uncle. I wasn't a religious person by any means, but I had this odd sensation Roger was watching me from somewhere.

Maybe Kat was in tune with my thoughts, because she squeezed my hand and glanced up toward the ceiling. My gaze followed. I could see why people believed in God. The gothic revival church was spectacular, exuding confidence, reverence, and tranquility. Standing in the middle, I fixed upon one stained glass window and then another, feeling small and insignificant in the grand scheme of things.

Roger hailed from a prominent family and was a well-respected businessman. In the nineties, he'd served in the House of Representatives for a couple of terms. The funeral wouldn't be along the scope of Edward Kennedy's, but it would be attended by many prominent and important people, and the governor of Massachusetts had agreed to give a eulogy. News crews were camped outside.

After taking in the church, I let my focus wander to the front.

More people started to arrive, and I figured we should try to locate my mom and aunt. Barbara stood in the front pew, next to my mother. Both wore simple black dresses with a single strand of pearls and both welcomed and hugged friends and associates.

"You ready?" My mom rubbed my back to be supportive, but it was disconcerting that Nell Tisdale was toning it down completely for my benefit. Not once over the past several days had she tried to divert all the attention to herself. She wasn't even speaking today. Only my father and I were included in the program for remembrances.

The church was finally at capacity, and violins, violas, cellos, and a clarinet began to play Mozart. Usually, music soothed me; today, it was as if every note swirled around my head and pulled each thought in six different directions. A commotion at the entrance alerted me Roger's casket had arrived. Slowly, the pallbearers, including my father, led my uncle's remains to the front.

At least the casket would remain closed. The accident had been horrific, and my aunt couldn't bear for all to see Roger at his worst. She wanted people to remember the vibrant man she knew and loved, not the Roger that morticians had to glue back together and slather in makeup to make him look halfway human.

Kat gripped my hand, and I nodded, afraid if I spoke, I'd break down.

The cardinal welcomed everyone and spoke briefly. The clock was ticking. In minutes, it would be me who had to stand before this crowd. I prayed I'd be able to keep my emotions in check. *Just get through it. You can break down later, Cori. In private.*

The psalm, Old Testament, and gospel readings were over before I had a chance to breathe, it seemed.

Then it was my turn.

Kat squeezed my hand, and my mom patted my back as I slipped by to make my way to the front.

I'd spoken at author events over the past few years, and I lectured at Adams University, but when my eyes panned the sea of black I couldn't kick the sensation I was an alien who had popped onto the wrong planet.

"Uh…" I cleared my throat and glanced to my left, where Aunt Barbara was smiling and nodding at me. "I want to thank you all for coming today to celebrate the life of Roger Ginnetti." I stared down at my notes, frozen. Everyone was silent, except for the occasional sniffle. My eyes scanned the crowd, searching for women who looked out of place, wondering about their connection to my uncle.

Stop, Cori!

I cleared my throat again. "Roger touched many through his charity work, businesses, and his overall zest for life. The past few days have been emotional, and so many have shared their personal stories about how Roger affected their lives. My uncle was blessed to have so many wonderful friends and associates, and it's an honor to stand before all of you." I dabbed my eyes with the handkerchief my father had slipped into my pocket.

"I was fortunate, growing up. Not only did I have two loving and supportive parents, but my aunt and uncle were like parents to me also. It was Uncle Roger who first put a basketball in my hands. He taught me how to box, so I could always defend myself. More importantly, he taught me the meaning of family.

"For me, our family is perfectly normal because I'm used to all the crazy. When I was in junior high, some of my classmates gave me a hard time. My mom, as many of you know, is a famous writer, and at the time, Roger was in the House of Representatives. I came home from school one day mad as hell because some kids had taunted me after I won a writing contest. They thought my mom had rigged the competition. Roger pulled me aside and said, 'I know it isn't easy being the center of attention, and you're at an age where you want to fit in, but here's the deal; you can never get rid of your family. When the chips are down, it's your family who'll always be there for you. No matter what.' It took me years to truly understand what he meant."

I looked to my aunt, who dashed away a single tear. "Roger's life wasn't easy. Before he became the man most of us knew and admired, he endured personal losses that would have broken many people. His only sister died before she could drive a car. His father passed the day before Roger's nineteenth birthday, and his mother died less than a year later. Each tragedy could have destroyed his beliefs and his passion for life. But Roger wasn't any man. He was a fighter. Every loss and hardship he experienced made him stronger and kinder. Ever since I can remember, Roger was always telling me, 'Get in the game.' Life for Roger wasn't something to be endured. It was something to be lived to the fullest."

I let out a long breath. "Roger was taken too soon, but he lived his life to the fullest. I'm saddened to say good-bye, but I'm thankful to have known and to have been loved by him. I've never been overly religious." I gave a slight shrug and looked up to the left at a stained-glass window. The priest smiled knowingly and many chuckled. I looked down at my uncle's casket, half expecting Roger to pop out and wrap his arms around me, saying, "You got this."

"His absence will be felt by many here and elsewhere. He was so much to so many: an uncle, brother-in-law, friend, a confidant, a businessman, politician, neighbor, a Red Sox fan, and an overall sports nut. And a loving husband." I nodded toward Barbara. "To me, he was my second father, and I'm not ready to say good-bye. So Roger"—I peered upward—"this isn't good-bye. I look forward to our talks and to shooting hoops when we meet again." As I walked past his casket back to the front pew, I whispered, "Take care of Charlotte for me, please."

Chapter Seventeen

The Saturday after the funeral, Sam, Lucy, and Harold came over for the weekly barbeque/Red Sox party in our backyard. The television on the deck was playing the pregame show, which no one paid attention to, although we always switched it on out of habit. Kat was inside, preparing snacks.

Lucy, as usual, manned the grill, and Harold was off to the side of our fenced yard, messing with his phone, probably tweeting about books.

Sam nudged me with an elbow. "I still remember that time during our senior year when Roger rushed into the basketball gym for the playoff game."

I smiled and took a swig of Harpoon IPA. "When I called to tell him about the schedule change, he promised he'd catch the next flight and wouldn't miss it. I didn't believe him."

"Where'd he fly from?" She squinted up at a plane overhead, or was she just saying hi to Roger?

"Japan. He hired a private jet."

"I can still see him running, his tie spilling out of his pocket." She smiled.

"I doubt he slept for twenty-four hours."

"All the cheerleaders used to call him our lucky charm," Sam said. "He was our most supportive fan. By the end of that game, his face paint had melted. I always wondered whether he had to toss the suit out afterward."

"He did. A custom-made suit, no less. Not that he gave a shit. All that mattered was we won. Do you remember the time he dyed his hair?" I laughed. "For a month his hair was green and yellow. I have that photo in my office." I clutched my beer bottle and brought it to my lips for a long tug.

"It was a nice touch when everyone sang 'Sweet Caroline' during the service."

I grinned. "He mentioned it once. I had to send him off right."

"Oh, Vanessa emailed me to see how you were doing."

"Really? Why didn't she contact me?" I swatted a fly away from the lip of my beer bottle.

Sam shrugged. "She was always an odd one. Besides, she mentioned you were probably drowning in people expressing their sympathy. She just wanted to see how you were handling it."

"That was kind of her. Tell her hello for me."

Kat and Lucy brought platters from the kitchen and started organizing food on the table off to the side of the deck.

Harold barreled over and showed Kat something on the screen of his cell. Occasionally, super famous authors would tweet him or something, making him swagger for days on end. But this time, the animated way he pounded his finger against the screen made it seem like whatever message was on his phone wasn't good.

Kat's eyes darted over to me, panic clouding her face.

"What's wrong?" I asked. The sun broke through a cloud and I couldn't see their faces well, so I shielded my eyes to get a better glimpse.

Kat and Harold stood frozen, staring down at me. Sam shifted awkwardly in her leather sandals.

Lucy craned over Harold's shoulder, and her expression confirmed my fears. Whatever was on Harold's cell phone was bad.

I stomped up the four steps and yanked Harold's phone out of his hands to find out for myself.

"WAS BUSINESS TYCOON ROGER GINNETTI A SERIAL CHEATER?" blared the headline article of *The Boston Globe*. It cited dozens of tweets from those "in the know." Ex-lovers. Spouses of his lovers. Spiteful business associates.

It wasn't breaking news to me or Kat, but his affairs had never been outed before, not even when he was running for office, although of course that had happened ages before social media. Now, no one had privacy. And the public craved one scandal after another, no matter how untrue.

"No one will believe that," Lucy said. "Everyone loved Roger. Who would start such a vicious lie?"

My eyes locked with Kat's. Was it still possible to shield Roger's memory from this? What about my aunt? How could I protect Barbara from the humiliation?

Sam joined us on the deck. She must have picked up on the truth mixed in with the fury of my expression, because she gasped and covered her mouth.

"Did your aunt know?"

Harold and Lucy remained mute. Harold gawked at his hairy Neanderthal-looking toes poking over the rim of his Tevas. His nails were in desperate need of a trim. Lucy continued to turn the same brat over and over on the grill.

"I need to call Mom," I said, ignoring Sam's question.

Everyone nodded as if I were asking permission. Maybe they didn't know what else to do or say without pushing my hothead button.

I slipped around the corner in the yard, for privacy. "Call Mom," I instructed my cell. The phone rang, and as soon as someone answered, I muttered, "What the hell?"

Mom sighed. "Come to my house tonight. We'll talk. The press is all over Barbara's." She hung up.

I kicked the side of the house, loosening one of the Heron Blue boards. I remembered the exact color because Roger and I had picked it out and painted the house together last summer. "Fuck!" Hopping on one foot, I kept repeating the word.

"It always amazes me when you slip into your stupid jock mode." Kat leaned against the cedar fence Roger and I had replaced two summers ago.

Cautiously, I put weight on my foot. Nothing was broken, thank goodness, or Kat would never let me live it down.

"You want to talk?"

"Not now. Mom wants us to come over tonight. The press is at Barb's."

Kat looped her arm through mine. "Come on. Let's eat and try to forget this for a few hours."

"How can I forget this? He hasn't been in the ground for seventy-two hours and already the social media vultures are tearing him to shreds."

***

"I'm not surprised it's coming out now." Mom stirred her bubbling homemade spaghetti sauce on the stovetop. Steam fogged the reading glasses that dangled on a silver chain around her neck. Occasionally, she would slip them on to read her grandmother's handwritten recipe card. "How it was kept quiet for so many years is astounding, considering how often people update their social media feeds."

"Do we know who leaked the story?" Kat asked as she chopped up carrots and cucumbers for the salad.

My father and I sat on barstools on the opposite side of the counter. Barbara was upstairs resting.

"There was that minor leak when he was in office." My father stroked the two-day stubble on his chin.

"What?" I snapped my head in his direction. "No one ever told me that."

"That's why he didn't seek reelection. For a time, he wanted to go all the way." Dad strummed his fingers on the granite countertop.

"All the way? You mean, president?"

He shook his head. "No. Governor."

Uncle Roger wanted to be governor? How did I not know this?

"What's the plan?" Kat stayed focused on the matter at hand.

"Ignore it 'til it goes away." Mom pinned me with her *you understand* glare.

"Ignore it?" My voice cracked, making it clear I didn't.

"We can't deny it, since it's true, and Barbara doesn't want to talk about it publicly. This is a no-win situation. So we ignore it. And if you so much as tweet or anything, I'll cut your fingers off." To emphasize her point, she wielded a paring knife. "The public will want a feeding frenzy, but if we don't engage, they can't have it. Not completely."

The knife didn't intimidate me. Her glower did.

I raised my palms. "I promise, but I have an interview in the next couple of weeks. What do I say if asked about it?"

"Say it's a family matter and you have no comment. Who's the interview with?"

"A writer from *Huffington Post*. Harold arranged it weeks ago. It's for the Mother's Day event coming up."

"Oh, good Lord. Maybe you should cancel." She dried her hands on a dish towel. "Can Harold reschedule?" She reached for her phone.

"No," Barbara said, leaning against the doorjamb. "No one is changing anything."

Kat and Mom exchanged worried glances. Dad rested his wobbly chin on his chest.

Silence screamed in my ears.

"You hungry?" Mom asked. "The sauce is nearly done, and the garlic bread is about to go in." She wrenched her head to the hot oven.

"No thanks." Barbara took a step to the counter and filled a wineglass to the top. "Smells good, though, Nell." My aunt came from tough stock. It was clear she was doing her best to hold the overwhelming sadness in check. I still hadn't seen her full-on cry, and I'd wondered if she ever would, if she'd ever allow herself to break down.

She and Roger had a different relationship, but I'd never doubted their love and companionship. The friendliness they showed each other made the situation bearable for the rest of us. I could count on one hand how many times Roger's affairs were alluded to when both or one of them was present. If my memory served, no one had ever mentioned it outright.

"Have you two started preparing for London?" she asked.

"Getting everything together for the visas," Kat said.

"Is there a lot?" Dad asked.

"More than I thought. Harold is all over it. He's color-coded everything. I never knew he had a mania for organization—well, besides his book collection. He has every book he's ever purchased and read listed in a spreadsheet. But not just any spreadsheet—it has dropdown boxes and other fancy shit. He even has spreadsheets for the characters, timelines, places, and quotes for his graphic novels."

"It's paid off for him. He's landed an agent, and a book deal is on the horizon," Mom said, a hint of pride in her tone.

I worried a thread on my sleeve. "Hopefully we get all the London stuff taken care of before he becomes famous."

"Puh-lease. Harold will never leave us. We're his family." Kat shooed the idea away.

Barbara rested against the counter. "I've been doing some research. You can get a visa if you plan to run a business. Of course, you need to have some coin to prove you can support the business and yourself." She shrugged off that concern.

Mom picked up on her meaning first.

"Are you referring to Kat and Cori or to yourself?"

Barbara met her sister's eyes. "Me. I'm already invested in Anselm's business, and he wants to open another studio. Kat and Cori could help me set it up this summer."

"Wait a minute. Are you talking about settling there permanently?" I sprang off the barstool.

"Not necessarily. I'm talking about getting away for a bit. Staying busy." She stared out the window.

"Define *a bit*?" Mom pushed.

Barbara sipped her wine and didn't respond.

My father studied her face. "How long have you been thinking about this?"

"Since Anselm's visit."

"That was well over a year ago, and you didn't tell me! Not once!" Mom whacked the countertop with a wet dishrag.

"I wasn't sure about it. It was just a nice thought to daydream about. Now, I'm seriously considering. I need to get out of this house. Away from... away from the memories. I need a change, Nell." She closed her eyes. "I've needed a change for years, but I was always needed here."

Barbara had been the de facto head of the family even before grandfather died. She held everything together. She was the one who patched up any quarrels or misunderstandings, picked us up when we fell, and was the first to celebrate triumphs.

"It'd be great for Kat. She'd be close to Paris. Every artist should spend days or weeks wandering Paris, visiting the museums. Anselm has a lot of connections. Nell, you can visit whenever you want." She rounded to me and placed a hand on my cheek. "And you can spend your time off from writing wandering the streets Charles Dickens explored. Imagine that."

"So you're suggesting we stay longer than the summer?" I asked, blinking excessively.

"If you'd like. My home will always be open to family—even if that home is in England. But if you want to come back to the States, I understand. All of you will get along fine without me."

Everyone was stunned into silence. She made it sound like it was a done deal—that Kat, Barbara, and I weren't visiting London this summer; we were moving to London. How could I say no, though? Even if she didn't admit it, she needed family. And after she'd been there for us following the accident… I wasn't sure what to think. With Roger's death and this new information to process, my head was spinning.

Chapter Eighteen

Three weeks later, Kat and I were in the hot tub.

"How long have you known?" I asked.

Kat cocked her head. "About what?"

"Barbara's London plan."

She didn't bother pretending. "We'd talked about it months ago. Barbara's been so unhappy for years. She loved your uncle, but the relationship wasn't fulfilling. You had to know that."

I did, on some level. And I was sure my mother understood as well. Barb did what she did best: made lemonade out of lemons.

"But was she going to leave if…?" I didn't have the heart to finish the sentence. Not that I needed to.

"I don't think so. Her plan had been to travel back and forth. She wanted me to eventually run the studio in Boston.

Roger was aware. He wasn't thrilled, but he understood." Kat prodded me with an elbow. "Talk to me. This is a lot to process. I'm not surprised it's taken you this long to broach the subject. Ideas have to marinate quite some time in your mind before they sink in."

I rested my head against the edge of the hot tub, taking in the vastness of the night sky. "Geez, Kat, I don't know what to think right now. My initial thought was she wanted to run away from everything. The funeral, the empty house, the press… but she had that look about her, the one that said she'd made up her mind."

"I believe she has. She wants me to be co-owner."

I snapped my head up. "That's huge. I have no doubt she'll be just as successful in jolly old London as she is here." My smile, I feared, didn't hold much warmth.

"What about us?" Kat asked.

"What do you mean?" My voice brimmed with concern. "You don't want to go alone, do you?"

She splashed water in my face. "No! How can you even think such a thing? How do you feel about us moving there for longer than ten weeks?"

I laughed. "Oh, God." I placed a palm on my thrumming heart. "Now I see. This was your plan all along. You mentioned two months to get me used to the idea, didn't you? Knowing if you sprung something so huge on me, my gut reaction would be to say no. But you and Barbara have been plotting behind the scenes. Is the Anselm part really happening?"

"Yes, of course."

"Am I right about the rest?"

"Maybe." She studied the gibbous moon as if she was trying to memorize the image for a future painting.

I positioned myself in front of her. "Tell me."

"Maybe."

"That means yes."

"Maybe."

"What about my classes?"

"How much would you miss them?" Her eyes quizzed me.

"Good question. Years ago, I hated teaching, but it's grown on me." I laughed. "The pay sucks and hardly covers a third of our bills." I shrugged.

"I don't care about the money. I want you to be happy. Successful. To follow your heart. What does your heart say?"

"You have my heart. Wherever you go, I'll go. Barb's right. Every artist should see Paris. But not just Paris. All of Europe. And if we lived in London, the continent would be our backyard."

"Not just artists. Writers. Think Hemingway, Crane, Pound, Fitzgerald, and Miller, just to name a few."

"Ha! Are you trying to alleviate my fear or intimidate the shit out of me?"

She took my pruned hand and placed it against her cheek. "You need to stop comparing yourself to others. Write the stories you want to write, no matter what."

Her dark eyes gazed into mine. She wasn't trying to seduce me, but the way the moonlight reflected off the water onto her skin… I wanted her. Her dark hair was pinned on top of her head, but a few strands hung down her neck and face. The water covered her naked breasts, lapping the freckles along her cleavage, tempting me.

We hadn't made love since that awful night the cops had arrived on Barbara's doorstep.

Kat leaned against my palm. Her soft lips kissed the base of my hand.

"Let's do it," I said.

The desire in my eyes must have confused her. "Do what?"

I grinned. "Help Barbara set up the studio. Let's get away from here for a bit. If I've learned one thing from Roger and —" I broke off, still not wanting to say the word. "Life is short. I don't want my life to be defined by the opportunities I skipped. We've had enough sorrow to last a lifetime, I don't want to add cowardice to our woes."

Her eyes widened. "Really?"

"Really! I think it would be good for you. For me." I tapped my chest and then rested my hand on hers. "For us."

Kat pulled my head to hers and we kissed tenderly. At first it was a celebratory kiss, but it soon turned into more. We were hungry for each other.

"Take me inside," she panted in between kisses.

I hopped out of the hot tub and snatched up the bathrobes, holding one open for her to step into before I put mine on.

Kat gripped my hand and led me to the front room. I sensed Kat wanted to avoid the walk past the nursery. Roger's death had stirred up too many emotions. However, this wasn't a night for remembering. It wasn't about forgetting either. It was about the two of us. Our love. Our commitment. And our wanting to make the other person feel good. Feel alive.

Winter's grip hadn't yet released its stranglehold, and she flipped on the fireplace. On the floor, she spread out a blanket from the couch while I lit a few candles. We stared awkwardly at each other from opposite sides of the room, searching for something else to set the mood. We acted like we'd never made love before. As though neither of us could process the next step. Who should make the first move?

"I love you," I whispered.

"I know." Kat wasn't usually shy. I found it oddly sensual. She pulled me into her lair as if she was Aphrodite.

We rushed across the room to each other, into a passionate embrace. It didn't take long for either of us to disrobe. Kat slammed me face-first against the wall, and it took great effort to twist my neck to continue kissing her eager mouth. Stunned by her zeal, my libido kicked up several notches.

She spread my legs with her knee.

"Fuck me. Oh God, Kat, fuck me. I need you inside me."

Kat entered me, pumping her fingers.

"I need to kiss you," I begged.

She spun me around, knocking over a small table and reading lamp. Neither of us paid much attention to the carnage. We fell onto the couch, kissing. Once again she separated my legs and inserted her fingers—I estimated she had four inside—frantically thrusting deep.

My head lolled back over the couch's armrest, and I gasped.

Kat's teeth grazed my nipple, which hardened instantly as she took it all the way into her mouth. Down below, she continued to thrust inside me.

"I've missed you," I said. "I've missed feeling like this."

Kat sat up, although her fingers dove in deep. "I want to watch you come." She glanced down at my pussy and slowly trailed her gaze up my writhing body. "I love how you move." She slid on top of me, never slowing the speed or strength of her penetrating fingers.

"You do this to me." My back levitated as if by magic. "You're the only one who's ever made me feel this way. So alive."

I was close; Kat sensed it and pushed in deeper, maneuvering her fingers upward.

A spasm zipped through me, and I groaned and pushed my head into a cushion.

Kat's fingers were moving furiously now, fucking me as if our lives depended on it.

"Kiss me," I was practically begging.

Her lips on mine brought me to the threshold of bliss, and one more forceful thrust took me beyond.

Kat didn't pull away. She didn't stop fucking me.

I came again—hard, spilling all over her hand. And I kept coming.

"I need to taste you," I said.

Before she could telegraph her move, we were on the floor and Kat's legs were spread open for me.

I laughed. "This is the painting I want you to create for me."

Kat propped herself up on her arms, angled her head all the way back, and raised her ass. "How's this?" she asked in her bedroom voice.

"Perfect. Don't move." I snapped a photo with my phone, admiring how well it turned out considering the low light. Smartphones these days were amazing.

"And now one with the two of us. A naughty selfie, so to speak." I positioned and snapped.

"Got it?"

I nodded.

"Good, now get to work."

I saluted her. "Yes, ma'am."

She pulled me toward her, and we tumbled onto the blanket in front of the fire. My cell phone skittered under the couch, but I'd worry about that later.

I could taste my own wetness on her tongue. "God, I love that."

Kat nodded, knowing what I meant.

My fingers trailed up and down her side, and she mewled softly in my ear. Watching her body twist under mine in the twinkling candlelight was one of the best feelings. It excited me to get her so completely revved up.

When I took her nipple in my mouth, while entering her below, the catch in her breath nearly made me come again.

How in the world had I managed to win over such an amazing woman?

Kat wrapped my hair around her fingers, tugging slightly and bringing me back to the task at hand.

"Where'd you go?" she asked.

"Thinking how amazing you are."

She flashed that sexy, crooked smile—not the one she used on people to get her way, but the one she reserved just for me.

"Show me how much you love me."

I did.

All night long.

***

The following morning, I scanned my iPad for more "news" about Roger. A handful of women had trickled forward so far, keeping the story fresh.

"Why do you bother reading that crap?" Kat placed some French toast on my plate. "Leave it alone. You can't do anything to stop it."

"But…" I munched on a slice of veggie bacon.

"But what?" Kat removed her apron and sat down to eat, wearing only a tank top and panties.

"I just hate it."

"That the news is out there now? Your mom's right. It's amazing it never leaked completely before. Your uncle was rich and powerful."

I sighed. "That doesn't mean he deserves this."

"Deserves what? Roger would be the first to tell you it's all true."

I angrily sliced into the French toast. "I know," I said through gritted teeth. "But he'd never want Barbara to deal with this."

"True, but I think something else is bothering you."

I squirmed in my chair.

"Tell me." She stroked the back of my hand with a finger.

"I hate how it makes me feel, seeing it splashed all over the newspapers, on Facebook, Twitter, and God knows how many other platforms I've never even heard of for weeks now. The man is dead. Why can't they leave him be?"

"Is it more than that?" She cocked her head, giving me the time I needed.

"It's just, all my life I've been conflicted about Roger. Seeing these stories, they make it clear what he was and it's hard to remember I love him. And I don't want people to think the rest of us are like him. Those thoughts make me feel guilty. He's always been there for me. But…"

Kat viciously forked a piece of cantaloupe, avoiding my eyes.

"What are your true feelings?" I asked.

Slowly, her eyes rose from her plate. "I... you know how close I am to your aunt."

I nodded.

"She's like a mother to me."

I motioned for her to say it quick, like ripping off a Band-Aid.

"I've never respected him. Not completely."

"I know." I cast my eyes downward at my plate.

"That's not to say I didn't love him, and it's not to say you should feel..." Kat froze.

"Go on."

"It's not my place to tell you how you should feel."

"What a cop-out!" I flung the rest of the flimsy bacon into my mouth. No matter how hard Kat tried, she could never get it crispy like real bacon.

She jiggled her eyebrows. "Yep, but I'm sticking to it. What you need to remember is no person is all good or all bad. Loving Roger doesn't make you anything like him."

I wiped my mouth with my napkin. "I need to get going. Have you seen my phone?"

Kat shook her head. "Not since last night. Have you looked on the floor?"

"Yeah. I thought it was under the couch." I stood. "I'm sure it'll show up. I have my backup." I patted my pocket, leaned down, and kissed the top of her head. "See you at the book signing tonight."

"Wouldn't miss it for the world."

Chapter Nineteen

The bookstore in the heart of the financial district buzzed with excitement. Harold zoomed here and there, ensuring all of our requests were met, including tea with lemon for Mom.

"We bump into each other again."

I whirled around to face Vanessa. "Are you stalking me? First the bar and now here."

She held up a copy of *I Know Why the Caged Bird Sings*. "Nope. I popped in to buy a book for my mom." Vanessa, in jeans and a pink Sox shirt, surveyed the store. "You really did it."

"What?"

"Succeeded. Who would have thought all those years ago, you'd be this famous?" She smiled, but it was hard to tell if it was genuine.

I wanted to say, "Serves you right for dumping me," but didn't. Instead I went the honest route. "I think most are here for my mom."

"Ah, still riding Nell's coattails." She bumped my shoulder playfully. "If I'd known about this event, I would have planned my trip back better. Mom would have loved seeing you and Nell." She tossed her arms around my neck. "I'm sorry I have to run."

"Next time, let's plan on bumping into each other and catch up."

"Deal. Good luck tonight." She vanished behind a book display, presumably heading to the cash registers.

I spied Kat in the classics section and joined her.

"You ready?" Kat rubbed my back.

Was I?

She didn't push for an answer, luckily.

"I need to pee."

She tittered. Even back in my basketball days, moments before tip-off, I always experienced the sensation I had to piss, even though the majority of the time nothing happened when I sat on the toilet. The sensation always continued until I made my first basket.

"I'll see you after you finish signing books. Depending on the line, Barb and I may go to the bar next door." She playfully shoved me toward the bathroom.

The restroom, mercifully, was deserted. I ran cold water and soaked a paper towel to sponge my face and the back of my neck. The room started to spin, and I glommed onto the counter with both hands. "Oh God."

Someone entered.

I turned to face a slight woman whose features were unremarkable on all fronts.

She covered the lower half of her face with a purple silk scarf and mumbled through the fabric. "It's you."

Puzzled, I nodded.

The woman lowered the protective purple barrier. "You're Cori Tisdale—you're speaking here tonight."

"Guilty as charged. That is if I don't faint." I laughed nervously, wishing I could take the statement back. Something about the way she looked at me made me think she knew me inside and out.

She approached carefully. "You okay?" Her eyes darted every which way.

"Yeah, I'm fine. Pregame jitters."

"I'm not surprised. It's packed out there. I don't know how you do it."

I swiped the towel across my brow. "You trying to psych me out or up?" I joked.

"Sorry! I didn't—"

"It's okay. You'd think after all this time I'd be used to speaking in front of people."

"They say even Broadway stars get butterflies before every performance, and they go on night after night." She smiled encouragingly. "You can do this." Her voice was sweet and her expression childlike. I wondered what Charlotte would have looked like at her age.

"Thanks. I think I can do it now, after talking with you." I stuck my hand out. "Nice to meet you."

She latched onto my hand, pumping it up and down. "This is so exciting. I'm a big fan—huge!"

I clasped my other hand around our conjoined hands. "I can't thank you enough. But now... showtime." I winked and she blushed deeply. I disengaged our hands and departed.

Mom sat in an upholstered chair in the front. When she noticed me, she smiled, playfully tapping her watch.

I stopped in my tracks until Roger's voice boomed in my head encouraging me to kick some ass. Pinching the bridge of my nose, I smeared on my crowd-pleasing face and took my seat.

"Welcome, ladies and gentlemen. Tonight we're honored to have Nell and Cori Tisdale speak. Afterward, they'll sign copies. And I should mention that all the proceeds from tonight's events will be donated to the neonatal intensive care unit at—"

I tuned out the rest of the introduction, fearful she'd mention Charlotte's death or the ballyhoo concerning Roger. I didn't want to focus on our woes. Tonight was about raising money to help other babies.

The host shifted in her chair. "Nell, your latest novel has been compared to *Tell the Wolves I'm Home*. The main protagonist in your novel is much younger than Cori, but was Cori and the loss of her daughter—your granddaughter—the inspiration?"

I imagined twisting the woman's head off and tossing it into the Charles.

Mom squeezed my thigh before answering.

I sucked in a ragged breath. *This is for you, baby girl.*

***

Sixty-three excruciating minutes later, the question and answer session ended and we made our way to the signing table.

"Nell! Cori! Can I get a picture of you two?"

Mom, the consummate professional, ringed my waist with one arm and posed. Several flashes popped, blinding me.

"Stop smiling like a serial killer." Mom jabbed her elbow into my side.

I tried extinguishing the unnatural smile.

"Just a few more."

People jostled each other to get a photo.

Harold sensed I was at my breaking point. "Okay, folks. You can get more photos when you get your book signed."

Mom whispered, "You're almost done."

Kat, off to one side, mouthed, "I love you."

The line snaked all the way through the largest bookstore in Massachusetts.

"Shall we?" I proffered my arm to Mom. "Your fans are waiting."

She laughed. "Oh, I think one or two are here for you," she whispered so only I could hear.

I whispered back, "I hope not. Signing books always gives me a hand cramp."

She rolled her eyes.

Those around us beamed, clearly enjoying seeing mother and daughter bantering back and forth. If only they knew.

The minutes clipped along easily, and much to my surprise, every person in line had at least one of my books.

Someone plonked down all four of my published works. I glanced up and smiled at the woman who had talked me off the ledge in the bathroom. If it wasn't for her purple scarf, I wouldn't have been able to pick her out in a police lineup; she was so shy and mousy looking.

"Well, hello again."

"You were great this evening," she gushed.

"Why thank you. Couldn't have done it without your support." I winked.

The comment caught Mom's ear. "Hi, I'm Nell."

"Mom, this woman found me in the bathroom—"

"Let me guess. My daughter was in the midst of a panic attack." Mom chortled.

At first the woman glared, but her expression eased when I joined my mom in laughter.

"You know it. Every single time."

Mom read the spines of the woman's hardcovers and reached behind her chair to extract a copy of her new release, autographing it. "On the house. Anyone who comes to my daughter's aid is a friend."

"Wow! Thank you."

The next person in line cleared her throat, and mom ushered her forward to her side of the table.

I started to sign the woman's books. "Who should I make this out to?"

"How about *To my new bff*?"

"Now why didn't I think of that?"

A grin split her face in half. "I have a podcast where I interview authors. It'd be an honor to host you."

"Is that right?" I caught Harold's eye, and he moved quickly to my side. "This is the man you want to talk to. He handles all media requests."

Her eyes lit up when I uttered media requests. "Wonderful. I can't thank you enough."

"Don't thank me. Thank fate." I nearly gagged on the word, unsure why I said it. Interacting with fans always forced my bumbling nature to the fore.

Harold whisked her off to the side.

Even though the woman was as nice as they came, my energy was severely flagging. Acting normal and charming, on tonight of all nights, was no mean feat. My eyes sought out Kat, but she must have been in the bathroom, or at the bar next door with Barbara.

"Next," Mom chirped, sounding brighter than I'd ever heard her. She jabbed me in the ribs with one elbow before turning back to the never-ending line of fans.

Chapter Twenty

The following morning, I returned from my run to find Harold and Kat at the kitchen table, pouring over the paperwork the lawyers needed for our visa applications.

"Oh, Cori." Harold glanced up. "The woman from the signing last night—she's the blogger, In the Shadows, who came to your defense months ago when G-Dawg went on the attack."

I peeled a banana, resting against the counter on the far side to spare them from my runner's stink. "No shit. In the Shadows is really a person."

"Way shit."

Kat met my eyes, and her thin lips cautioned me about teasing Harold. He was still fragile from being dumped.

"So is she legit? If I remember correctly, you and Barb wanted to check her out. Make sure she's not some crazy à la Kathy Bates in *Misery*."

"She seems okay to me. A bit over the top, but she has passion. Her blog and podcast are still relatively small potatoes, but I think it'd be worthwhile. We talked briefly, and she's sharp. Knows the publishing world."

I tossed a hand in the air. "Book it, then. I stumbled across a photo of Obama doing a podcast in some dude's garage the other day. If podcasts are good enough for the president, they're good enough for me."

"How very open of you," Kat joshed.

"You know me. Always on the lookout for the next trend." I finished off the banana. "We still on for late lunch at my mom's?"

"Yes. I might be late. I'm meeting Gertie for coffee beforehand. And don't forget dinner with Phineas tonight."

I groaned. "How could I forget?"

"I'm not looking forward to it either. I'm sure he'll have some comment about the Roger news. We haven't seen my parents since the story broke."

***

Kat's parents were the opposite of mine, not accepting, old-fashioned, and more frigid than a hundred-year-old corpse on Everest. It was hard to believe my vivacious and loving wife came from two such repressed people. Not just sexually, but socially.

Phineas Finn, a dentist, was a dead ringer for Lurch in *The Addams Family*. Whenever I was in his presence, I had to squelch a desire to say, "You rang?"

Mrs. Finn, in her starched shirts with lace collars, made me think of *Little House on the Prairie*.

Before the accident we had regular dinners once a month with the Finns at the same Italian restaurant, but over the past year we'd only dined together a few times. I hated the place. Back in the fifties, it was *the* hot spot. Now it was so run down that even tourists stayed away, yet they acted like it was a Michelin star joint. Today, though, a lone individual sat at a table near us. I could only make out the back of the person's head, denying me a chance to cast a warning look to the individual about dining at the restaurant.

Within a minute, my throat, clogged with dust, threatened to close. Vegetarianism hadn't caught on with the chef either, so the only option on the menu for me was a limp salad with rancid dressing.

Phineas and his wife perused the menu like they'd never seen it before, the way they did every time, even though they both ordered the same thing on every occasion.

It drove me insane!

Kat patted my thigh quickly to escape her parents' eyes. She wore a long-sleeved shirt and an unflattering skirt that fell below her knees. Nonetheless, she looked sexy, and I envisioned getting on my knees and going down on her under the table. Would her parents notice?

I winked at Kat so the Finns wouldn't see. Her cheeks reddened. Kat hardly ever blushed, but when she was around her parental freaks she wasn't her usual self.

Phineas cleared his throat. Not because he espied the wink. That was just his cue he was ready to order.

William appeared as if he was a cardboard figure that had popped up from the floor. I nearly jumped out of my skin.

He held his pencil expectantly and waited patiently for each of us. Were Kat and I the only two normal humans in this joint? William had waited on us each time for years. Did he really have to wait for us to say what we wanted? And not once did he say, "You want your usual?" He never cracked a smile. Never joked. I was starting to wonder whether Phineas had kidnapped him and the others who worked here to keep up the façade of Finn family tradition. It was like having dinner at a haunted mansion. Granted, we usually met her parents well before the dinner hour, since they never liked to be out much after dark, but still.

William made himself scarce after receiving the orders. Phineas eyed me and then Kat. Margaret kept her eyes down, which was her norm.

"Cori, I was sorry to hear about your uncle's passing."

I nodded, unable to speak. For weeks people had been saying this to me, and I still hadn't found the words to respond. What could I say? Several times I'd mumbled thanks, but I had no idea what I was thanking them for, and from the embarrassed look on the other person's face it became clear the best response was no response.

Phineas sat up, looking like someone had just slammed a broom handle up his ass. He licked his puckered lips and blinked. "Times like this remind us how important legacies are."

Kat glugged her iced tea. I stared at the man, waiting for it.

Phineas had a warped sense of himself. He claimed his family was one of the greatest, if not *the* greatest, in Massachusetts. I was fairly certain they lived off Margaret's inheritance; her family connections were truly impressive. The Finns had been privateers during the 1800s—successful, yes, but still crooks.

"And after everything that's been said about your uncle, it saddens me to say this, but..." He focused on Kat, his only child. "It's time for you to come home."

My jaw dropped so swiftly it was as if the lower half had snapped off the hinge.

Kat blurted out, "What?"

He swiveled his head to me, looking more and more like an animated Disney figure on the Haunted Mansion ride. "Cori, I know this is hard to hear, but your family is no good for my daughter. You two have been friends for years, but it can't continue."

Friends?

I wanted to scream, "We're married, you fucking freak!"

He continued, "If I had known the whole truth, I never would have allowed your association with my daughter."

I wished he would stop saying *my daughter*, like Kat was some type of possession. She was a woman in her thirties with a successful career and had lived outside of their house for over a decade. The man was insane. Clearly insane.

"Association?" I muttered under my breath, but he heard it.

"Yes, association. Margaret and I have always been careful about who we let interact with our only child. We thought you came from a good and decent family. As it turns out, Cori, your uncle was filth."

I hated how he kept saying my name like he always did. Was that his way of connecting on a human level? "Filth?" I said, much louder than my normal tone around Phineas. "Who in the hell do you think you are?" I gripped my fork at the top, the tines biting into my flesh.

Phineas visibly flinched. It was clear from his demeanor that no one had ever talked to him like that before.

"You think you're better than everyone. Ha! You, Phineas"—I stretched a finger toward him—"have no clue what it's like in the real world. You keep yourself locked up in that creepy house of yours on Beacon Hill and pop into your dental office around the corner, which probably sees what… twenty or thirty patients a week? I know." I rapped my chest. "I used to do your billing. You are so far out of touch, old man." I was just getting started. "Call my family filth? Not once did you or your wife hug Kat when she was a child. Not once! You kept her under lock and key. And even during all of those years, you never got to know your only child." I punctuated each word by thumping a fist on the table.

I looked to Kat. "She is the most amazing woman I've ever met. So loving, kind, funny, intelligent, and a gifted artist. And you had nothing to do with it. You"—I stabbed a finger in his direction and then Margaret's—"never encouraged her. Never loved her. Never supported her. You treated Kat like a precious object that had to be protected at all costs, like all the other fucking objects you keep in that twisted place you call home.

"My family and I"—I slapped my chest with a palm—"know and love Kat as a person, as the beautiful person she is. My uncle would have done anything for Kat. He went to all of her art shows. How many have you attended? Zero. Not once have you said, 'Kat we're really proud of you.' Hell, Roger helped set up each and every one of her shows. One of her best pieces hangs in the lobby of his office building.

"We invited you to our wedding, but you didn't bother coming. Your only daughter's wedding, and you were a no-show. What'd you say? That it wasn't your type of thing. *Thing*. Kat isn't a thing, but you don't see or understand that. When she was in the hospital, you never visited. Yet she still tries to include you in her life… in our life. We get together to catch up, and to be honest, it's a waste of time. You never ask anything about Kat's life. Or about us. You just get on your fucking soapbox and expound on how great you are, how lucky we are to be in your presence.

"You, Phineas Finn, are a blowhard." I turned his name into at least six syllables. "And you are completely clueless about what it's like to be a parent or to be human. Yet you still have the gumption to sit here and tell me I'm no good and my family is no good. And you want to whisk Kat away and lock her up in your mansion. What the fuck? It's the twenty-first century." I waved to the world outside the window. "Not that you've noticed. You've been living in the past. Not your past, but the past of when great families established Boston." I waved to the nearly empty restaurant as proof, and then I turned to Kat. "Your daughter is a grown woman. You have no control over her. Not anymore." I leveled my eyes on his. "So fuck off, Phineas!" I threw my napkin onto the table, stood up, and put my hand out for Kat's.

Phineas was gobsmacked. His mouth opened and closed, and his freakishly tall, pasty white, scrawny frame seemed to rock in his seat, but no words came out of his mouth. Even

Margaret shook a little, but there was an odd glint in her eyes and I hoped she was starting to see the light.

Kat gripped my hand and followed me outside. We walked several blocks without speaking. By the time we reached Boston Common, it dawned on me what I'd done. What I'd said.

My chin dropped to my chest. "Oh, Kat. I'm so sorry. I don't know what got into me. You're always telling me to rein in my knee-jerk jock reactions." I collapsed against a lamppost and placed both palms on top of my head. "And I just went Super Jock on your father. On Phineas! Oh, this is bad. So bad!" I struggled for air, like I was hyperventilating. I put my hands on my knees. "Say something, please," I begged, righting myself.

My wife gazed into my eyes, shell-shocked.

"Do you want me to apologize? I will. I'll get down on my hands and knees and beg for his forgiveness. I'll even kiss his ass—literally. Just tell me what you want me to do. Please. Tell me what you want me to do to fix this."

Kat rested a hand on my chest. "Never." She hesitated. "Not once has anyone ever spoken to my father like that." Her voice was completely devoid of emotion, not giving me a clue about what thoughts swirled inside.

"I know. I'm so sorry." Tears blurred my vision.

"I don't know what to say…" Her eyes widened, and a small smile tugged at the corner of her lips. "Except thank you."

I swiped my eyes with my sleeve. "Thank you?"

"Thank you." Kat yanked my head to hers and kissed me. I paused, but then kissed her madly, fairly certain we were making a scene in the oldest park in the United States and not giving a flying fuck. I thought I'd lost Kat, that she'd leave me for humiliating the Finn patriarch. She'd always pleaded with me to just stay quiet around Phineas and not ruffle his feathers. Just pretend for one hour once a month that he was as great as he thought. Go through the motions for her sake. She recognized Phineas wielded some power over her, but she never hinted at walking away—not entirely. Her request wasn't much, really. Considering all the time she spent with my family, it really didn't seem like she was asking too much of me. And now I'd gone ballistic on him, and she didn't even hate me for it.

My legs almost buckled. "You aren't livid?"

"No, I'm not." Sensing I was struggling to stay upright, she gestured for us to sit on a bench. After we settled, a swan boat cruised by, and Kat didn't let it out of her sight. "I grew up minutes from this spot, and not once did my parents bring me here. We never went on one of these boats, never had a picnic here. Never did anything." Tears brimmed in her eyes. "When I was little, I would sit in my room and peek through the closed curtains, wishing someone would rescue me. Like in the fairytales, you know?" She smiled wanly. "I was the princess and I prayed someone would climb through my window and ferry me away on a magic carpet or something." She laughed, and a bit of snot shot out. Kat rummaged through her bag until she retrieved a small packet of Kleenex. She dabbed her eyes, her mascara running. "When I busted out, I thought I'd left it all behind. But today, when my father demanded I move back home, for a brief moment, I thought I had to. Panic seized me. And all those memories… those dark memories…" She lowered her chin to her chest to gather her thoughts.

When she raised her head again, she gazed at the people milling about. "And then you…" She paused and cleared her throat before continuing. "You stood up for me. Rescued me." She batted her lashes. "My hero."

Neither of us spoke. Kat's attention returned to the swan boats.

"When I was a kid, I wrote a report on these boats. We had to write about something iconic in the city." She waved to the water. "Did you know they started back in 1877? Robert Paget started them. His descendants still own and operate the business." She smiled. "*Lohengrin*, an opera by Robert Wagner, was the inspiration. A swan pulls a boat carrying a knight, and do you know what his mission was?"

I shook my head.

"To rescue a maiden."

I chuckled. "I had no idea. I never thought to find out about them; they've always been here during the summer."

"I remember writing that report and then begging Mother to let me ride one. She never did. We were both terrified of Phineas and his rules and ways."

"What do you say, Mrs. Tisdale? Want to ride one now?" I stood with my hand extended. We'd legally changed our names after our wedding. Now I was Cori Tisdale-Finn. I never considered it as taking Phineas's last name, but as taking Kat's. Professionally, we both used only our maiden names.

"I'd love to, Mrs. Finn." She laughed and motioned for me to wait a second while she pulled out a compact to fix her makeup. When presentable, she clasped my hand and we made our way to the line of tourists and families.

We sat in the back of the boat, on a wooden bench. The driver, located in a large fiberglass swan, was directly behind us.

The entire time we were on the swan boat, I couldn't take my eyes off Kat. I didn't even bother to take in the sights. Sheer delight sparkled in her eyes and her smile. From the moment I'd met Kat, she came across as a free and loving spirit, but there was always a hint of darkness inside. After the accident, the darkness deepened. On the swan boat, that darkness leached out entirely. Beautiful wasn't the right word to describe her. Serene didn't cut it either. The only word that came to mind was Kat. She was Kat—pure and simple.

The ride ended, and I gripped her hand in mine, steering her away from the crowd. "Do you have any plans tomorrow?"

Kat's eyes crinkled as she thought. "Not that I can think of. Why?"

"Because I have an idea. When's the last time we had a break from everything? Writing, painting, family?"

"But I have meetings on Wednesday."

I put up a palm. "I know. It's Monday night. Let's check into a hotel and go to a ridiculously expensive restaurant. And then tomorrow, let's pretend we've never been to Boston and explore for the first time."

"I've always wanted to have dinner at the top of the Prudential."

"That's perfect!"

"Can you get reservations for tonight?" Her voice was dubious.

I laughed and put a hand on my chest. "Me, no. But Nell Tisdale can finagle a table at the Top of the Hub." I whipped out my cell phone. "Mom, I need help." She was all ears, and I rattled off what I wanted.

"Consider it done," was all she said before the line went dead.

Ten minutes later, I got a text: *Nine tonight*.

And Phineas had badmouthed my family. Pfffft! I blocked that thought from my head.

"Darling, let's go get some clothes for our date." I bent an arm at the elbow for her to hook her arm through.

Kat rested her head on my shoulder. "Thank you."

"Don't thank me. I have ulterior motives."

She withdrew playfully. "Really? What are those?"

"Just you wait."

***

"Oh, my God, it's stunning." Kat leaned closer to the window and took in the lights of the Back Bay, more than fifty floors below.

Even I was giddy. "It really is. I haven't eaten here since I was a kid."

The waiter set our cocktails down. I ordered the Boston Bee, with Absolut wild tea vodka, lemon juice, agave nectar, and ginger beer. Kat's drink, the Boston's Bully Boy Smash, had Bully Boy White Whiskey, lemon, mint, and sugar cane.

I hoisted my drink. "To visiting Boston with the most beautiful woman on the planet."

Kat grinned and clinked her glass against mine. "The planet? I think you're exaggerating."

We stood at the window by our table to soak in the view. I eyed her red dress, which had a slit up the side that almost reached her crotch. I made a show of peering down the front. "Not exaggerating. And just in case you didn't notice, I think three couples may be getting divorced after tonight. Did you see that one man who was ogling you? He nearly fell off his chair! I feel like Richard Gere in *Pretty Woman*, when he escorts Julia Roberts to the opera. Except you're hotter."

"Than Richard or Julia?"

"Both!"

Kat snorted and quickly covered her mouth. "That probably dampened my hotness factor a smidge."

"No way. You could fart and belch at the same time and you'd still be the most beautiful."

"You do have a way with words."

Our appetizers arrived: French onion soup with vegetable broth for me, and clam chowder for Kat. We retook our seats.

"How's the chowder?" I asked after a minute.

"I believe they pronounce it chowdah here." Kat was really taking to the idea that we were pretending we'd never been to Boston before.

"Is that so? What other Boston-speak do you know? So I don't embarrass myself." I played along.

"Water fountains are called bubblas."

"That's wicked," I replied with a wink.

Kat sampled her chowder and closed her eyes. "No, *that's* wicked." She pointed to the bowl with her spoon.

Her foot inched up my leg, under my dress, and didn't stop until it hit *the* spot. I glanced down at my lap and muttered, "Check, please."

Kat slapped my arm. "No way! You have to sit there and behave while I devour my two-pound lobster and then the Boston cream pie."

Her toe continued to massage me.

"Do you think anyone would notice if I came at the table?" I asked.

"I would," she said with a sexy look in her eye. "And I'm the only one who matters."

"Very true. Always."

Her foot stilled, but remained on my seat for a moment. I stroked her bare calf, stifling a moan. "How do you do it?"

Kat held her spoon midair and her eyebrows nearly met in the middle.

"How do you make it feel like it's the first time whenever you touch me? God, I'm frickin' gushing over here, if you know what I mean."

She smiled like the devil. "I think I'm going to take my time eating tonight." She licked her spoon, and my insides throbbed.

A woman next to us cleared her throat so loudly it sounded like she was hacking up her lung. Her husband's face was redder than Kat's dress, and it wasn't from embarrassment. Fight number four, maybe.

"Take all the time you need. I'll make you pay for it later."

Kat placed both forearms on the table and leaned over just enough for me to get an eyeful. "I'm counting on it."

The waiter approached to ask if we were done with our soup. Neither of us spoke, but he made the correct decision and bussed away our bowls without saying another peep.

"You have the most amazing eyes," Kat said. "I always know what you're thinking."

"Ha! I'm pretty sure most everyone here is thinking the same thing at the moment."

"And what's that?" She laced her fingers together and propped her chin on her hands, elbows still on the table.

"I want to fuck you." I bent closer. "And the best part is I'm the only person in this room who will. Ever." My voice was low, but my passion had kicked into high gear.

"I do love it when you talk like that. I remember when we first met. You could barely string two sentences together." Kat's eyes feasted on my face, and her toe explored again.

I let out an almost undetectable gasp that was meant only for Kat.

Her toe orbited my clit. I steadied my breathing as much as possible and stared intently at my wife. Would she take me there? At the top of the Pru?

As if she was in tune with my thoughts, she nodded ever so slightly.

Oh. My. God.

I wondered whether anyone suspected what was happening under the table. Surely the waiter had picked up on the fact that we wanted some *alone* time. He seemed to have stalled before bringing out the next course.

Kat continued.

All of the chatter and clattering in the room magically faded. It was only Kat and I in the posh restaurant overlooking the Boston skyline, and we only had eyes for each other.

The closer I came to the brink, the more intent Kat's concentration became, not just her toe, but also her expression. Kat wanted me to explode in my panties, which more than likely wouldn't stem the tide. Sayonara to the chair and my two-hour-old dress.

I closed my eyes and stilled my body as much as possible, but I couldn't stop the hint of a shudder.

"Here ya go," said the waiter, placing the lobster in front of Kat. All of the bustling crashed into my ears again, snapping the door shut on my orgasm.

"I can't wait to taste it," Kat said to me, grinning.

The waiter nodded crisply and set my grilled eggplant and zucchini in front of me before he fled. Could he smell my juices, or did I have a nearly fucked glow?

Kat moistened her lips. "Good?"

"Y-yes," I stuttered. "Bon appétit." I sipped my glass of ice-cold water, tempted to dump it over my burning body to tamp down my desire, which was only intensified by Kat's performance.

"Yes, you too, my love." Kat cracked a lobster claw, dipped the tender meat into the garlic butter sauce, and placed it on her tongue. Her eyes closed, her shoulders heaved slightly, and her chest hitched up.

"Good?"

"I think I've died and gone to heaven."

She repeated the performance. A crowbar wouldn't have been able to pry my eyes off her.

"You aren't hungry?" She pointed to my plate with the shell cracker.

"I'm getting my fill; trust me."

"Anything I can do to improve my performance?"

I mulled this over. "My first thought was for you to slip out of your dress, but actually, I think this, right now, is perfect."

"Why's that?" Kat placed another delectable morsel on her tongue, savoring it for both of our benefits.

"Because my brain is going into warp speed imagining all the ways I'm going to rip your clothes off."

"Do tell."

Surreptitiously, I glanced around the crowded restaurant. Waiters hustled and bustled with plates, carrying bottles of wine or champagne. Diners in suits and dresses conversed, laughed, or ate in silence. It didn't take much imagination to pretend we were sitting in a fancy schmancy gin joint/upscale restaurant in the roaring twenties, the time period of the latest novel I was working on.

And my beautiful wife wanted me to talk dirty to her.

It was fucking hot.

"I want to fuck you up against the glass window of our room, and I insist you keep your eyes open. No one will be able to see you so high up, but it'll be like you're on display for the world. I don't want to share you completely, but I want to share how I make you feel. Share that gorgeous face when you come. Create our own sensual art in the sky. And you'll be able to see all of Boston lit up just for you. All the brilliant and twinkling lights shining for your enjoyment."

Kat's eyes told me to keep going.

"I'm going to take you from behind, fast and hard. I can picture it now. My hand slickened with your juices, thrusting in and out. You begging for more, but I want you to come in front of the glass before I taste you." I motioned to a piece of lobster she was dangling in front of her face and smiled at her mouth hanging agape. "Eat up, darling. You're going to need your strength."

Kat stuck her tongue out, and then licked her lips before she sucked the lobster inside.

Surely people were noticing us now, and I wondered whether they recognized us. The Roger news had died away, for the most part. But after the funeral my face had been splattered all over the major news channels, clips of my speech, before they'd cut away to the scandal about his sex life.

Still, I doubted people recognized me. Kat had insisted we have our hair and makeup done for dinner, so my hair was swept up and my usually makeup-free face was expertly painted like a runway model. I didn't resemble the heartbroken niece who'd given her uncle's eulogy weeks ago.

The pain of Charlotte's and Roger's deaths would never diminish, but sitting here with Kat made me realize the cruel fact that life marches on. I could march with it, or I could let it pass me by. Roger wouldn't want me to be a spectator.

Kat must have noticed the drastic change in my demeanor. She set aside the lobster cracker and mini-pitchfork. "What's wrong?"

"Nothing." I swiped away a tear. "I've never felt more alive."

"Then why are you crying?" Kat patted my hand.

"Happy tears, Kit Kat."

Kat snapped her fingers.

Surprisingly, a waiter appeared within three seconds. "Yes?"

"Can we get a bottle of champagne, please?"

"Of course, madam."

"Madam?" Kat teased when the coast was clear.

"Goes with the territory, I think." I waved to the room.

"This place is so very unPhineas-like." She narrowed her eyes.

"You deserve the best."

The waiter popped the cork and Kat clapped her hands, making him smile. His eyes wandered over her body. Let him look. My hands would be all over her soon.

"Any dessert?"

"Yes," Kat purred. "The Boston cream pie and the black forest cake."

"Excellent choices." He bowed and walked back two steps before flipping around on his heel and marching toward the kitchen.

"Funny, lately our lives have been filled with choices, and I think each one has been excellent," Kat said. "Your uncle would be so proud of you."

"I think he is with me. Everything he taught me." I mimicked his voice, "Get in the game, Cori." I laughed. "God, I can't tell you how many times I heard him say that or imagined him saying it."

"Is that your plan then? Tonight?"

"Trust me. I plan to blow your mind."

***

I kicked at the tangle of sheets at the foot of the bed. "That was amazing."

Kat eyed the smudges on the glass. "Do you think housekeeping will guess how all those finger marks and face splotches got onto the window?"

I closed my eyes, remembering flashes of Kat pressed against the window. My fingers thrusting inside her. The lights below. Her moans.

The entire room was in shambles. We'd made love repeatedly, not wasting an inch of space in the one-bedroom suite, which was twice the size of the one-bedroom apartment I'd had in college.

"How in the hell did you manage that move on the chair?" I gestured to the upholstered chair.

"I've been doing squats. My thigh muscles are in the best shape."

"Hands down, this night is in the top five of sexual escapades."

Kat raked her fingers through my hair. "Not the best?"

"Close. I still think our wedding night is the night to beat." I kissed her nipple. It hardened immediately.

Kat covered it with a hand. "No! I need a break."

I laughed. "I don't know about you, but I'm going to walk funny for the next three days."

"Ah, yes. The *I've been fucked* walk. You do it so well."

"My compliments to the artist." I mimed tipping my hat.

Sleep beckoned, and there was no fighting it. My eyes closed. Kat must have already slipped into dream world. Her entire body spasmed and then stilled completely.

Chapter Twenty-One

"Wow, you actually slept through the night." Kat kissed the top of my head, and I snuggled into the crook of her arm.

"Not sure very many could stay awake after last night's activities." I wrapped my arm around her, showing no desire to get out of bed.

She laughed her completely satisfied laugh. "I'm starving."

"Order room service. Mom's picking up the tab," I mumbled into her chest.

Kat playfully jabbed her elbow into my side, but that didn't stop her from picking up the phone and placing an order. When she hung up, she said, "You have twenty minutes before they arrive."

"Good. I want to keep my eyes closed and enjoy being in your arms."

Kat continued to hold me until room service knocked on the door. She slipped into a robe to answer, while I remained in bed with the covers pulled up to my chin. A young man in a waiter's version of a monkey suit rolled the cart in. I detected his eyes taking in the scene, but he was trained not to show any emotion. I was fairly certain he'd walked into many rooms the morning after a fuckfest.

"By the window?" he asked Kat.

She nodded, reaching into her purse for the tip. She gave him two twenties. Hush money, maybe? He thanked her as if getting cash from half-naked gorgeous women happened every day. It probably did.

The door shut quietly.

"Nice tip," I said, sitting up, stretching my arms, and releasing a contented yawn.

She shrugged. "He was a cutie, and oh my gosh, did you see how young?" Kat handed over the double espresso, and then she poured a cup of Darjeeling for herself.

"I swear, each year college freshmen get younger and younger." I meandered to the table, both hands clutching the tiny cup. Spying fresh blueberries, I popped three into my mouth.

"I'm sure it's just that we're getting older." Kat settled at the table, after righting both of the chairs, which had been toppled over the previous night.

"You, my dear, don't look a day older than when I met you." I kissed her cheek and donned a robe, not wanting to sit bare ass in a hotel chair.

Waffles, French toast, eggs Benedict, and an omelet filled with lobster and crabmeat for Kat sat on the table, along with fresh fruit.

"I doubt we'll eat it all," I said.

"Don't worry. Harold will be here in twenty."

"What? Why?"

She hitched her shoulders. "He texted an hour ago saying we had to talk."

I crinkled my eyes. "That sounds ominous."

Kat scooped in a mouthful of her omelet and groaned with satisfaction. "I could get used to living like this."

A knock on the door interrupted.

"How in the world is he always early when meeting us, yet he was never on time when we worked at the coffee shop?" I asked. "Not once."

"Seriously, you don't know? He's always hopeful he'll catch us in the middle of sex. Harold's harmless mostly, but he's still a man."

Kat let him in while I pulled the toppled desk chair up to the cramped table. Now it made sense that she'd ordered eggs Benedict.

He wore a Mind the Gap T-shirt and jeans. His eyes darted around the room, and I wondered what perversions were racing through his mind. More than likely, he wasn't far off the mark. When he spied the food, Harold took a seat at the table and tucked a white linen napkin into his collar.

"Help yourself," Kat said before I had a chance to say anything rude. The woman knew me better than I knew myself.

He glommed onto the eggs. Watching Harold eat was like sitting in the stands of a hot-dog-eating contest. Once he took his first bite, he consumed food quickly and with precision. If I didn't know his history, I would have assumed he was a foster kid who'd learned to eat fast or not eat at all. However, his mother was a sweet little old lady who'd had him late in life and coddled him before he even popped out. When I asked him why he rushed, he said the one thing his mother was strict about was no books at the dinner table. He'd learned to eat like Mario Andretti so he could be excused to read.

After he sopped up the remnants of hollandaise with a bit of toast, I asked, "What's up, Harold?"

He set his fork on the nearly spotless plate. "Have you checked in with your mom?"

"No. Why?" I crossed my arms.

He fished his iPad out of his bag and efficiently manipulated the screen before placing it down in front of me. Kat stood behind me and peered over my shoulder.

"What the fuck?" She snatched the tablet off the table. "How did you get these?"

"Cori's email." He remained quite calm—the complete opposite of Kat.

I lightly rapped my fingers on the table, unperturbed he'd read my emails. It was part of his job, after all. "Care to tell me what's going on?"

Kat still clutched the iPad, and I'd yet to see why her panties were in such a bunch; however, I was confident she currently wasn't wearing any under her robe.

Kat flipped around, her eyes bulging with fury.

Now I was worried. "What?"

Kat stared at the table and shook her head. Without saying a word, she set the iPad down.

I skimmed the email and digested snippets. "What is this?" The sender had assembled different fonts—no, I leaned closer —Photoshopped letters from magazines, proclaiming undying love. "Is this a joke?" My eyes and brain couldn't focus on the proof before me.

Harold sat with his hands folded on the table, and Kat paced the room, sputtering incomprehensibly.

I leveled my eyes on Harold. "Do I even want to open the attachments?" I groaned. "What's going on? The attached…" I still didn't want to see them.

"The painting," he answered with a professional calm. "And photos of you lecturing, running—doing everyday things. There are a few of Kat, but only when she's with you. I think the person has been trailing you. There are photos of you two in public over a span of time, including dinner last night." He gestured to Kat's red dress on the floor.

"What painting?" I glowered at poor Harold.

He flinched. "Yours."

"Which one? I'm married to an artist, and my aunt owns a studio."

Harold stretched a skinny finger in my direction.

"I haven't shown any works with Cori," Kat defended.

Harold cleared his throat. "I think the painting in question was meant to be private."

I rubbed my eyes. Kat sank into the couch by the table and pulled her knees to her chest. Her feet stuck out from her billowed robe.

"Is there a photo of the painting?" I laid a hand on the tablet screen. "Attached to the email?"

Harold nodded once.

"How? It's under lock and key in our home."

"Someone must have broken in." Kat stared at the ceiling, her eyes brimming with frustrated tears. "There's more."

My heart hammered in my eardrums.

"Do you remember the photo you snapped—of us? You said you wanted me to paint it for your personal collection." Kat avoided my eyes by looking out the window.

I started to put the pieces together. "My phone. I thought I'd misplaced it, but it must have been stolen from our house." Last I'd seen the cell, it was under the couch. "It had a pass code."

Harold didn't bother to state the obvious. Anything digital could be hacked.

I sat dumbfounded.

Kat squeezed my shoulder and took a seat next to me. She pinned her eyes on mine. "You're handling this much better than I thought." She spoke slowly, as if worried if she brought reality to my attention I'd flip-out and go into full-blown jock mode.

"I don't even know what to think. If it wasn't so sick, I'd say it was Mom playing a joke. I mean—this shit is crazy. Like someone is short forty-eight cards of a full deck." I squinted at the screen again. "I mean the person is obsessed with me. My life. Not you. Who in the hell would zero in on me and not you?"

"So you wish I was the target?" Kat flinched.

"No, of course not. I just can't wrap my head around it. A stalker—really? This doesn't happen to people like me. I'm not Sandra Bullock."

Kat grimaced. "I don't even want to think about it." She stiffened. "There are photos of you sleeping in our bed."

My skin crawled. "What do we do?"

Harold shook his head. "Your mom is on her way."

"What are you? The prep team?" I would have laughed, but this wasn't funny. This was my life. Someone was forcing their way into my life.

"Who does this?" I hopped out of my seat.

Harold squirmed in his chair.

I wandered to the window and traced the outline of Kat's smudged face from last night. "Does this person have any decency? Scruples? Following me, breaking into our home. What's next? Kidnapping? Being stashed in some basement, never to be seen again?" Neither of them spoke.

I rested my forehead on the cool glass and stared down at the people and cars twenty floors below. I pretended I was Gulliver, trapped in an unknown and confusing land. I squashed everyone down below between my forefinger and thumb, feeling somewhat more in control.

"I think we've lost her," Kat told Harold.

"Seems to be the case." Harold sounded forlorn.

A knock sounded on the hotel door. All of us eyed each other.

Harold stood. "I'll get it." He cautiously peeked through the glass and whispered, "It's your mom."

"Let me in, Harold," Mom barked from the other side.

She strolled in, took in the chaos of the room, and smiled. "My, my, my. Good thing your stalker doesn't have photos of this… yet." She waved to the destroyed room. Our dresses and underthings tossed about. The toppled chair by the window. The vase and flowers spilled on the carpet.

Shit, did the waiter have a hidden camera on him? Was he the stalker? Or perhaps just on the stalker's payroll? Did stalkers hire freelancers?

"How'd you find us?" I asked.

"I made the reservation, remember?" She set her purse down on an end table. "If we don't play this right, the whole world will soon know your every move. The letter demands a meeting or all of the photos will be leaked—the racy ones."

"It said that?" I blinked.

Both Kat and Harold nodded.

"Fuck!" I squinted down at the street again. Was that a crowd by the entrance, waiting for us to leave? Were we too late?

"If these photos get out, you'll be super famous, and not for getting beamed in the head by a baseball."

Would no one forget about that damn ball?

Shit! Would no one forget about *this*?

"You don't really think the person will go public with the photos, do you? I mean, it has to be a bluff, right? Do stalkers like to share?"

Mom exhaled. "I have no idea. We need to prepare for all contingencies."

Contingencies. My life now boiled down to contingency plans because some psycho had set their sights on me. I perched on the edge of the couch and held my arms tightly against my body. "So now what?"

"Get dressed." She pointed to Kat and me. "You've had your fun. Time to take care of this. Barbara's waiting in the garage in Roger's Bentley."

"Why'd she bring Roger's Bentley?"

The car was his baby, which he'd only ever taken out on Sunday drives, not for busting out his niece from whatever the fuck I was embroiled in; however, he might have, if he were still alive.

"Seemed like the perfect car for this situation. Goodness knows it got Roger out of a few scrapes."

I huffed. Right now, I didn't want any comparisons to my uncle and the seedy side of his life I'd ignored for years.

"Don't start with me. I'm not the one teetering on the brink of unfathomable embarrassment. The pictures are explicit, but what if the person has a video of you two?" Mom smiled. Only my mother. She was truly enjoying the situation.

I smothered my ears. "Don't say that."

Kat guided me by the arm toward the bathroom. "We'll be out in a moment," she said over her shoulder.

Mom snapped her fingers. "Harold, start tossing their stuff in that shopping bag."

From the confines of the bathroom, the sounds of Harold and Mom rustling through the room, sweeping things into a bag, filled me with guilt. Here I was, a woman in her thirties, being rescued by her mommy. I stepped outside for a pair of jeans right as Harold plucked Kat's crotchless panties up off the floor. We locked eyes, and then I retreated behind the door once again.

"Who's doing this?" Kat collapsed against the bathroom counter and placed her hands on my shoulders. "You okay?"

"I'm stunned. A blackmailing stalker? Really? This doesn't happen to people like me. Roger—yes. Even my mom, who has novels in every airport bookstore, but I'm Marilyn Munster."

"What?"

"Marilyn Munster—the only normal one in *The Munsters*." My voice cracked.

Kat shook her head and disrobed.

I'd yet to make a move toward getting dressed. It was as if I were frozen in ice and couldn't move.

"Hey! Are you two having sex again? Get moving!" Mom shouted from the other side of the door.

"She's loving this, isn't she?" I slipped into my jeans.

"Nell Tisdale lives for moments like this." Kat hiked up a pencil skirt.

"What? Blackmail?" I yanked a T-shirt over my head and raked my hair into a clumsy ponytail.

"Protecting her only child. Don't ever mess with a momma bear." In one motion, Kat swiped her makeup into an overnight bag we'd purchased yesterday in preparation for weekend trips in Europe. "Let's roll."

I managed a small smile. "You're enjoying these spy shenanigans, aren't you?"

"Kinda."

Harold and Mom waited by the door. Harold had his eye glued to the peephole. Mom leaned against the doorjamb, looking slightly amused by his antics, which were straight out of one of his graphic novels.

"Ready?" She straightened.

Harold's hand shot up. "Someone's out there," he whispered.

Mom whispered back, "I know. He's with us."

"Really? He's huge." Harold stared at my mom as if she were the head of the CIA.

"Did we get everything?" Mom asked.

Harold's pale brown eyes scoped the room. "Wait." He trotted toward the bed and reached for something under the covers.

My mind flashed to the object, and I shouted, "Don't touch that!"

Too late. Harold turned around with a leather strap-on dangling from one finger, the six-inch dick twitching in the air.

I covered my mouth while Mom broke into hysterics.

Harold wore the oddest expression. Was he disgusted? Turned on? Confused?

Kat grabbed it from him and shoved it into her purse. Then, for some inexplicable reason, she turned to my mother, the woman who'd given birth to me, and confessed, "I surprised Cori last night."

"I'm sure you did." Mom chortled.

"Seriously, is this happening?" I crumpled against the wall.

"Breathe." Kat rubbed my arm.

Mom tried to wipe the smile off her face. "You ready?"

"Just get me out of this," I mumbled.

In the hall, I shook hands with Floyd, a man Roger had employed from time to time, and tried to act normal. He was a PI, bodyguard, and chauffeur all rolled into one.

"Let's hit the road." Floyd motioned for us to go ahead.

"Not that way." Mom rolled her eyes. "The service elevator. Such an amateur." She tsked. "Who knows where your stalker is?"

"How'd you get access to the service elevator?" I asked over my shoulder.

Floyd and Mom remained silent. My gut said this wasn't Floyd's first time breaking a client out of this posh hotel. Had Roger used the service elevator?

In the garage, Barbara had the Bentley right next to the door. I hoped my aunt hadn't waited in this exact spot for her husband.

The four of us squeezed into the back seat, and Floyd rode shotgun.

Barbara adjusted the rearview mirror to peer into the back seat. "Roger would have loved this." Her eyes glistened with happy nostalgia, eradicating my earlier hope.

Dammit, Roger! The shit he'd put her through. How was he such a wonderful uncle and a completely crappy and selfish husband? I would never understand that completely.

"Now get on the floor, just in case." She gestured to me. "And, Kat, stay out of sight."

I rolled my eyes, but complied. Kat, who was several inches shorter than I was, scrunched down in the back seat mostly out of view. Mom placed a floppy old lady hat on Kat's head and Jackie-O sunglasses over her eyes. Seriously, had they been waiting to do this all their lives?

"Love the new look," I said.

Kat fluffed her voluminous dark hair, which poured out of the hat like a chocolate waterfall.

"I don't know about you, but I want to track down the son of a bitch who broke into our home," I said.

Mom nodded to Floyd, who returned the gesture. He about-faced and was on his phone, rattling off directions like a marine sergeant.

"And then what?" Kat asked.

"Sue the shit out of the asshole. After I pummel the crap out of him."

Kat grimaced.

"He broke into our home while we were sleeping," I squawked.

"Why do you think it's a man?" Mom asked.

"Good question. But I don't have any issues kicking a woman's ass either. Not at the moment."

"Whoa! Before you channel Clint Eastwood, take a step back. Like I said earlier, we have to play this just right. That's why Floyd's here. No matter what, we want to keep this out of the press and off the Web. Otherwise, this will dog you the rest of your life."

"At the moment, I'm more concerned about the crazed person who wants me as a play toy."

"I get that; I do. But think about everyone involved. Who knows what this person will say or do?" Mom held my eyes. "We don't know how many photos the person has, but we've seen a preview, and it's clear this person has been able to blend in seamlessly for months, if not years."

"So what?" I sat up to the best of my ability on the floor of the car and leaned against the door. Barbara made a sharp turn, and I had to brace myself with both hands. "You want to dangle me in front of this creep in the hope of catching the bastard?"

"Floyd is going to track down the person and put a stop to this madness."

"You mean?" I made a gun with my fingers.

Mom burst out laughing. "God, no. Once we know who we're dealing with, we'll loop in the authorities."

"Why aren't we looping in the authorities now? This person broke into my home and has photos of me sleeping in my bed next to Kat, not to mention photos of intimate moments. Every aspect of my life has been invaded." I tossed both hands in the air, immediately regretting it when Barb made another turn and my head bumped into Kat's knees.

"Floyd is back-channeling. We want to keep this off the radar, if possible. If all of this is released so closely to the news breaking about Roger, who knows how the public will react. They might not see you as a victim. Not completely. We need to control the narrative—you're a victim, not a sex-crazed addict, even though all the acts are with your wife. However, the photo of you dancing with Inez suggests you may not be completely innocent, and the revelations about Roger are still fresh in people's minds. Furthermore, there are segments in society who think all homosexuals are deviants. We need to get in front of that narrative and get the public on your side." She turned to Harold. "You saved the day by retrieving that strap-on. We didn't need housekeeping finding that."

Chapter Twenty-Two

"I need to shower," Kat announced as soon as we arrived at my mother's house.

I nodded.

"Harold picked up some clothes for you two. Your bags are in Cori's room." Mom patted Kat's back.

Barbara and Floyd disappeared into the office. Dad was nowhere in sight, and Harold had slipped off, probably to the library, which was his refuge in good times and bad.

Mom waved to the barstool in the kitchen. "Sit."

I did.

"Want anything to eat? French toast?"

I shook my head. "No thanks. I ate earlier." I leaned on the kitchen countertop, propping my head up with my palm. Mom stood on the other side, igniting a burner for the teakettle. "I'm worried."

"I'm sure you are. This is beyond creepy," she said with her back to me.

"That's an understatement. I mean, I may be on camera now."

Mom fluffed her hair.

"Seriously, Mom."

"Doesn't hurt to look nice." She flipped around to avoid my glare.

I sighed. "It's not just the stalker. I mean, that's a huge problem, but Kat and I have been through so much. And now the nude photos of Kat, of me. What if Kat disappears—?"

"Don't even think it." Mom cleaved the air with her hand, her back still turned. "That's not how you were raised."

"Shit. You never prepped me for this. Someone breaking into my house, snapping photos of private things, threatening to share it with the world unless I become—what? A sex slave?" I covered my face with both hands. "Why is this happening? I'm not a bad person, and Kat doesn't deserve this. Not one bit. She's suffered so much, and now this is hanging over our heads. Will we ever feel safe again in our own home?"

Mom must have walked around the island, because her hand was stroking my back. "We'll protect both of you. Nothing will happen to you or Kat."

I sat up. "You're right. I need to focus on Kat. Protecting her at all costs. Who knows what this crazy person is capable of?"

"And I'll protect you," Kat said, interrupting our conversation.

I turned to her. She was dressed in my dingy Harvard sweatpants and T-shirt. "Hi, beautiful." I smiled.

Mom quietly cleared out.

"Come here." I opened my arms and held her. "We'll get through this together."

She sniffled. "I know. But it still sucks."

I drew back and gazed into her eyes. "It does, but there's no one else I would want to go through this with. And let's keep the big picture in mind. Soon, we'll be in London." I swiped a stray wet strand of dark hair off her cheek. "A new chapter in our lives, Kit Kat."

Once I pulverize this stalking asshole.

***

"We received a video from Cori's stalker. The person makes one demand." Floyd sat on the couch in his impressive office overlooking Boston Common, his legs wide open and a hand on each knee. He and his crew had been monitoring my email, social media, and phone.

Harold hummed the James Bond theme song.

"What's the demand?" Mom asked, ignoring Harold's attempt to lighten the mood.

"I think you need to see it." Floyd fiddled with the laptop on the table to his side.

Dad, Barbara, Kat, Harold, and Mom all swarmed the screen. I stood to the side, not wanting to see but unable to look away.

A figure in a black hoodie with a pixelated face spoke, obviously using a device to distort the voice—unless my stalker was a rogue robot.

"Hello, Cori." The idiot had the balls to wave like we were long-lost friends. Were we? "I know you probably have some

283

questions, and the only way forward is for us to meet. Please know I don't mean you any harm…" A nervous giggle choked the rest of the thought. The person stiffened. "Let's meet. Talk. Get to know each other."

"No way," I muttered under my breath.

"Once I explain, I know you'll see things the way I do. Fate has kept us apart—and Kat."

Harold made a fist and smashed it into his other palm.

"I'll kill you, ya fucker." I made a gun with my fingers.

Mom placed a hand on my shoulder. Floyd had stopped the video, and the look on his face questioned whether we could stomach the rest. All heads nodded.

"Kat isn't the person for you, but you can't see that. You and I have chemistry that can't be denied. I didn't realize it until recently. Before, I was content watching from afar, but now… I know we were meant to be more. I can't walk away. And I won't let you slip through my fingers. Not again."

Harold flashed two middle fingers, jabbing them at the hooded individual on the screen.

"I want us to meet. Privately. If you don't agree, you won't like the consequences. I know you value your privacy—we all do. And I know you don't want people thinking you're anything like Roger. I don't want to release the photos, but if you don't agree to meet, I will. I'll be in touch in twenty-four hours. What will you decide, Cori? Us? Or the end?" The screen went black.

"What do you think they mean by *the end*?" Barbara spun around to Floyd.

"*Slip through my fingers*? Do I know this person? Someone from my past?"

Floyd motioned for all of us to take a seat. "We don't have a lot of time. Cori, did you encounter anyone recently or bump into someone you hadn't seen in ages and share a moment, no matter how small?"

"A moment?" I rubbed the top of my head. "I told off Kat's dad."

"You told off Phineas?" Mom's jaw fell.

I shrugged.

"You're missing a key point. The person wants to be with you and I seriously doubt my father has been harboring romantic feelings about you." Kat mimed crossing his name off the list. "Think, Cori."

"I—" I jolted out of my chair. "I don't really meet a lot of people. The only people I associate with, besides the people in this room, are Sam and Lucy—and I'm 110 percent positive it isn't one of them."

"What about the book event?" Barbara prodded.

I stopped pacing. "I bumped into Vanessa there."

Floyd raised an eyebrow.

"An old girlfriend. She lives in New York now." I massaged my eyes. "She was in town for Mother's Day and popped into the store to buy a gift. *I Know Why the Caged Bird Sings*."

"That's an odd book for Mother's Day," Mom said with a pinched face.

I shook my head. "I can't picture her going to these lengths, though. She barely paid attention to me when we attended the same school—let alone when we dated."

"I'll check her out just in case. Who else was at the event?" Floyd tapped the side of his head, indicating I should dig deep.

"Hundreds of people showed up. Where would I even start?" I drummed my fingers on top of my head.

"Where was this?" Floyd clicked his pen.

Harold rattled off the name of the bookstore.

Floyd met my eyes. "Did anyone ask any off-the-wall questions? Approach you, before or after?"

"After the talk, lots of people wanted photos, and we signed books. More people requested photos then. There were so many the line went out the door."

"Did anyone stand out? Besides Vanessa?" He waved his hand in an attempt to stoke a memory.

"She left before the event started." I closed my eyes to concentrate.

"What about that one woman—the one you bumped into in the bathroom?" Mom snapped her fingers.

"Her? You've got to be kidding." I pooh-poohed the idea with a swat of my hand.

"Why?" Mom crossed her arms. "She was really interested in you."

"Everyone there was a fan. That's why we hold these events."

"But she didn't even have a copy of any of *my* novels. Only yours."

"So? That means she's a fucking stalker, because she's not one of your fans? That's low, even for you."

"Of course not!" Mom scoffed.

Harold snapped his fingers. "She's that blogger who rushed to Cori's defense when G-Dawg—"

"Who's G-Dawg?" Floyd motioned for us to slow down and tell him everything.

"G-Dawg is the blogger who tried to set me up." I scrunched my face.

"Tell me more." Floyd sat up in his chair, pen ready.

Harold filled him in on the details.

"Wait. Didn't Roger contact you months ago about G-Dawg?" Barbara asked.

Floyd shook his head slowly, as if understanding his answer would upset Barb while also implicating Roger. Had Roger guessed G-Dawg's identity, but he didn't want any of us to know? And he was the one who'd suggested we focus on G-Dawg. Knowing how protective he'd been all my life, Roger probably thought he could control the situation without looping Floyd in.

"Okay, G-Dawg tried to set up Cori, but it didn't catch fire," Floyd said, avoiding Barb's eyes, clearly not wanting to open the Roger can of worms at the moment.

"Roger said you would handle it." Barb fiddled with her purse strap, not able to put the Roger bit to bed, so to speak.

"Who's the other blogger?" Floyd once again didn't bother zeroing in on the Roger aspect.

"One blogger, In the Shadows, gushed about Cori and her writing," Harold said.

"In the Shadows?" Floyd asked.

"That's her screen name," Harold said. "Cori has a podcast with her next month."

"How'd that happen?" Floyd asked.

Harold filled him in.

"Um, consider the booking canceled." I crossed my arms. "If this Shadows person is the one stalking me, one of us won't be alive next month."

Floyd frowned and motioned for me to pipe down. "And this blogger, showed up at the book signing on Mother's Day asking to do a podcast?"

"No, there was more," Mom pushed. "You're forgetting the bathroom."

"The bathroom?" Floyd and Kat parroted.

"Before I do public speaking events, I kinda freak out. I went to the bathroom to calm my nerves. A woman found me in there and talked me off the ledge. She was kind and supportive, nothing like the fucker on the video."

Mom huffed. "Later, during the signing, she cozied up to Cori like they were best buddies. What was it she said when you asked how you should sign her name?" Mom's eyes blazed.

I swallowed.

Every single person in the room waited for my answer.

"She said I should address it to my new bff."

***

Floyd hotfooted out of the room to confer with his team, and I parked my ass on the windowsill, away from everyone, ruing the day I had decided to become a novelist. Maybe I should have stayed at Beantown Café, out of the public eye.

Mom and Barb whispered behind their hands. Dad stared off into space, and Harold had his eyes closed.

Kat motioned for me to make room on the ledge. "You okay?"

Before I could respond, Floyd returned gripping a paper. He gathered us around the table and laid a photo down for all to see. "Does she look familiar?" It was a photo of the woman from the bathroom while I signed her book.

Kat's hand shot up to cover her mouth, and we all craned our necks to give the photograph our full attention.

"Gertrude—she's in one of my painting classes." Kat swiveled to me. "Do you remember when I mentioned a woman in my class I wanted to fix Harold up with?"

"You were going to set me up with a girl named Gertrude?" Harold ignored the fact that the woman was stalking me. He hovered over the grainy photo. "Not bad. I would have dated her."

I glared at him. He shrugged.

"Why didn't I notice her at the signing?" Kat rubbed her chin.

"She had a scarf that covered her face. I didn't think anything of it at the time. Also, you and Barb left early."

Kat closed her eyes, shaking her head.

"I don't understand why she sought you out in the first place. If she's obsessed with me, why take a painting class with you?"

Floyd sat in one of the chairs around the conference table and steepled his fingers under his chin. Could the man only think while sitting? "My guess would be she wanted to surround herself with people who knew you. In the video, she said she initially thought staying on the periphery would suffice."

Floyd shifted his beady eyes to Kat. "How long have you two been friends?"

Kat closed her eyes. I could see her mentally counting the days. "Over a year now. Do you mean that right from the start I was a pawn for her to get close to Cori?" She furrowed her brow. "She was so nice, so supportive. A friend when I really needed one."

"Yes," Floyd said softly, although his face didn't divulge any additional information.

Barbara consoled Kat.

"G-Dawg," Harold said.

Every head turned to him, as if we all expected him to say, "Colonel Mustard in the library with the candlestick."

"What?" I asked.

"G-Dawg… Is Gertrude G-Dawg?" Harold asked.

"That could make sense. Perhaps she started the controversy with one profile so she could swoop in with a different identity and rescue Cori." Floyd rubbed his chin.

"Like a knight rescuing a princess." Kat's wan smile tore at my insides.

"But the social media fiasco ended before it really had a chance to start. Why?" Mom demanded.

"Roger," Barb said.

"What do you mean?" I asked.

"Roger told all of us that he'd recruited Floyd's help. But what if Gertrude had weaseled her way into Roger's life, too, not just Kat's?" Barbara left the rest unsaid.

The look of anger on Barb's face, and my mom's supportive hand on her back, confirmed one thing: Gertrude and Roger had been close, probably lovers. This woman had been chasing me, through my family, for months, and I'd had no idea she even existed.

"In the Shadows referred to being in Cori's shadow. When the G-Dawg thing went down, we thought it was a reference to Cori being in Nell's shadow—we had no idea it meant someone was watching Cori from the shadows." Barb shuddered. "For how long?"

"I think I'm going to be sick." I sprinted toward the bathroom.

Chapter Twenty-Three

"I don't like this. I don't like it one bit." Mom paced my front room.

Floyd, along with the police, hustled around the entire house, setting up the equipment.

"I'll be fine. I promise." I stepped into Mom's path and placed a hand on each of her shoulders. "I want to do this. I need to do this."

"But—"

Kat raised a reassuring hand. "She's Super Jock."

"What?" Barb screeched.

I grinned at Kat and jabbed a thumb at my chest. "That's right; I'm Super Jock."

"Don't get too cocky. Super Jock's kryptonite is her temper. Can you control your emotions enough to reel this bitch in?" Kat narrowed her eyes.

"I promise not to lose my shit."

"Seriously. You have to stay in control." Kat's eyes bored into mine.

"Bring me a bible. I'll swear on it."

"You aren't religious."

"Okay, I swear on my honor."

"I've seen the photos. Your honor has been completely blown out of proportion," Mom jeered.

Floyd cleared his throat. "Okay. This place is wired. There are more cameras than you can shake a stick at, so don't worry about trying to get her to face a certain way or to speak louder. Just act natural. Even the smallest confession will go a long way."

I nodded. "Got it."

Floyd motioned it was time for everyone to scram. I gave Kat a peck on the cheek, unable to think of anything to say.

She smiled knowingly. "Remember, she's desperate, which makes her vulnerable. Use that brain of yours and keep your knee-jerk reactions in control, please."

I put both hands on her chest and shoved gently. "Go. Trust me."

"Please, be careful."

"When am I ever not careful?"

***

I sat on the couch, holding a book in my hand, but all the words spun on the page. Instead, I concentrated on my breathing. In and out.

The doorbell rang, and I glanced around the room, hoping the cameras were fully functioning. I didn't want to have to do this a second time. And I certainly wanted to make sure the police were watching and ready to intervene if she went really nuts.

A diminutive woman stood on my front stoop, an odd smile affixed to her face. My instincts screamed for me to punch her right in the kisser, but my promise to rein in those instincts prodded me to say, "Come in."

She barely resembled the woman I'd met at the signing. Today, she had on a tight shirt, fashionable jeans, makeup, and newly highlighted hair, as if she was on a first date. I might have noticed the woman who stood before me now—but never the woman in the bathroom. Was she a master of disguises?

"Would you like something to drink?" I waited patiently for the bitch's reply, doing my best to maintain a non-threatening pose—hard for a woman close to six feet tall who was standing next to a tiny fucker who deserved to have her teeth bashed in.

"Water would be great." The conniver smiled the most bashful smile I'd ever seen.

"Ice?" I channeled Kat to play the perfect host.

"No, thanks."

I ducked out of the room, focusing on the task at hand instead of threading my fingers around her pale neck. Step one: fill a glass under the water spigot of the fridge. Step two: spit in it. If only she'd asked for ice; that would have camouflaged a loogie floating in the water. I contemplated sticking my tongue in the water, but the freak would probably enjoy that, so I nixed the idea.

My shoulders shook and my hands trembled. I looked toward the ceiling to steady my nerves. Letting out a cleansing breath, I waltzed back into the room. "Here you go." I did my best June Cleaver impression.

Gertrude thanked me sweetly. *Don't try, bitch. I got your number.*

We sat quietly on opposite corners of the couch, facing the front window, waiting for the other to break first. I willed myself to stay silent. *Get Gertrude on her back foot.*

Gertie worried a string on the seam of her jeans. "Thanks for agreeing to meet to discuss, uh…"

For a stalker, she was quite bashful. How did she ever work up the nerve to break into my home while we were sleeping? How often had she been creeping around?

"It's okay. Take your time." My voice sounded nothing like me.

Gertrude's shoulders relaxed, and she took a sip of the water. "Please know I never meant to cause you any pain. The thing with Kat—"

"What about Kat?" The woman had no business saying my wife's name. My hackles raised, but I steadied my breathing, focusing on the big picture: a confession would get this fucking cunt out of my life permanently. I needed irrefutable proof she was fucked in the head and a danger to society.

"Let's talk about us—not *her*." She changed gears.

I kept my eyes on Gertrude's face, not showing any emotion.

"You have everything going for you." She waved to the furnishings and bric-a-brac in my front room.

I shifted in my seat, crossing my arms and immediately remembering Floyd telling me not to do that. *Keep it friendly and non-threatening.* I uncrossed my arms, trying to find a place to rest that would make it look like I was acting normal.

"There's only one thing missing." Gertrude set the water glass down on a coaster on the coffee table. She placed her hands on her knees. "This doesn't have to be messy. I believe in quick, like a Band-Aid."

I forced my muscles to soften. "What do you mean?"

Gertie fiddled with the fringe of the afghan on the back of the couch. "Oh, I don't want to say it aloud. I know it won't be easy for you, but in time, you'll see it's for the best."

"I'm curious. How do you know? That you and I"—I waved to her and back to me—"are meant to be together?"

"I just do," she gushed. "I've been watching you from afar for so long. You always amaze me. Like how calm and collected you were at your uncle's funeral."

She was at the funeral? Was nothing sacred?

I pursed my lips, afraid my voice would betray my desire to squash her like a blood-sucking mosquito.

Gertie's voice recaptured my attention. "I wanted to be near you from the moment I first laid eyes on you."

Near me? I nearly squeaked. "When was that?" My voice was thick.

"When you spoke at an event in Philly."

"You're from Philly?" My mind tried to pinpoint when I'd last been in Philly. It was for a book tour, but I couldn't quite put my finger on which tour. My first novel or my second? Or maybe my third?

She nodded proudly. "Never left the city until the day I followed you home."

Jesus, she was a sick fuck.

Silence fell between us.

"I'm so sorry—I never meant to hurt you."

I licked my lips. "Have you released the photos, then?"

She shook her head. "Oh no. I don't want to do that."

"Then how did you hurt me?" I spoke softly, fearful she'd realize I wanted her to speak for the cameras. I had no desire to hear any of the details, but proof was paramount. "You don't seem like the type who would hurt a fly." I tried to coax her into confessing.

"I'm not. Not normally," she mumbled to her folded hands in her lap.

"Are you referring to the G-Dawg trick?" I was in control of my nerves once again.

"I knew you'd put that piece into the puzzle. It's hard to fool a Harvard grad." She smiled ingratiatingly.

It took everything I had to force the next question out of my mouth. "Why did you back off before the G-Dawg thing had a chance to take root?"

"I was scared. Turned out I couldn't stand people saying those things about you."

She seemed sincere. Maybe it wasn't Roger who put a stop to it, after all. But if so, why did Roger say he'd passed it on to Floyd? Something wasn't adding up.

"So you came to my defense, like a knight rescuing a princess."

"Yes, I did." She beamed. "I like how you put that. When I came up with the screen name Finndale, I thought it was cute. It wasn't until the others pounced that I realized it was too obvious or that others might assume it was you. When I crafted the name, it felt as if you and I were merging into one. I used to pretend I was Kat—that you cherished me like you do her. I want to cherish you, Cori."

For a moment, I thought she was going to try to touch me, and I had to will myself to stay still. I couldn't believe the words coming out of her mouth. She was legit batshit crazy.

"So you stopped because too many people were being mean to me? Was that the only reason?" I couldn't leave the Roger aspect alone. I wanted to divert her attention away from me as much as possible.

Her gaze met mine, but she quickly glanced away. "Uh…"

Leaning forward, I placed a finger on her thigh, swallowing the bile storming its way up my throat. "If you want us to work, we need open communication. If there's something else, some secret, I need to know. That's very important to me."

Her face relaxed.

"Did you share the secret with anyone?"

"Kinda."

"Kinda how?"

"I can't say." She stared at the spot where my finger had been moments ago.

I replaced my hand. "Why?"

"I don't want you to hate me." Her hand twitched as though she wanted to reach for my finger but didn't have the guts.

Oh, I hate you, Gertie. I hate you more than I ever thought possible.

"I don't think I could ever hate you," I said, trying to mimic Kat's purr. "Remember in the bathroom—how you calmed me down?"

She swiped a tear off her cheek. "How could I forget?"

"I haven't forgotten either." I couldn't force myself to follow up with a wink, even though I could almost detect Kat praying for me to from where she and the others were watching everything unfold on the screen next door. "I trusted you that night. I need you to trust me now. Relationships are a two-way street, right?"

"But—" She screwed up her face, clearly unable to trust me or her intuition.

I put a finger to my lips. "Shush. It's okay. Take your time. I just need you to open up to me, Gertie." I almost gagged on her name.

She squirmed, and her gaze ping-ponged around the room. Was she looking for cameras, starting to piece together that I was teasing out a full confession?

"You promise not to get mad?" Her voice sounded so childlike—like it had in the bathroom at the signing.

"I promise."

"It was Roger."

Sometimes I hated being right. "How'd you meet my uncle?"

She blushed. "It wasn't hard. He... had a weakness."

Blood stormed through my ears and turned everything red behind my eyes. "You sought him out and seduced him," I whispered.

"I didn't want to. I don't like men, but I had to—to get close to you. Please tell me you understand. Please." She clasped her hands together as if praying.

I snapped my eyes shut, slowly counted to ten, and opened them again.

She was rocking on the couch, hugging her chest with both arms. "You promised."

"I remember. But I still need to know everything. How did Roger figure it out?"

"He used to call me G-Dawg. Kind of a nickname. It was silly of me, really."

That seemed like Roger. Did that mean she'd wanted to get caught, though? If she stalked me as much as the pictures suggested, she must have been aware of how much time I spent with my family. I switched gears. "Were you responsible for revealing Roger's affairs?"

Gertie scooted into the corner of the couch. "I did that for you," she whispered.

"How was that for me?"

Her face contorted in panic. "I wanted to free you—from the shame of his lifestyle. Kat told me how much it tormented you, the way he cheated on your aunt all the time."

Kat told her that? How close were these two?

I couldn't push her on this subject without transforming into Super Jock—the out of control side.

"It was such a relief when Roger died," she said and immediately flinched. "I mean, it was hard on you, but it was hard on me as well. After the G-Dawg trick, he tried ending things with me, but I wouldn't let him. I wanted—no, needed to stay close to you. I knew I had to be extra careful so he wouldn't guess how much I cared about you. Do you know how hard that was? All I wanted to talk about was you, but I couldn't.

"The day he died, he accused me of stalking him. Calling and texting at all hours. Thank God for the accident or I would have had to do something about him. If he contacted the authorities—it would have been bad." She laughed good naturedly as if she wasn't completely fucked in the head. "He had no idea the entire time I was with him, I pretended he was you. It was so hard—being with him when I really wanted to be with you. For so long, I didn't think this"—she waved a hand between us—"you and me in the same room, would happen. And for a while, I was okay with that. I liked to leave you gifts. Did you get them?"

The tulips! And the cookies on the front porch! I remembered the neck of one of the tulips had been snapped. Was that meant to symbolize Kat? I nodded slowly, not knowing where to go.

"Tell me about your friendship with Kat," I said after a minute.

"I wanted to figure out why you loved her so much, to learn how to make you happy."

On the inside, my body juddered. The idea that planted in my mind truly made me sick. "Do you like Kat?"

She shrugged.

"Many people think she's beautiful."

She nodded noncommittally. Was she trying to spare my feelings? I was completely used to people lusting after Kat and not giving me the time of day.

"Would you consider a..." I couldn't believe I was about to utter the next word. "Throuple."

"A throuple? You'd never go for that. I know you too well." She clutched a pillow to her chest.

I put two hands up. "Kat and I have experimented some, with Clementine—"

Her face flared red with anger. "Don't lie to me! I know Clementine is your vibrator. And I've heard all about Harold's throuple and your feelings about it, and Kat's." She straightened, pulling herself together a little. "I don't like it when you lie to me."

"I'm not lying. That was the first step to wanting to broaden our… our sex life. I know you and Kat were close, but she and I had conversations no one was privy to." I blocked out the knowledge that Mom, Barb, and Kat, along with Floyd, Harold, and unfamiliar police officers were listening to every word I said. If I survived this, how would I ever live it down?

"I don't know. I don't like to share." Gertie pouted and met my eyes. I kept my gaze firmly fixed on her.

How did I even get to this point—trying to compromise with a stalker? And why? Surely this was enough. What other information could I get out of her?

"Why do you love her so much?" Gertrude asked. "Especially after she let you down." The bafflement in her voice was genuine.

"Let me down?" Despite my best efforts, the words came out with too much force.

"She should have stayed home that night. And it wouldn't have happened."

The word *happened* wiggled an unthinkable thought in my brain.

"What do you mean? What happened?" The words rushed out of my mouth anyway. I didn't know how. Sheer willpower I guessed. Or rage.

"I didn't mean to do it, you know. But it was snowing, and she shouldn't have gone out like that. Taking your unborn child out in that weather, all alone, and at night too. I read an article that said you guys used your egg. I just meant to follow her—to keep an eye on her, ya know, make sure nothing bad happened."

I stopped breathing.

"Then her car fishtailed a little, but she still didn't turn around. When she pulled into Taco Bell, I lost it. She was pregnant with your child, and she'd driven in a snowstorm for a taco." Gertie's voice grated like heavy-duty sandpaper on metal and she shook her head, tsking.

Kat hated Taco Bell. But I loved it, especially when I drank, and even though Kat's memory of that day was minimal my gut told me she had gone to Taco Bell to surprise me.

Everything. The accident. Kat. Charlotte—all of it was my fault. If it wasn't for this nut job stalking me, Kat's trip to Taco Bell would have been forgotten by now.

Gertie continued speaking in that soft, childlike voice. "I knew I had to do something. Just teach her a lesson, so she'd be more careful. I only rammed into her car a little bit to push her off the road."

The room spun viciously, and I gasped for air.

"After I hit her, I waited at the scene, out of sight, so the cops wouldn't see my banged-up car. I wanted to be there when you heard the news she was dead, so I could comfort you from afar. But she didn't die. I followed the ambulance. When you arrived at the hospital and saw me in the waiting room, I felt like you understood. Like you were saying thank you. Thanking me for ridding you of a woman who would never make you happy. I thought for sure you would see the light and leave the selfish bitch after what happened, but you didn't." Her tone hitched up a notch. "Why didn't you leave, Cori?" It became a screech. "After everything I did for you!"

I snapped.

I seriously fucking snapped. I lunged to Gertie's side of the couch, pinning her beneath me and pressing my hands around her throat. "I'm going to fucking kill you!" I yelled, tightening my grip.

Floyd and several police officers stormed through the front door, yanking me off the sicko.

"Let me at her." I flailed about in Floyd's arms. "She murdered my daughter!"

Floyd hefted me off the floor and hauled me into the kitchen.

"She killed my daughter!" I bellowed.

Chapter Twenty-Four

Our family, including Harold, Sam, and Lucy, sat around the dining room table in my parents' home. It'd been over a year since Gertrude had been arrested, charged, and locked up in a mental institution, but that wasn't the reason for tonight's gathering. It was our last family dinner before Kat and I boarded the 7:50 a.m. flight to London the following morning. After having to put London on hold, it was a relief to finally be able to move forward.

Mom raised her glass of red wine. "To Kat, our gifted daughter. May this experience be just what you need."

"Here, here." Dad clinked his pint glass with Kat's.

Harold toasted with a purple concoction—I was afraid to ask what that was. Sam started to roll her eyes, but her wife's glare stopped her before her eyeballs could complete the arc.

"I can't believe the time has come," Barbara said, swiping at one eye.

"Jeez, Barb, you're acting like you're never going to see them again. You'll be in London the following week," Mom chided, trying to keep a stiff upper lip. "I'm the one being left behind."

"Left behind? You and Dale are coming over for the entire month of August. Two and a half weeks from now." Barbara countered. The two sisters carried on bickering back and forth.

Secretly, I hoped my parents would fall in love with London and stay.

Harold turned to me with glee on his face. He was flying with Barb, and he had packed and repacked his bags days ago. Kat and I were looking forward to a week alone before getting to work.

"I hope your place is big enough for when we visit." Sam circled a finger toward herself and Lucy.

"You don't mind the couch, right?" I ducked, knowing she'd lob something across the table at me. An olive pinged me right between the eyes. "Nice shot."

Sam bowed in her seat.

"You two could always crash in my room." Harold's voice wasn't seductive, but the hopefulness in his eyes was comical.

"In your dreams, perv." Lucy laced her fingers through Sam's. "Not after you ruined my proposal."

"Hey now," I came to Harold's defense. "Sam ruined that all by herself."

Another olive shot across the table.

Sam stabbed the air with her hands. "Bull's-eye."

Barbara's sniffling hushed the rest of the group. "I know we've been planning this for ages, but now that it's here, it's…" Barb sipped her drink with a shaky hand.

Mom nodded. The two sisters eyed each other, not speaking but connecting on their secret sibling wavelength.

"August will be here before you know it." Kat looked to my mom and dad. "Our family dinners will take place in quaint pubs."

"Hell, yeah," I said. "I'm making it my mission to ferret out all the best pubs."

"Way to aim high, Cori." Mom scoffed in her typical Nell Tisdale way. It was an indication of how hard this separation would be on her. I was her baby, and now I was flying the coop, crossing the pond for an unspecified amount of time. After the Gertrude affair, the police investigation, and the trial, Kat and I had no desire to return.

"It's only a five-hour flight. I'm game with helping you find pubs." Sam looked to Lucy. "You in?"

"I'm in." Luce pushed her glasses into place. "As long as we can find a babysitter." She cradled her tiny baby bump, eyeing Mom and Barb expectantly.

Mom and Barb nodded their agreement.

Kat met my eye with a nostalgic grin. Sensing the change in her mood, we all straightened in our chairs.

"To new beginnings." Kat raised her glass. "And to family. Always."

***

The wind swirled around us, making it nearly impossible to determine which direction it was blowing from.

Kat flipped her dark locks away from her face to take in the view. "I can't believe we're standing on Tower Bridge."

"I can't believe they'd take their kid out in this wind," I said, nodding to a family pushing a baby in a buggy. As soon as I said it, I kicked myself and examined Kat's face for any sign of sadness, but her gaze was fixed on the skyline of London.

That could have been us, I thought for a moment, *me and Kat and Lottie, even despite the wind.*

We had landed at Heathrow several hours ago, and our first stop after checking in at the hotel was the bridge.

Glad Kat hadn't reacted to my gaffe, I pointed to the right, unwilling to let my memories cloud the moment. "The Tower of London is right there."

Kat soaked in the view of the medieval structure on the northern side of the River Thames.

I read a paragraph from the guidebook and gave Kat the highlights. "Elizabeth I, before she was queen, was sent to the Tower. Obviously, she wasn't killed. According to this book, fewer than ten people were executed inside the Tower. One victim was Anne Boleyn. They say her ghost haunts the chapel." I scanned the page. "Tower Hill, to the north, is a totally different story. More than one hundred were killed."

Kat's gaze wandered, taking in the mix of historical structures and glass buildings. A nearby plaque supplied the names of the best-known structures. The Gherkin, the Monument, the top of St. Paul's, the Tate, City Hall. Kat tapped the plaque. "The Shard isn't on here."

I double-checked. "Must be too new." I studied the narrow, glass pyramid skyscraper on the South Bank. "We're having dinner there tomorrow night."

She gripped my arm. "We are?"

"Yep. On the thirty-third floor. Anselm reserved a table for half an hour before sunset. That way, we can watch this bridge light up." I held the railing with both hands and leaned over to see the top of the bridge.

Another gust of wind tousled Kat's hair, and I ringed an arm around her waist. "Can you feel that?"

She spat hair out of her mouth. "Taste it, more like."

I smiled. "Not that, silly. *That*." I spread my arms as another gust blew over us. "Do you feel it?" I waved to the horizon. "The winds of change. Promising new adventures in London and beyond."

A City Cruises boat chugged along the water below, heading underneath the bridge, drawing our attention. The baby, swaddled in her mother's arms, saw it too. She laughed —that delightful, gurgling baby laugh—and clapped her small hands.

I turned to Kat, expecting to see that same old sadness in her eyes, but my beautiful wife just smiled as she slipped her hand in mine.

"To new adventures… in London and beyond," she said, and we continued on over the bridge, both of us keeping our eyes on the happy baby ahead.

Author's Note

Thank you for reading *Confessions from the Dark*. If you enjoyed the novel, please consider leaving a review on Goodreads or Amazon. No matter how long or short, I would very much appreciate your feedback.

You can follow me, TB Markinson, on Twitter at @IHeartLesfic or email me at tbm@tbmarkinson.com. I would love to know your thoughts.

About the Author

TB Markinson is an American living in England. When she isn't writing, she's traveling the world, watching sports on the telly, visiting pubs, or reading. Not necessarily in that order.

Her novels have hit Amazon bestseller lists for lesbian fiction and lesbian romance. For a full listing of TB's novels, please visit her Amazon page.

Feel free to visit TB's website to say hello. She also runs I Heart Lesfic, a place for authors and fans of lesfic to come together to celebrate and chat about lesbian fiction. On her 50 Year Project blog, TB chronicles her challenge to visit 192 countries, read 1,001 books, and to watch the AFI's top 100 movies.

Printed in Great Britain
by Amazon